BATMAN™
GOTHAM KNIGHT

BATMAN™
GOTHAM KNIGHT

LOUISE SIMONSON

Based on the screenplay by
Brian Azzarello, Alan Burnett, Jordan Goldberg,
David Goyer, Josh Olson, and Greg Rucka

·

BATMAN CREATED BY BOB KANE

ACE BOOKS, NEW YORK

THE BERKLEY PUBLISHING GROUP
Published by the Penguin Group
Penguin Group (USA) Inc.
375 Hudson Street, New York, New York 10014, USA
Penguin Group (Canada), 90 Eglinton Avenue East, Suite 700, Toronto, Ontario M4P 2Y3, Canada
(a division of Pearson Penguin Canada Inc.)
Penguin Books Ltd., 80 Strand, London WC2R 0RL, England
Penguin Group Ireland, 25 St. Stephen's Green, Dublin 2, Ireland (a division of Penguin Books Ltd.)
Penguin Group (Australia), 250 Camberwell Road, Camberwell, Victoria 3124, Australia
(a division of Pearson Australia Group Pty. Ltd.)
Penguin Books India Pvt. Ltd., 11 Community Centre, Panchsheel Park, New Delhi—110 017, India
Penguin Group (NZ), 67 Apollo Drive, Rosedale, North Shore 0632, New Zealand
(a division of Pearson New Zealand Ltd.)
Penguin Books (South Africa) (Pty.) Ltd., 24 Sturdee Avenue, Rosebank, Johannesburg 2196,
South Africa

Penguin Books Ltd., Registered Offices: 80 Strand, London WC2R 0RL, England

This is a work of fiction. Names, characters, places, and incidents either are the product of the author's imagination or are used fictitiously, and any resemblance to actual persons, living or dead, business establishments, events, or locales is entirely coincidental. The publisher does not have any control over and does not assume any responsibility for author or third-party websites or their content.

BATMAN: GOTHAM KNIGHT

An Ace Book / published by arrangement with DC Comics

PRINTING HISTORY
Ace mass-market movie tie-in edition / June 2008

ISBN: 978-0-441-01613-6

ACE
Ace Books are published by The Berkley Publishing Group,
a division of Penguin Group (USA) Inc.,
375 Hudson Street, New York, New York 10014.
ACE and the "A" design are trademarks belonging to Penguin Group (USA) Inc.

PRINTED IN THE UNITED STATES OF AMERICA

10 9 8 7 6 5 4 3 2 1

For my husband, Walter Simonson,
artist, writer, and altogether cool guy

ACKNOWLEDGMENTS

The stories in any shared universe are built on the contributions of a number of people. *Batman: Gotham Knight* melds the visions of hundreds of creators involved in the production of Batman comics, animation, and movie continuities.

I'd like to thank:

Bob Kane and Bill Finger, who gave Batman and many of his enduring villains lots of amazing adventures.

David S. Goyer, Christopher Nolan, Jonathan Nolan, and the other producers, directors, writers, and designers of the movies *Batman Begins* and *The Dark Knight*. This book is set in the Gotham City they envisioned.

Animated feature producer/director Bruce Timm and segment writers Brian Azzarello, Alan Burnett, Jordan Goldberg, David Goyer, Josh Olson, and Greg Rucka. Their linked stories provided the framework for this novel.

Dennis O'Neil and Neal Adams, for amazing Rā's al Ghūl stories.

Gerry Conway and Don Newton, for Killer Croc adventures.

Chris Cerasi and Ginjer Buchanan, super-editors.

Walter Simonson, Thomas Kintner, Les Parker, and Steve Hoveke, whose assistance was invaluable in the completion of this project.

1

The first body washed in on the brackish tide in the early morning.

Melissa Delridge, an early riser who liked to get in her exercise before the day turned hot and muggy, managed to call 911 before she began throwing up. She was still on her hands and knees, on the jogging path beside the Gotham River, when the first squad car screamed up.

Nobody saw the Batman arrive.

Nobody saw him leave.

Everyone was looking at what was left of the John Doe. He'd been dead a long time, and he looked like he'd been part of somebody's breakfast.

The Gotham City Police Department headquarters was a massive multistoried edifice in central Downtown. Built as part of a WPA project during the Great Depression, the building, with its graceful art-deco facade, was old, ill equipped, and outdated. It was a structure under siege, and it took its position seriously.

Public parking was prohibited in a fifty-foot area

surrounding the building. At night, floodlight illuminated the base of the building. The more accessible lights were shot out regularly, and GCPD maintenance was kept busy replacing them.

With the exception of the doors to the public waiting areas, all other entrances were electrically controlled. Bullet-proof Plexiglas-shielded doors and windows provided the police with maximum visibility. These helped keep out the bad guys and protect the good.

Batman slipped in through the window of Lieutenant Jim Gordon's office, left open—if anyone asked—to catch a few night breezes.

Lieutenant Gordon, head of the newly created Major Crimes Unit, was at his desk. When he heard the soft rustle of fabric, he swiveled in his chair and leaned back. He'd been waiting.

"I haven't ID'd our floater yet," Gordon said.

"I have," Batman said. "Through his fingerprints."

"How the hell did you get his fingerprints?"

"Stealth and cunning." Batman smiled grimly. "He's Jeremy Greensmith, originally from Des Moines. Real estate agent; good husband, by all accounts; father of two teenagers; and for the past four years, missing, believed dead.

"Somehow he ended up here in Gotham—a homeless bum, living a life of psychotic episodes punctuated by moments of fearful clarity. He prowled on the fringes of Port Adams, panhandled, and drank himself into stupors when he could afford the booze. Liked by his fellow travelers. Vanished from the area about two weeks ago. Not that his disappearance was reported to Missing Persons."

Gordon frowned. "And his fingerprints were in the system?"

"Not exactly."

Beneath his sand-colored mustache, Gordon's mouth twitched in wry amusement. Batman's resources beat GCPD's all to hell.

"Greensmith's not the only disappearance," Batman continued: "Other bums around Downtown have vanished in the last few weeks. Word on the street points to that old urban legend—that crocodiles kids have flushed down their toilets have grown up and are taking anyone who gets too close to a manhole.

"Nobody in Downtown goes near a manhole these days."

"Appreciate the heads-up," Gordon said. "I'll pass it on. Tell my unit to keep their eyes and ears open."

Batman shook his head in disgust. "I should have noticed what was happening earlier. I haven't been paying enough attention." He tossed a sheaf of papers on Gordon's desk. "Here's what I have."

Gordon glanced down at the papers.

When he looked up, Batman had vanished into the night.

The Aparo Tower was more than amazing, Dander thought as he looked around the rooftop observation deck on the eightieth floor. It was a honkin' massive art-deco *masterpiece*. It was worth the trouble he'd had sneaking up here.

The teenager leaned back against the railing that encircled the building's rooftop observation deck and drank in the scene around him.

The Tower took up a complete city block, rising in steep steps to a large flat roof. In the center of the roof was a bronzed elevator tower, six stories tall, adorned with winged lions. At night, lit by several spotlights, the lion sculptures gleamed like massive golden idols.

He'd heard that the elevator tower had been designed originally as a mooring for dirigibles. Dander rolled his eyes. *What idiot had thought* that *would be a good idea? I mean . . . how would passengers get down from one of those big balloons? Especially with winds whipping across the roof like they were now.*

A gust tore at his T-shirt and threatened to tear the knit cap from his head. He grabbed it before the wind could take it and stuffed it in a pocket in his jeans. The wind whipped his dark hair into his eyes. He brushed it back and craned his neck up . . . and up.

A decorative brass needle topped the elevator tower and added another fifteen stories to the building's official height. Dander knew it was actually an antenna that beamed radio signals out over Gotham City and the surrounding suburbs. Considering what Gotham was like, even in the best of times, that was a good thing. It helped to be up on breaking news in Gotham. Sometimes it kept you alive.

Dander sighed. Even when you were up this high, you couldn't see the stars. Smog hung low, shrouding the tip of the antenna. It smelled faintly of diesel fumes and reflected back the ambient light of the city.

He shrugged. Modern times in Gotham. These days, the mooring tower was just a decorative building that housed elevators, and those elevators mostly brought tourists on an eighty-story ride up to the observation deck. Considering Gotham's reputation, it always surprised him that people from around the world flocked to his city to take in the sights.

Dander looked around. There were plenty of tourists. Men, women, and children. All shapes. All sizes. Old, young, and in between. Gaping at the view and gawking through the pay-per-view binoculars. He heard a babble of languages. Spanish. French. Italian? Some Mideast language . . . Pakistani or Indian, maybe. And . . . Russian?

His eyes followed a group of Japanese tourists, cute girls maybe a few years older than he was, fluttering like a flock of exotic birds toward the side of the building, exclaiming at the view and pulling out their cameras.

He turned, wanting to see what they saw, and the panorama caught him.

Gotham City had been built on three large islands running north to south with a few smaller ones thrown in for good measure. The city was hundreds of years old, a mishmash of architecture with newer buildings built on the ruins of older ones.

Like Rome, Dander thought, and laughed at himself. He'd gotten that from eleventh-grade World History. He'd skipped so many classes, he couldn't believe he remembered any of it. But he'd thought building new cities on dead ones was cool.

Now, as he looked, the familiar dirt, the crumbling infrastructure, the fetid alleys fell away into darkness. From up here, nighttime Gotham was defined by light. But he knew that somewhere beneath it all were the bones of the old city.

Below him, lit windows delineated the shapes and angles of the office buildings and apartments of Midtown. Spotlights illuminated the roof towers of the Wayne Enterprises corporate headquarters. Cars inched through rush-hour traffic in bright rows of white headlights and red brake lights. A monorail gleamed softly as it swung in a gentle arc toward the main hub far below.

On the island the natives called Uptown, stadium lights glared. *Gotham Knights must be playing,* Dander thought. Nearby were the bright lights of Amusement Mile. Something was always going on in Uptown. Uptown was fun. It was a happenin' place to be. But, right now, Uptown didn't interest him.

Dander crossed to the opposite railing and looked toward Downtown, past South City Park, toward a slash of darkness. This was the Narrows, a dagger-shaped island in the middle of the river. Lights out nearly everywhere. Though sometimes at night, fires raged out of control through its ruined buildings.

The Narrows used to be a crime-ridden slum surrounding the infamous Arkham Asylum, a hospital for Gotham's criminally insane. It used to be so dangerous that not even the cops would go there.

Then, a few months ago, a mad doctor named Crane, who called himself the Scarecrow, had freed most of

Arkham's inmates and tried to poison Gotham's water with a fear-inducing toxin. Batman—a striking new presence in Gotham—had foiled the maniac's plan but hadn't recaptured the Scarecrow. Yet.

Some escapees were back in the asylum. But others still stalked the Narrows, lurking in its squalid passageways and burned-out buildings. While others had crossed the river into greater Gotham.

Now the Narrows was sealed off from the rest of the city. Arkham Asylum was spotlit—the precious jewel of the Narrows. Gotham's finest, wearing Kevlar vests and packing automatic weapons and riot gear, patrolled its corridors and guarded the bridges that connected the island with greater Gotham. Cops, inside the asylum and out, had made the place a fortress against the lunatics who still roamed unchecked across the rest of the Narrows. Without a heavily armed escort, nobody went onto the island. And nobody got off. Dander figured that's what people meant when they said, "closing the barn door after the horses were gone."

Because the worst of the crazies were out there somewhere—nuts like the Scarecrow and his fruitcake friends. In Gotham, there were lots of shadows where criminal madmen could hide.

Even from Batman.

Dander leaned over the edge and squinted. Batman was probably out there right now. He'd never seen the crime-fighting hero himself, but Batman's exploits were all over the news. That was why Dander was up here. To scan the city and see if he could maybe catch a glimpse of the armored vigilante the media was calling the Dark Knight of Gotham.

Nothing.

Maybe I'm too high up, Dander thought. *Batman would be down below, where the crime is.* He eyed the pay-per-view binoculars thoughtfully, wondering if they would help.

Downtown, to the south, beyond the Narrows, more spotlights defined the soaring spires of Gotham Cathedral. City Hall was Downtown. So was the headquarters of the Gotham City Police Department. And a batch of museums.

Institutions that stood for morality, order, and the rule of law. Until recently, they'd been a kind of joke. Maybe, now, that was changing.

Maybe.

With so many real cops pulling extra duty and the rent-a-cops distracted by the possible presence of psycho killers skulking among the tourists, it had been easy for a normal-looking teenager to sneak onto the elevator along with the paying customers and take a ride to the top. I mean . . . Dander wasn't a *tourist*, right? It seemed wrong for a native Gothamite to pay tourist rates. Besides, where would he get twenty-five bucks for an elevator ride? Even if he had that kind of money, he sure wouldn't blow it just to stand on top of a building. Even an amazing one like—

Boom!

The noise slammed into him from behind and shoved his body forward into the protective railing that edged the roof. He felt his heart stop. His brain went blank as the floor beneath him rocked and shuddered.

The lights on the observation deck went out.

He whirled and saw people stumbling away from the elevator housing in semidarkness. They shoved toward the edge of the roof, giving the tower a wide berth. Smoke curled up into the night.

An alarm began to shriek.

In the dim, ambient light reflected from the lowering clouds, Dander could see the cleared circle around the elevator tower and what was left of its once elegant brass doors. Twisted metal . . . opening onto an empty shaft.

Dander almost missed the dark figure standing in the shadows beside the shredded door.

His heart leapt. *Batman! He's here! There was an explosion, and he's come to rescue us!*

Then the figure moved into the light.

That's definitely not *Batman!* Dander thought. Batman wore black, sure, but he also had a long, flowing cape—everyone said so. And a mask with ears like a bat. And he was tall and scary and built like the Terminator.

This guy was tall, yeah, but his body was skinny and kind of slumped and soft-looking. He was covered from head to toe in a black rubbery-looking suit that hid his face and did nothing to flatter his paunchy belly and spindly legs. His back looked lumpy, humped, and misshapen. A dark utility belt circled his middle, riding below his gut. A holster hung from it. Bulging goggles gave his face a pop-eyed, froglike appearance.

The truth was, the dude looked a lot like a large, black, semimature tadpole. If it hadn't been for the futuristic blaster he held, Dander might have laughed.

But the business end of the gun was pointed toward the crowd. Dander wondered if the gun had fired the explosive that blew up the elevator.

Tadpole-man tossed a black satchel onto the ground several feet in front of the shredded elevator doors.

"Ladies and gentlemen!" he said in a loud voice muffled by the rubber that covered his mouth, shouting to be heard over the shriek of the alarm. "This is a robbery. You've seen the kind of damage my weapons can do. None of you want to experience that kind of damage personally. If you cooperate, everything will be fine. You'll be safe at home in time to watch this story unfold on the evening news. You'll be able to brag to your friends that you were among the first victims of the Man in Black.

"Now, line up in front of me, remove all your valuables, and place them in this bag. You have two minutes."

2

"I'd rather be trawling the sewers." Bruce Wayne, billionaire industrialist and sole heir to the Wayne family fortune, grimaced as he shrugged into his dress shirt.

"But what Teresa Williams is doing is important, sir." Alfred Pennyworth, the Wayne family's longtime butler and Bruce's supporter and confidant, hid a knowing smile. He held the tuxedo jacket ready for Bruce to slip over his broad shoulders. "As you, yourself, have said. In her own way, Ms. Williams's crusade symbolizes hope for Gotham. As much, in some ways, as does Batman's."

Bruce buttoned up his shirt. "And, so, here I am. Putting on a monkey suit and going to a fund-raiser."

"Eating canapés while Gotham burns?"

He tied his bow tie. "You're preaching to the converted, Alfred. Still . . ." He sighed.

The city had condemned a tract of slum buildings in an area known as Hob's Oven, built two hundred years ago on the north shore of Downtown, overlooking the Narrows. Mayor Hill had called for land-reclamation proposals.

Community activist Teresa Williams had pitched the creation of decent low-to-moderate-income co-ops and apartments to replace the condemned buildings. They would provide reduced-cost housing to city workers like teachers, policemen, and firemen, as well as displaced former residents. The plan had plenty of advocates. It also had its detractors, several of whom had come up with alternative bids.

But the unions were behind the Williams proposal, and their influence had led the city council to give her plan a chance. All Williams had to do was come up with the funding within the next three months. That's where Gotham's wealthy and powerful came in.

The philanthropic Wayne Foundation had already made a hefty donation. But Bruce knew his presence at the fundraiser as Gotham's most eligible bachelor would ratchet up interest in the cause and help ensure positive media coverage.

Seeing Bruce's put-upon expression, Alfred suppressed a grin. "Don't fret, Master Bruce. The night will still be young when the party's over. And the criminal element never seems to sleep."

Bruce was reaching for his jacket when the buzzer in his pocket vibrated. He and Alfred simultaneously pulled out identical earbuds and inserted them in their ears.

The silent alarm was linked to traffic on the GCPD police-band emergency-response channels. An increase in chatter was a surefire warning of more-than-ordinary trouble in Gotham.

The police bands were jammed with reports of an explosion atop the Aparo Tower. The electricity was off, and the elevator was no longer working. Tourists were trapped on the roof.

Bruce turned, dashed out his bedroom door, down the hall, and onto the stairs, without a glance at the priceless paintings and antique treasures that adorned his Gotham City penthouse apartment.

Alfred folded the tuxedo jacket over his arm and followed more sedately, down the sweeping staircase and through the magnificently appointed rooms to the secret passage that led to the private bunker far below.

By the time Alfred stepped onto the floor of the bunker and threaded his way past the equipment and vehicles, Bruce had nearly completed his transformation from debonair billionaire playboy philanthropist to vigilante creature of the night.

His body was encased in black Kevlar biweave body armor with a stylized bat symbol embossed on his chest. His gloves hid switches that controlled the rigidity of his armor, triggering an increase in density that would deflect most bullets. The heels of his calf-high boots held a hypersonic sounder that could summon a swarm of bats. The streamlined utility belt around his waist contained a collection of useful, nonlethal criminal deterrents. Even his flowing cape supported several unusual functions.

He slid the impact-resistant black cowl, with its interior protective Kevlar panels, over his head and locked the strap. The cowl, designed to mask his upper face, was shaped to evoke the head of a bat. It was also his information-retrieval and communication center.

Antennas, hidden in the mask's ears, gave him access to police and emergency radio bands. Night-vision lenses helped him see in the dark. Nose filters prevented inhalation of airborne toxins. High-gain microphones let him eavesdrop on distant conversations, including those taking place inside buildings. A private channel let him stay in touch with Alfred.

Bruce glanced at the high-speed Tumbler he and Alfred had begun to call his Batmobile. "It's rush hour. It won't get me there fast enough or take me high enough."

Alfred raised an eyebrow. "Then I suggest we take the helicopter."

They took the private elevator to the roof, where their newest toy, a modified black R-44 Raven, waited.

Bruce swung into the passenger seat and strapped on his seat belt. Alfred's eyes sparkled as he slipped into the pilot's seat beside him.

During the past year, Alfred had learned to fly both rotary and fixed-wing airplanes. He was now a licensed pilot, but he hadn't yet had the opportunity to take this baby out on anything more than a test run. This was going to be fun.

Alfred grinned as he set the rotor spinning.

I might be sixtysomething, but I'm not dead, he thought, as the motor caught and the rotor began to turn slowly overhead. *And, if I were dead, being behind the joystick of this little darling might just bring me back to life.*

The rotor revved faster, and the chopper lifted off the ground. It pivoted toward the roof of the Aparo Tower and took off.

3

On the roof of the Aparo Tower, the tourists were nervously shuffling into line. Some were translating the Man in Black's command for those who did not understand English. Women were removing their earrings and other jewelry with shaking hands. Men were taking off their watches and pulling wallets out of their pockets.

The Man in Black wants valuables, Dander thought. *That lets me out. I haven't got any valuables. Except—* He felt in his pocket for his cell phone.

Dander figured the Man in Black must be one of the guys who had escaped from Arkham. Any sane dude who could invent a small gun that could fire a blast hot enough to blow apart an elevator would patent the thing and rake in the dough. He wouldn't use it to show off and steal low-end jewelry and petty cash.

One by one, the tourists stepped forward and dropped their valuables in the Man in Black's satchel, then went to huddle in a group beside the destroyed elevator tower.

Slowly, Dander began to sidle toward the back of the line of tourists. Then he dropped into a crouch behind them.

Hidden from sight behind their bodies, he pulled out his cell phone and dialed 911. *Not that the cops won't hear the alarms,* he thought. *But it won't hurt to clue them in on what's happening up here.*

Kneeling behind a group of tourists speaking guttural German, he whispered frantically into the phone, answering the emergency dispatcher's questions. "A man in black, a black-rubber suit . . . yeah, that's what it looks like . . . a robbery . . . the Aparo Tower roof . . . blew up the elevator, maybe with a blaster that fires explosive—"

The dispatcher's next question was drowned out by a loud *whup whup whup.*

Dander snapped his cell phone shut, stood, and glanced around. The tourists craned their necks, squinting into the overcast sky. The Man in Black swiveled his head.

The *whup whup whup* grew louder.

Dander frowned. It sounded like a helicopter . . . maybe one of those air-tour jobs that flew out of the small heliport near Ranelogh Ferry Building. Or maybe it was an accomplice, coming to get the Man in Black. Or maybe . . .

The smog-laden clouds overhead roiled. A strong gust of wind buffeted the watchers.

A black shape plunged toward the roof.

Batman!

Dander raised his fist and pumped the air. *Yes!* He pushed to the front of the crowd so he could see what happened next. That guy was the *coolest.* He didn't want to miss a minute of this confrontation.

Batman's head was encased in a horned cowl that covered his eyes but left his mouth and chin exposed. He wore formfitting black armor and a flowing cape.

Batman landed on his feet, crouching. Then he stood slowly and faced the Man in Black. He looked tall and strong and fearless, and his cape flowed in the wind.

"Put down the gun," he said. His voice was deep and commanding.

The Man in Black sneered, "Bite me."

He raised his arm, pointed his gun at Batman's chest,

and fired. *Crack! Boom!* The blast hit Batman full in the chest, knocking him backward several steps. The missile that struck him erupted into flames. For a minute, he was engulfed in a conflagration. Then the fire went out.

Batman smiled coldly.

Better the Man in Black than me, Dander thought. *If Batman smiled at me like that, I'd wet my pants.*

Dander couldn't tell if the Man in Black felt as scared as he would have felt, since his face was completely masked. But the guy's hand shook as he leveled the gun at Batman a second time. "Don't . . . don't come any closer!"

Dander rolled his eyes. *Like that's gonna work.* One of his teachers had said insanity was doing exactly the same thing over and over and expecting to get different results. Well, the Man in Black *was* probably an escapee from Arkham, so he guessed it figured he was nuts, but—

Maybe the Man in Black wasn't as nuts as Dander thought. At the last minute, he swung the gun away from Batman and pointed it directly at Dander.

"Back off," he said. "Or I blow the kid to Kingdom Come."

Dander wanted to smile coldly like Batman had. He wanted to be tough and defiant. He wanted to say, "Go on! I ain't scared of you, man. Make my day!"

He opened his mouth, but no words came out. Dander wasn't wearing armor as Batman was. If the Man in Black fired, his explosive bullets wouldn't flare and die against Dander's chest. They would make his chest look like the exploded elevator—only bloodier. Then he'd fry like bacon.

Dander stared at the hand holding the blaster. The Man in Black's rubber-encased hand was shaking. It looked like his finger was tightening on the trigger. *He isn't going to wait,* Dander thought. *He's gonna do me right now!*

Batman raised his arm in a fluid motion and pointed at the Man in Black. Something shot from his hand. The roof was dark, and it happened too fast for Dander to be sure exactly what he had seen. A laser beam? No. It was some kind of thrown projectile, like a *shuriken*!

Whatever it was, it sliced through the back of the Man in Black's gun hand and lodged in his wrist. The robber yelped in pain and dropped his blaster. He yanked the blade—was it a knife?—from the back of his wrist and hurled it to the ground.

Then he drew another gun from the holster at his waist.

Batman raised his hand and pointed.

This time there was a faint whirring sound, and before the Man in Black could point the gun at anyone, it flew out of his hand. Batman caught it deftly.

The rubber-masked bandit turned and sprinted for the edge of the roof. He leapt on top of the railing.

Batman shouted, "Don't!"

But the Man in Black dove off the roof, into the sea of lights below.

Batman ran to the railing. Dander and the tourists rushed forward, torn between shock and horror and their need to see what happened next.

The Man in Black plummeted toward the streets. Then, with a loud roar, a gout of fire kicked from the hump on his back. He lurched upward, then, in a controlled dive, dropped steeply toward a dark alley. The sound cut off, and the Man in Black vanished.

Whoa! Dander thought. *The hump on his back is a jet pack.* The dude could fly.

Batman had one foot on the railing. It looked like he was going after the robber. *How?* Dander wondered. Heck, for all he knew, Batman could fly, too.

"Wait!"

Dander snatched up the knifelike object that had been lodged in the Man in Black's rubber-clad wrist. It was about eight inches long, made of dark metal, and it looked kind of like a boomerang, except that it was shaped like the symbol on Batman's chest.

"Here!" He held out the weapon. "You saved my life. Thanks. What you did . . . how you did it. It was amazing!"

Batman smiled. He took the Batarang and placed it in a pocket in his belt. "You called the police."

How'd he know that? Dander wondered. Maybe Batman listened to police emergency calls and recognized his voice. Heck, for all Dander knew, Batman could read minds. "Yeah," he said. "I called but—"

"You kept your head and told the police what to expect. You might make a good cop yourself someday. Well done."

Wow! Then Dander frowned. "The Man in Black got away. He didn't look like he was planning on giving up."

Batman smiled grimly. "Then we have that in common. I don't give up either." He pointed to the weapon lying on the floor of the observation deck. "Don't let anyone touch his gun. It's evidence . . . for the police. They'll be here in another few minutes."

He dove over the side of the building and into the air. His cloak fluttered in the breeze as he fell. Then, suddenly, the cloak appeared to stiffen.

And then he was gone, gliding silently into the night.

4

The dive into free fall was always a leap of faith.

Batman pressed the switch in his glove that sent an electrical current through his cape, causing the molecules to realign in a predetermined pattern. With a sharp crack, the cape stiffened into its preset glider configuration.

His body jerked as the glider caught the wind and abruptly halted his downward momentum. The wind whistled past his head. He engaged the infrared lenses built into his cowl.

Batman's chest ached where the rubber-clad robber's missile had slammed into it. He knew from experience that his ribs were already darkening from the severe bruising. His experimental fire-retardant Nomex survival suit had originally been designed to protect advanced infantry armed forces units and was relatively bullet resistant. A missile fired at close range would leave him battered and bruised, but alive.

Fortunately, it had worked as designed. Still, he thought he might have to break down later and take a couple of aspirin.

He glided over city streets, scanning for the Man in

Black. But at this time of night, there were plenty of pedestrians walking the Midtown streets. The visible infrared track from the Man in Black's body heat beneath him reached street level. There, it merged and was lost among the hundreds of crisscrossing patterns of human activity. The criminal had already entered the city's honeycomb of dark alleys and was gone.

Batman had recognized the characteristic MO of the robber.

The man's name was Jacob Feely. He was featured in one of the many dossiers that cataloged the Arkham escapees, listing their odd and dangerous proclivities.

Feely was a brilliant but paranoid tinkerer who obsessively created devices—most of which were dangerously explosive. He was so afraid he'd be taken advantage of that he had refused to patent his creations and sell the designs. Instead, he had used his inventions in petty robberies, stealing funds to finance his obsessive habit of inventing more explosive devices. He was a criminal who dreamed big and thought small.

Feely had been incarcerated in Arkham for nearly five years, following his attempted robbery of a theater audience, which resulted in several deaths and the partial demolition of the theater.

For some reason, Feely was now wearing a head-to-toe rubber suit and jet pack, but he was still unmistakable. And he was certainly clever. If he hadn't been dangerously and criminally insane, with a habit of blowing things up and killing anyone he thought was a threat, he might have been a good fit for the research division at Wayne Enterprises.

Now that Feely had escaped from Arkham, he was up to his old tricks. He needed funds to fuel his inventing habit, he was paranoid, and he wasn't a patient individual. He'd been thwarted in this robbery, but he would try again soon. And he would blame Batman for his problems.

Batman vowed silently that, the next time Feely surfaced, he would send the inventor back to Arkham, where he belonged. Where he could take up knitting, for all Batman cared!

He pressed a button, activating the secure communicator function in the cowl. He gave Alfred a quick rundown of the events on the Tower roof and told him about Feely's escape using a personal jet pack.

"The real surprise of the evening is that Feely didn't set himself on fire with that thing. I'll change for the fundraiser back at the apartment. I'll arrive fashionably late, but that will probably enhance my playboy bachelor image."

The kid on the roof held it together pretty well, Batman thought as he caught a thermal and turned the glider toward his penthouse. Probably from somewhere around Crime Alley—he'd recognized the accent. Not as bad an area as the Hob's Oven property the city had condemned but heading in that direction. The teenager was the sort of kid who'd benefit from the kind of improved neighborhood Teresa Williams was lobbying for. Maybe Hob's Oven would be a first step . . .

Batman glided down toward the secret bunker he had installed not too far from the penthouse building. He keyed the opener and, when the door slid back, he slipped inside to meet Alfred.

His mouth twitched into a smile when Alfred put aside the newspaper he had been reading and rose to help him strip off his armor.

He pulled Feely's gun from a pouch on his belt and handed it to the older man.

"Feely's getting the equipment he needs for his little projects from somewhere, Alfred. That's a sample of one of his inventions—probably a recent one, since he's been free only a few months. It fires some kind of explosive pellets. He lost a couple of guns tonight, so he'll probably have to build new weapons. My bet is he'll want to upgrade to armor-piercing projectiles. If you have some spare time, you might try to locate his sources."

Alfred smiled. "I've read the paper and finished today's crossword puzzle, sir. My evening is open. While you're at the fund-raiser, I'll check for sources here in Gotham."

"Good." Bruce finished peeling off his Batsuit and walked toward the elevator. "It would be good if we could get to Feely before he tries to fry anyone else."

Bruce Wayne climbed from his limo in front of the Gotham Historical Society, where the gala fund-raiser was in full swing.

There was a light breeze, but not one scrap of paper was blowing in the street. The litter baskets on the corner were freshly painted. And empty. He sighed.

He glanced up at the high, arched floor-to-ceiling windows, set like large jewels in the marble facade. The glittering attendees were clearly visible inside—Gotham's wealthiest, most powerful, and most philanthropic—here to donate to a good cause.

Those people lived in a completely different city . . . a completely different world . . . than the residents of Hob's Oven or Crime Alley. It was heartening that at least some of them were willing to try to bridge the gap.

Bruce stopped for a moment, smiling and bantering with the lifestyle and society reporters who thronged the sidewalk. He posed, allowing the photographers to snap his picture as he answered the reporters' shouted questions.

"What's your relationship with Sondra Beemer?"

"Gorgeous, isn't she? She's on the cover of this month's *Fashion*, and deserves the spot."

"You were seen at Vinnie's Italian with Lavinia Lazar. Have you seen a screening yet of *Fast Race to Death*?"

"No, but I hear she's sensational."

"What about Dr. Sophie Yaeger? You had lunch with her at Rudy's. She's up for a Nobel Prize in physics."

"Brilliant as well as beautiful. I tried to hire her for Wayne Enterprises, but, alas, her heart belongs to pure science. I'll have to see if I have any influence with the Nobel committee."

Bruce smiled and charmed. He assured them that each of their candidates for romance was just a very good friend. The truth was, as amazing as those women were, Bruce couldn't allow himself to get close to any of them. He enjoyed their company, and their quality and variety underlined his playboy image. Maybe he could have a serious relationship—someday. But, right now, his duty was to Gotham City.

He was shocked when a reporter asked a semiserious question. "What about the Wayne Enterprises research satellite that recently malfunctioned? Did Dr. Yaeger have any experiments aboard the project?"

He smiled. "You must be from the *Times*. That was the Wayne-6. We'll be launching a new communications satellite—the I-Brite 7—next week, if the weather's clear, to take its place. We'll take that opportunity to retrieve the damaged research satellite. It could have been hit by a meteor or debris, but our research division is concerned that there may have been a flaw in its construction. And, no, Dr. Yaeger's experiments weren't on aboard."

With a careless wave, Bruce walked up the marble steps, past uniformed policemen who stood at attention.

The mayor, the governor, and at least one senator are supposed to be here, Bruce thought. *It figures there'd be a visible police presence. Still . . .*

He frowned, wondering if the beefed-up guards were Gordon's idea. It was possible that the lieutenant had some information that Bruce didn't. Jim Gordon tolerated Batman because he got the job done. And, on some level, he even liked and trusted the vigilante. But Jim didn't confide in him. Not unless he had to.

He supposed it was only fair. Batman didn't entirely confide in the head of the GCPD Major Crimes Unit either. Perhaps one day . . .

* * *

Bruce shoved open the polished double doors and en-tered the foyer.

The noise struck him first. The background music of the chamber quartet playing in the corner. Haydn, he thought. Opus 33, No. 2. He smiled inwardly. He was partial to Haydn's "Russian" quartets. The music was filtered through the buzz of lively conversation. The clink of glasses added soft accents to the music as soberly clad waiters offered trays of cocktails and hors d'oeuvres around the room.

He strode across the inlaid marble floor of the foyer, into a high-ceilinged ballroom lit by a pair of immense chandeliers. Lavish silk-brocade curtains draped the gracefully arched windows. A hand-woven ballroom-sized Aubusson carpet softened the gleaming hardwood floor. A carved-marble fireplace provided a spectacular focal point, though he thought that the fauns were a little much. Delicate couches and chairs were arranged to facilitate conversation, their subtly striped upholstery reflecting the rose of the walls and the deeper burgundy of the curtains. Priceless paintings enhanced the room's elegance, while gilded mirrors reflected the glittering spectacle.

Sweeping the room with his eyes, Bruce spotted the senator deep in conversation with a wealthy art collector. Mayor Hill, as usual, was hidden behind a throng of cronies. Police Commissioner Loeb—not one of Batman's fans—was deep in discussion with the governor.

Bruce recognized Detective Crispus Allen, a handsome African-American cop approaching middle age. His gleaming head was shaven; his goatee and mustache were neatly trimmed. His dark, well-cut suit coat didn't quite hide the bulge of the revolver in his shoulder holster.

His partner, Detective Renee Montoya, stood beside him. She was younger than Allen, close to Bruce's age. Her dark hair was pulled back in a classic bun, with tendrils curling down from her temples. The emerald sheath she wore was high-necked and knee length, with a deep slit up the back seam. Her bulging evening purse barely concealed her handgun.

Bruce smiled. From what he knew of Montoya, the slit skirt wasn't mandated by fashion. She was ready to chase down the bad guys, should any appear. He did have some questions about how far she'd get in those spike-heel shoes, but he'd heard she was tough. She'd probably run barefoot after any criminal fool enough to bring himself to her attention.

Allen and Montoya were among Gotham's finest police officers, handpicked by Gordon to be part of his newly created Major Crimes Unit. In a police force that was rife with corruption, the MCU cops were the exception: honest, hardworking, and intelligent. Montoya and Allen qualified on all counts.

The detectives wouldn't recognize him. Their interactions had only been with Batman. Bruce knew that while Montoya found Batman fascinating, Detective Allen distrusted everything about him.

His vigilante persona was definitely polarizing.

Allen and Montoya were doing their best to blend in— no doubt, as ordered—but their very watchfulness, the way they scanned the crowd with flat, suspicious eyes, screamed cop. They were here officially, then, placed among the partygoers in case of trouble. Some powerful people were unhappy that Teresa Williams's proposal was chosen over theirs. It didn't hurt to be careful.

Fleetingly, he wondered if his appearance here as Bruce Wayne was a bad idea, if he would be of more use outside, prowling the rooftops as Batman.

"How come you aren't gawking at Bruce Wayne, like every other woman in the room?" Allen asked Montoya, as they scanned the crowd. "Look at them! You can see their heads turn to watch him as he walks across the room."

"And some of the men's." Montoya shot her partner a look out of the corner of her eyes. "That's one of the things

I admire about you, Detective. Your keen powers of observation." She shrugged. "Word is, Wayne's a pretty decent
guy for a playboy billionaire. What's not to like?"

Allen shook his head. "Whatever's attracting them, it's
more than the money. He draws women like iron to a magnet."

Montoya laughed out loud. "You actually sound jealous!
Believe me, Cris—as an attractor, his billions don't hurt."
She changed the subject. "Too bad Gordon was called away
to deal with the Aparo Tower mess. I'm surprised we weren't
called in, as well."

"Azeveda and Hartley drew that one. Since it included
hoofing it up eighty stories, I'm happy to take a pass." He
sipped at the seltzer in his highball glass. "I know Gordon's
sorry to miss this, though. He's a big fan of Williams. I am,
too. I have a copy of *Death Grip* in my pocket." Montoya
looked confused. "Her most recent book, Montoya. Don't
you read? I wonder if she'd sign it. It's for my cousin."

"*Sure* it is." Montoya rolled her eyes. "I've never thought
you'd go *gaga* over a celebrity."

Allen scowled. "Cripes, Montoya, I'm not *gaga*. It's just
Vanessa—my cousin—grew up the next neighborhood over
from Hob's Oven. It wasn't as bad, but it was bad enough.
When Van was a kid, Teresa Williams was already making a
name for herself as an assistant DA. Van hero-worshipped
her from afar. Still does. That's why she became a lawyer. If
I get an autograph, I'll be in like Flynn with her . . . forever!"

They spotted the author crossing the room toward Bruce
Wayne. Her hands were outstretched. Her delight at seeing
Wayne was evident.

And he was smiling back just as warmly.

Allen and Montoya watched as she took Wayne's hands
in hers. He bent to kiss her cheek.

"Heck," Allen grumbled. "Even Teresa Williams has
fallen under the playboy spell."

Montoya smiled crookedly. "Maybe. But it looks to me
like the admiration's mutual."

5

Teresa Williams took a step back and smiled at Bruce appreciatively.

"My, my," she said, "I sure do like to see a handsome man dressed up in a tuxedo. If I was thirty years younger and fifty pounds lighter, I'd be throwing myself at you like all the other women you know."

Bruce smiled down at her with genuine affection. "Give it a try, Teresa. I just might let *you* catch me."

She laughed, a big hearty laugh. "Don't tempt me, son." She was a grandmotherly woman with skin the color of a café latte, heavy on the cream. Her salt-and-pepper hair was cut short and curled tightly against her head. Tonight, she wore a floor-length red silk gown and large gold hoop earrings.

She had grown up in Hob's Oven, but she'd been blessed with superior intelligence and good role models. She'd made it out of the slum, had gone to college on a full scholarship, and had become a lawyer, then a district attorney. Now, in retirement, she was the author of a string of best-selling novels set in Gotham, featuring police detective Luke Sharp and D.A. Roberta Chilton.

She also worked tirelessly to make Gotham a better place for everyone.

Given her history, she was a heroine to Gotham's poor and a particular favorite of Gotham's finest and the legal community.

"I wanted to thank you personally for your generous contribution to the cause. Your family has a long history in this town, and I know you take your philanthropic responsibilities seriously."

Bruce grinned down at her. "Don't tell anyone," he whispered. "Wouldn't want to spoil my frivolous image."

Cardinal O'Fallon, tall, lean, and austere, came up and apologized for breaking in. He dragged Teresa off to meet a wealthy admirer and potentially large contributor. As she turned to go, Bruce spotted the real estate mogul Ronald Marshall watching her like a predator as she walked across the room.

Marshall, a relatively new high-end developer with properties scattered the length of Gotham, had submitted a plan for the urban renewal of Hob's Oven. This included creating an upscale sports complex featuring a driving range and tennis courts. The complex would include costly high-rise co-ops that would take full advantage of the river view, even as it threw a shadow across lower Midtown. As a sop to the displaced residents of Hob's Oven, he had proposed a mission center to aid the homeless.

Marshall's proposal had lost out to Teresa Williams's, and he wasn't known for being a good loser. So what was he doing here, at a fund-raiser to ensure the success of his rival's plan?

Bruce wandered over to see if he could find out.

"How's it going, Ron? I didn't expect to see you here, of all places."

Ronald Marshall was a big, square man with a long nose that had been flattened years ago. His heavy jaw jutted forward, giving him an antagonistic bulldog appearance. His receding dark hair was a bit too long and slicked back from a sharp widow's peak. Bruce knew his usual dress preference ran to open shirts, displaying his chest hair and thick gold chains, but, in deference to the formality of the occasion, Marshall had squeezed into a tuxedo that was just a bit tight across his middle.

The woman on his arm was too young and too thin. Her strapless, low-cut top stretched enticingly across impressive breasts of the man-made variety. Her beaded bodice caught the light from the chandeliers. Diamonds and rubies glistened on her neck and sparkled in her ears. She smiled at Bruce, enticing and vacant-eyed.

Marshall didn't bother to introduce her—he obviously considered her arm candy, of less importance than the Rolex he wore on his wrist. He reached across her and snagged a canapé from a passing tray. "I've pledged a contribution to Teresa's Hob's Oven Restoration Fund. I'm a great admirer. Admirable woman, Teresa."

Bruce smiled. "That's very generous. I'd have thought you'd be annoyed . . ."

Marshall shrugged. "I'm a generous man. And a good loser." He smiled, exposing a gap between his front teeth. The expression didn't reach his eyes. "And it's not like I don't have other irons in the fire—"

There was a soft *pop!* A pane in one of the floor-to-ceiling windows shattered. Shards of glass hit the floor and scattered across the carpet.

Bruce whirled, scanning the room. He glanced at the window with its shattered pane of glass. Someone outside had fired a silenced rifle into the crowd. But fired at whom?

Around him, men and women in fancy dress gaped, eyes wide with shock.

A woman screamed.

A gore-spattered waiter dropped his tray. Champagne and glass crashed onto the carpet as the man crumpled sideways.

Had he been hit? Was he the target?

The crowd shifted and Bruce saw the body. Saw the tan-

gle of red silk, spilling like blood across the carpet. He
stepped closer.

Teresa Williams lay on the floor. There was a small
black hole in the center of her forehead. Blood and brains
spilled from the large exit wound at the back of her shattered skull. Her blood was already soaking into the Aubusson.

Someone—a high-powered surgeon at Gotham General
Hospital; Bruce remembered meeting the man—knelt beside her. He felt for a pulse, looked into her staring eyes.

"She was dead before she hit the floor," he said. "A wound
like that . . . there's nothing anyone could have done."

Everywhere Bruce looked, he saw faces pale with shock
and horror. But instinct prompted him to look back over his
shoulder, at Ronald Marshall. For a fleeting instant, Marshall glanced toward the window. One side of his slit of a
mouth quirked in a smirk of satisfaction. Then his lips turned
down, into a classic grimace of outraged sorrow.

Bruce glanced toward the floor where Teresa lay dead,
then up at the shattered windowpane. Quickly, he com-
puted the angle of entry. He glanced toward the brownstone
across the street. The sniper would have been up there, firing from the rooftop.

"Crap!" Detective Allen's eyes flashed from the fallen
Williams to the shattered window. They'd been prepared
for trouble, just not this kind of trouble. He reached for the
SIG-P226 in his shoulder holster.

Renee Montoya yanked her modified Glock 19 from her
evening bag. "How can this have happened?"

They raced from the room, weapons drawn.

Allen was ahead. Montoya was slowed down by the
high heels she was wearing. Cop shoes hadn't been appro-
priate with the emerald sheath. Not if she wanted to blend
in, as ordered.

She had her cell phone to her ear, calling in the disaster,
shouting for an ambulance over the rising noise in the

room behind her. Not that an ambulance would help Teresa
Williams.

"Secure the premises," she shouted to the uniforms
guarding the door. "Don't let anyone leave. This is a crime
scene."

She put through a call to Lieutenant Gordon as she
raced down the steps.

On the sidewalk, soft-news reporters were speaking on
camera, smugly aware that, for once, they were at the fore-
front of a breaking story.

Montoya heard them as background commentary. "A
bullet just shattered the window of the Historical Society
where the gala fund-raiser—"

The reporters spotted the two detectives and surged forward. A correspondent for the *Gotham Times* shoved a microphone into Montoya's face and shouted a question she
hardly heard. She shoved it back with an abrupt, "No comment," and raced after Allen.

As she crossed toward the brownstone, an ambulance
screamed up to the curb. GCPD cars turned onto the street,
their red and white lights flashing, reflections bouncing off
the buildings' facades.

At the top of the brownstone steps, Allen punched the
doorbell to the unlit building, shouting that he was the police and ordering the inhabitant to open up. When the door
stayed shut, he yelled that he was coming in.

With a single shove of his shoe, he kicked the door
open, setting a burglar alarm screeching.

Montoya rushed behind him into the foyer. She kicked
off her heels and raced after him, in stockinged feet, up the
stairs. She helped him pull down the access ladder and hurried after him up onto the roof.

The roof was empty. To the naked eye, at least, there
was no sign that anyone had ever been there.

Batman, once again in full armor, crouched on the roof
of the Gotham Historical Society. He watched and listened

through the night as GCPD forensic investigators sifted
through the evidence in the Teresa Williams murder.

Detectives Allen and Montoya, as primaries, had worked
beside the uniforms to take the statements of party attendees, caterers, and waitstaff. Now, they stood to one side of
the roof, watching as Forensics gathered their evidence.

Lieutenant Gordon arrived, looking tired and disheveled
after hours spent on the Tower. Eventually he went back
downstairs, leaving Allen and Montoya in charge.

Every half hour or so, a news chopper circled overhead,
and Batman melted deeper into the shadows. He eaves-
dropped shamelessly, using the high-gain microphones
embedded in his helmet. Not that he learned anything useful.

The owners of the brownstone were vacationing on Cape
Cod and weren't implicated in the shooting. The shooter,
apparently covered from head to toe, left no discernible
trace of his or her identity on the brownstone roof. Not a
fingerprint, not a hair, not even a flake of skin. Whoever it
was had even been careful enough to remove the spent cartridge. The only solid bit of evidence was the bullet that
ripped through Teresa Williams's skull and slammed into
the ballroom floor. None of the potential witnesses saw or
heard anything unusual.

Gordon's unit was outraged. Teresa Williams had been a
favorite of Gotham's cops. They would leave no stone un-
turned to catch the killer.

Montoya and Allen blamed themselves because the murder had happened on their watch.

It was nearly dawn when Detectives Montoya and Allen
abandoned the brownstone roof.

They walked dispiritedly down the stairs, then looked
out the front window of the brownstone. They stared in disgust at the three-ring circus set up outside. News vans lined
both sides of the street, totally ignoring parking regula-
tions. Camerapersons shined spotlights and shot footage.

Reporters camped out, waiting for information and primed for action.

Allen groaned. "I guess we're lucky the uniforms kept reporters from chasing us up the stairs and following us onto the roof."

Montoya bent and grabbed the shoes she had abandoned at the foot of the stairs. "We can't hide in here all night— not that much is left of it." She slipped on her heels. "Let's go, partner."

The detectives opened the door, stepped onto the small stoop, and walked down the stairs, past the uniforms keeping guard. The minute they stepped onto the sidewalk, they were mobbed.

"What did you find?"

"Who do you suspect?"

"How did you feel?"

"Was this murder committed by the Man in Black?"

Montoya and Allen put their heads down and plunged into the crowd of reporters. They chanted a duet of "No comment! No comment!" as they muscled their way through the mob and down the street toward their car.

"Your turn to drive," Montoya muttered.

They climbed into the unmarked, slammed the doors in the reporters' faces, and flicked the locks, then fastened their seat belts. All the while, cameramen leaned over the hood and shoved their cameras against the windows, trying for footage that would hold the fickle attention of the TV news audience.

Only when the car began to move, slowly but firmly, did the reporters back off and let them pull away from the curb.

The detectives drove several blocks in brooding silence.

Montoya sighed and looked over at Allen. "What do you think, Cris? Was the Man in Black—the guy from the Tower mess—responsible for this shooting?"

"My gut says no," Allen said. "Sounds like a different MO. I think it was a different guy."

"I think so, too. Jesus," Montoya said, rubbing her eyes

tiredly. "That poor woman. All the good she was trying to do . . . gone. And you never got her autograph."

"No," Allen said. "But we're gonna get the creep who killed her."

From the Historical Society's roof, Batman watched and listened.

He agreed with Allen and Montoya's assessment. The shooter probably wasn't Feely. Feely's MO was to use weapons of his own invention, preferably ones that exploded dramatically. And Feely was driven by greed and fear. The shooter hadn't tried to rob the partygoers at the fund-raiser. Teresa Williams was no threat to the shooter, who therefore had no reason to kill her.

Wrong guy, Batman thought. Not that logic would stop some of the media from linking the two events. No, Teresa Williams had been deliberately assassinated. And her assassin was a hired killer carrying out a professional hit. Someone entirely different from the Man in Black. Someone unknown, and, so far, untraceable.

Batman didn't know who actually pulled the trigger. But he thought he knew the name of the man who'd hired him. He just couldn't prove it.

At least, not yet.

Alfred's voice spoke into his earbud. "Sir, I think I may have traced the source of several of Feely's components."

"Excellent," Batman said. "What have you got?"

6

People were the life's blood of Gotham City. This was never more evident than in Midtown during rush hour on a hot summer evening.

Those ending their workday thronged the sidewalks, jaywalked through stalled traffic, hailed cabs, clambered down steep steps into the subways, and glided overhead on the newly restored monorails.

Street vendors lined the sidewalks, hawking cheap wares—baseball caps, T-shirts, jewelry, small appliances—displayed on rolled-out mats, merchandise almost all of which had "fallen off the back of a truck." Food carts squatted on corners, offering classics such as hot dogs, pretzels, and ice cream, as well as an astounding variety of ethnic snacks. Street musicians had their hats on the ground and their instruments wailing. Beggars held out their hands, importuning passersby. Pickpockets lifted wallets from the pockets of the unwary. A teenage girl on a skateboard was trying to blast through the crowd but wasn't making much headway.

Corner newsstands displayed today's newspapers. Headlines of the conservative *Gotham Times* were split between

the murder of Teresa Williams and the attempted robbery
at the Aparo Tower, which had been foiled by Batman.
Page one of the sensationalist *Gotham Gazette* screamed
"Man in Black Strikes . . . Then Strikes Again!" It featured
pictures of the destroyed elevator on the Tower roof and
Williams's covered corpse being wheeled on a gurney toward a waiting ambulance.

Batman crouched on the roof of a four-story converted
tenement in the shadow of the decorative false front that
enhanced its facade. Even in late afternoon, the asphalt
smelled of tar and retained much of the midday heat.

A trickle of sweat ran from beneath his mask and down
his cheek. *Maybe I should talk to Lucius about adding
cooling coils to the Batsuit,* he thought.

He snorted, not believing he'd even thought such a thing.
Rā's al Ghūl, his old mentor and deadly enemy, would have
been appalled. Rā's was all about working through heat and
cold, through pain and fear, to attain an objective.

It was a search for self-mastery that Bruce himself had
embarked upon long before he'd met Rā's. And until Rā's
had found him in a Chinese cell on the Tibet border, that
search had been only partially successfull.

In his mountaintop hideout in the no-man's-land be-
tween China and Tibet, Rā's had honed Bruce, had trained
his body and toughened his resolve. But long before that,
Alfred had nurtured his spirit and taught him the importance of ethics and personal responsibility. Lucius Fox, a
recent addition to his support system, had supplied the state-
of-the-art Batsuit and most of the rest of the high-tech wiz-
ardry Batman had needed to reach his goal.

Rā's al Ghūl had seen Gotham as a latter-day version of
the biblical Sodom and Gomorrah. He had tried to get
his star pupil to help him destroy it, as a symbol of con-
temporary corruption and decadence, and as a way to

introduce Rā's's own vision of justice and order to the modern world.

As Batman, he had understood Rā's al Ghūl's agenda and thwarted Rā's's plan.

He felt a personal responsibility to the people of Gotham. His aim was to remove the criminal element that was undermining their city. If necessary, he would do it one wrongdoer at a time. He wasn't judge, jury, or executioner. He didn't kill. To the extent that he was able, he worked within the law.

And, in a strange way, he was grateful to the much more ruthless Rā's, who had helped him realize his destiny. He understood, now, as he surveyed the city of Gotham lying before him, that he would never be a man of peace, a living embodiment of the Way. He was a warrior; it was his karma. Even if he *did* feel the seduction of air-conditioning.

By such roundabout means did he come to be crouching on the roof of a 150-year-old building, sweltering in Neoprene and Kevlar, awaiting the arrival of a flying Man in Black.

This area of Downtown, southwest of Port Adams, was one of the oldest parts of the city. Its narrow streets had originated as twisted lanes, and before that had probably been deer trails. At present, it featured a mishmash of architectural styles, from brick-faced converted tenements to grand edifices of glass and steel that would have pleased Mies van der Rohe. To the west lay Cathedral Square, Gotham's government buildings, the courthouse, and the headquarters of the GCPD.

Across the street, to the south, a six-story Gothic-style office building, constructed during the gaslight era and decorated with gargoyles, was crammed against a row of brownstones—most of them mixed-use, with shops on the ground floor and apartments and businesses above. The streetlights were decorative wrought-iron affairs that echoed the long-departed era of gaslight above horses and carriages.

The brownstones continued for another block.

The block beyond held a crumbling warehouse slated for demolition to make way for a gleaming skyscraper. A sign proclaimed it was a Ronald Marshall project . . . just one of the many "irons in the fire" of which the builder had spoken.

Beyond that, the East Side Expressway swept past old, tumbled-down wooden docks that had been abandoned when the Port Adams area was refurbished.

And from the docks to the horizon lay the Atlantic Ocean.

Below, the rumble and beep of bumper-to-bumper traffic quieted. The rush-hour bustle began to fade. In the distance, the ocean sparkled as choppy waves caught the rays of the setting sun.

Still, Batman crouched in the shadows and watched and waited.

Last night, Feely had lost both his blasters in their confrontation at the Tower. One gun was in police hands. Alfred had dismantled the other into its component parts. In order to pull off another robbery, Feely would need to rebuild his cache of weapons. Which meant he'd need more parts. Which he couldn't afford to buy since his recent attempt to secure funds had been thwarted.

Knowing Feely's convoluted logic, obsession, and limited resources, Batman thought he'd try to steal the parts he needed. So he waited patiently, watching the little shop across the street.

It was in a small, one-story building. Its grimy front picture window was crammed with sparkly gewgaws, antique clothing on mannequins that had been out-of-date when Nixon was president, and fake brand-name watches. The shop sported a tattered maroon awning. Faded letters whispered the shop's name—CHARLIE'S NOSTALGIA AND POTPOURRI.

As far as Alfred had been able to determine—through a meticulous search of city records, building plans, code-violation citations, and, possibly, direct observation—there hadn't been a Charlie in the store for as long as records had been kept in the city's archives. Gautier de Villiers, a French expatriate, sat behind the counter. The store looked like any other cheap tourist trap, shabbier than most. In fact, there was very little in the way of munitions and high explosives that an interested party couldn't obtain there. For the right price.

Batman hadn't yet been able to track down the chain of command behind Charlie's. That day would come. But tonight, it was the likeliest place in Gotham where Feely might come to find the sort of armor-piercing shells that Batman felt sure he would now be looking for.

Batman's perch across the street gave him a view of the street and a direct line of sight into a side alley barely wide enough for a van to enter. The side door, toward the rear of the building, gave access to the real goods that Charlie's had to sell.

Batman knew that a lot of people, like the kid on the roof of the Tower, thought his life was a string of exciting smackdowns with evildoers. But the bulk of his activity involved meticulous research and hours of waiting, followed by short spurts of violence and danger. Mostly he waited, and waiting gave him time to think.

He considered what to do about Teresa Williams's murder. It smelled strongly of a professional hit. The sniper had done his job cleanly, efficiently, and then disappeared without a trace. There were few such killings in Gotham.

Gordon would have cops searching the International Crimes Database for similar incidents. Batman would have Alfred follow that route as well. Maybe it would lead to a break. Sometime, somewhere else, the sniper might have made a mistake.

That was one way to come at the problem. But Batman

thought he'd try another angle as well. Because he'd seen the brief smirk of satisfaction on Ronald Marshall's face after the sniper had struck.

All of Gotham knew Marshall was dirty. He'd been buying politicians, bribing judges, and greasing the palms of city officials for the last thirty years. But these were white-collar crimes, barely noticeable in the turmoil of rising violence that threatened to overwhelm the city.

Batman had planned to go after Marshall and his ilk eventually. After he dealt with the havoc created by the outbreak from Arkham Asylum. And the burgeoning mob war for control of Gotham that was beginning to erupt following the removal of Carmine Falcone as Gotham's underworld boss.

But, with that fleeting smile and the violent death of his old friend, Ronald Marshall had moved himself into one of the Top Three spots on Batman's takedown list.

A clock in a nearby tower struck eight.

The sun was sinking in the west, lighting the tops of Gotham's spires and throwing its canyon streets into dense shadow.

There was the smell of the sea in the gust of wind that stirred Batman's cape.

Lamps began to shine in apartment windows. Streetlights blinked on, casting a yellowish glow that did little to dispel the creeping gloom.

The hawkers of cheap goods rolled up their sidewalk mats. The last food vendor wheeled his cart onto the truck that would take it to an overnight storage facility and hurried down the street toward the subway entrance. Occasionally shoppers bustled in and out of neighborhood stores, but a pedestrian could walk down the sidewalk in a straight line.

The teenage girl on the skateboard was back, able now to blast along the sidewalk at a good clip, grooving to the music that her iPod pumped into her ears. Her hair, pulled into stiff ponytails, was bouncing to a hip-hop beat. From his hidden position, Batman could feel the bass notes through his mask. *She'll have a 40 percent hearing loss by the time she's thirty if she keeps that up,* he thought.

A beat cop stepped from the door of the brightly lit deli next to Charlie's, and she swerved to avoid a collision. The forward wheels of her skateboard caught in a hole in the sidewalk, and the board lurched to an abrupt stop and tipped sideways. Thrown off balance, she pitched onto her hands and knees.

"Ow! Darn!" She looked at her skinned palms, then up at the cop, who was scowling down at her. "Officer O'Hara! Sorry."

"Let that be a lesson ta ya, Meesh-girl," he said. "Don't let me catch ya not wearin' a helmet next time!"

A hint of movement—a darker shadow creeping through the darkness in the alley across the street—drew Batman's attention away from the cop and kid and back to Charlie's. He flipped down the night-vision lenses in his cowl, leaned forward carefully, and peered across the street.

Feely, dressed in his black-rubber suit, was working frantically, trying to open the shop door with some kind of high-tech picklock. It obviously wasn't working, and his frustration level was rising.

With a muttered curse, he flung the pick aside, pulled a marble-sized ball from his utility belt, and stuffed it into the lock.

It flared, sizzled . . . then exploded.

Feely went flying backward, knocked on his ass by the force of the detonation. "Whoa! Too much juice in that puppy," he muttered.

Across the street, Batman leapt to his feet. There was a hole in the side wall—four feet across—where the door used to be. *So that's how he took out the Tower elevators,* he thought. He'd been wondering.

An alarm howled, shrill and loud, from inside the shop.

Batman raised his grapple gun, sighted at the exterior fire

escape zigzagging down the side wall of the building next to Charlie's, and pulled the trigger. An expandable hook, attached to a strong monofilament, shot from the grapple gun's mouth. Batman hit a switch, the monofilament locked, and string tugged as the hook caught in an upper riser.

He hit another switch, and the monofilament rewound silently, dragging him upward, off the street and up the side of the building. He swung across the street on the monofilament and lowered himself silently onto the roof of Charlie's shop. He hit another control, released the grapple, and retracted it back into the grapple gun.

Below him, Officer O'Hara raced down the sidewalk, past Charlie's, and into the alley, trying simultaneously to turn on his flashlight and draw his gun. Feely struggled to his feet. O'Hara identified himself as a policeman and ordered the dark shape before him to halt and raise his hands.

Crouching, Feely lifted his arms high in the air.

Batman smiled grimly. Maybe, this time, he wouldn't need to make the arrest. Maybe O'Hara could manage it.

The flashlight flicked on. Its beam caught the black, misshapen, almost demonic-looking figure in its glare. Its goggles caught the light and reflected it back, like two glowing eyes.

The policeman's jaw dropped. "What the . . . ?"

The girl with the ponytails—Meesh—had raced after the cop to the mouth of the alley. She gaped at the rubber-clad figure.

"Smokin'!" she said, over the blare of the alarm. "It's the guy from the news—the Man in Black!"

Taking advantage of the cop's momentary shock, Feely dropped a hand over his back and flicked the ignition switch of his jet pack. Flames belched from the exhaust, and he roared skyward.

When he reached rooftop height, Batman dove off the roof's edge and grabbed him around the knees in a classic tackle, diving low to avoid the flames belching from the jet. His Batsuit was fireproof, but he didn't want to test it unnecessarily.

Batman's weight, added to Feely's, was more than the small engine could handle. It coughed and wheezed and, slowly, Feely and Batman sank toward the ground.

Feely struggled and kicked, trying to free himself. Batman could feel his grip on the man's legs slipping. The black suit looked and smelled like it was made of rubber, but it was slick, as if it had been coated with some kind of grease. The more Feely shouted and wiggled, the farther Batman slid downward. He imagined it was like trying to hold on to a greased pig.

Feely wrenched free a foot and stomped down hard on Batman's shoulder. Batman slid down even farther. Another kick, and he was falling toward the ground.

He landed in a crouch and looked up. Feely was hovering fifteen feet above him.

The cop aimed his Glock at the hovering Man in Black and squeezed off six rounds.

Blam! Blam! Blam! Blam! Blam! Blam!

The bullets whizzed past Feely's head and recoiled off the walls of the alley. A ricochet struck the jet pack a glancing blow. Its roar became a coughing whine.

Batman saw Feely reach into his utility belt and scoop out more of his explosive capsules. He tossed them toward the cop—smaller pellets this time, close to the size of peas.

"Get down!" Batman threw himself on O'Hara, sending him sprawling on the ground. He lay on top of the policeman, protecting him with his armored body as the pellets exploded around them, blowing small craters in the concrete ground of the alley, sending shards into the air, shocking their senses with a fusillade of light and sound.

Batman looked up. Through the dying barrage, he saw Feely swoop toward the young skateboarder, who stood shocked and staring at the mouth of the alley.

She turned and ran.

Batman and the cop leapt to their feet and chased after them. The girl blundered out into the street, trying to get away. Traffic was light and moving fast. A car slammed on its brakes to avoid hitting the girl, and a taxi, following too closely, rammed it from behind with a loud *wham!*

The Man in Black jetted after the fleeing girl. He grabbed her around her waist. She dropped her skateboard and screamed as the criminal dragged her into the air.

The cop braced himself against the alley wall and raised his Glock in a double-handed stance, ready to get off a few more rounds.

"Wait!" Batman grabbed the cop's hands and shoved the barrel down as Feely whirled in midair. He was facing them, holding the girl in front of him, using her body as a shield.

"Drop your gun!" Feely shouted over the coughing whine of his damaged jet pack and the shrill blare of the burglar alarm. "And you!" He raised one arm and pointed at Batman. "You keep away from me. Don't try to follow, or I'll blow the kid to smithereens."

The driver and cabbie climbed from their wrecked cars and gaped up at the flying man and his hostage. Customers gathered at the doors of ground-floor shops. Apartment dwellers hung out of windows, drawn to them by the noise.

The Man in Black thumbed a control. His jet pack coughed, spitting out a large gout of flame. Accompanied by a clattering, ear-shattering roar, he rose jerkily into the air, dragging the girl with him.

Batman dashed into the street, staring up after them.

The kid's eyes were wide with fright, and her mouth was open in a silent scream. She was a skinny little thing, weighing less than a hundred pounds. Heavy enough to slow Feely's rise, but not heavy enough to ground him—a lightweight compared to Batman in his body armor.

Even though the jet pack was damaged, Feely was climbing, his arms clamped around the girl's waist, holding her hostage. But his black suit was slick, and Batman feared Feely's upper-body strength wouldn't be up to the task of keeping her there for long.

He saw Feely's arms already starting to unbend as muscle fatigue began to set in. Feely shifted his hold, trying to ease his cramping muscles and get a better grip.

His jet pack sputtered and lurched. The girl shrieked as she slipped down farther. She grabbed on to Feely's arms, trying to keep herself from plummeting to the ground.

"Give it up, Feely. Put the girl down," Batman shouted. "That jet pack isn't powerful enough to carry the two of you."

"Keep away," Feely shrieked. "Don't follow me, or I'll drop her!"

He's going to drop her anyway, Batman thought. Feely's voice, muffled by the rubber covering his mouth, was already thready with the strain of holding the girl. Then he dropped one of his arms and began to fumble in his utility belt for more of his explosive capsules.

Feely hurled a handful of pellets down at Batman. Batman dove and rolled across the street toward the gargoyle-covered apartment building, trying to look like a man who was in a panic to escape. As he rolled, he reached into his own utility belt, pulled out a few smoke pellets, and tossed them into the middle of Feely's latest barrage.

Dense smoke filled the street along with light and noise. It billowed upward in a thick cloud, enveloping the Man in Black and his helpless hostage.

In a move made fluid by hours of practice, Batman pulled his grapple gun from his utility belt, aimed it upward, where he knew a stone gargoyle leered from a decorative ledge, and squeezed the trigger. The grapple hook flew upward, caught in a crevice where the gargoyle's wing met the wall, and locked.

He retracted the monofilament and flew upward, off the street and up the side of the building. When he was above the smoke, he stopped his upward momentum, dropped onto a narrow ledge, and retrieved the grapple.

He could hear Feely's angry shout and the coughing roar of his jet pack as it struggled to rise above the smoke.

A gust of wind cleared the smoke. He could see Feely, about ten feet below. His back was to Batman, and it looked as though he was trying to peer down over the girl's head to see where Batman had gone.

"I guess I took care of him," Feely chortled. "Blew him up! Blew him to smithereens!"

"Then . . . then . . . put me down! You don't need me anymore!" The girl was pleading with him, tears rolling down her cheeks. "Please! I don't want to fall! I don't want to die."

Feely ignored her entreaty. His jet pack spouted a gout of brighter flame and they lurched upward. The child shrieked as she began to slip free from his grasp. She screamed, a thin, desperate howl of horror.

Batman leapt into midair at the rising Feely. He twisted sideways and grabbed the girl as she slid from Feely's slippery arms. Together, the girl and Batman began to fall.

With the touch of a control stud, his cape stiffened and became a glider, and he swept toward the street with the terrified girl in his arms. He touched down in the middle of the intersection, near the wrecked cars and the cratered macadam, and put her gently on the ground.

"Thanks!" She sniffed and swiped at her eyes with the back of her hand. Then she looked up at him and smiled crookedly, trying for cocky bravado. "Wait till I tell my friends. Glad I have all these witnesses; otherwise, nobody'd believe me. Wow! Batman! Thanks."

Batman flashed what he hoped was a reassuring smile. "It was my pleasure."

He glanced toward the mouth of the alley, where Officer O'Hara was on his cell phone, looking up as he called in the details of the incident. In the background, the alarm from Charlie's Nostalgia and Potpourri was still blaring. Adding to the noise was the distant *whoop-whoop* of approaching cop-car sirens.

Batman looked skyward. The Man in Black had disappeared. Again.

7

Batman raised an arm and sighted the grapple gun at the roof of a nearby brownstone and fired. The hook caught on the raised ledge. He activated the retractor and was hauled upward once more.

He pulled himself up over the edge and onto the asphalt roof. He kicked in his amplifiers and stood listening, trying to hear the telltale rumble of Feely's jet pack over the noise from the street below. There! Four o'clock! The once-ominous roar of the jet engine had become a whine interspersed with a coughing sputter. He squinted southeast and spotted a flicker of flames dancing unsteadily above the roofline.

He raced across the blacktop, vaulted a wall, sailed over an alleyway, and landed on the roof of the next building. When fully fueled and undamaged, the jet pack was powerful, but its compact shape meant a small fuel reservoir. Batman hoped some of the sputtering meant that Feely was running out of gas. He just might catch him this time.

The Man in Black looked back and cursed. Batman's cape had flared out behind him, and its shape was silhouetted against the lit skyscrapers of Gotham. He jabbed at his controls. The jet pack's flame flared, bigger and brighter, and its motor whined louder as he pushed its failing engine to the limit. He zoomed over a narrow street and over another block of tenements, slammed one against the other. His jet engine was choking now. Batman followed, but more slowly.

The Man in Black stood on the edge of a brownstone roof, then launched himself over a final avenue.

From the shadows beneath an old water tower, Batman watched as Feely cleared the street, lined with parked cars but nearly devoid of pedestrians. He sank, lurched roughly over a chain-link fence topped with razor wire, and hovered noisily above the roof of the crumbling warehouse slated for demolition. He whirled around and stared into the darkness behind him.

Batman slipped deeper into shadow. Instinct told him that Feely had been moving purposefully—that he had a plan. Batman bet that plan involved going to ground in some dark hole where Batman would no longer be able to find him. He wanted to lull Feely into a sense of false security, give him the impression that he had outrun his enemy.

His ploy worked. Feely powered down the jet pack and landed on the roof with an audible thump. He trotted across the crumbling surface, not completely at ease, but comfortable enough to give his struggling engine a rest.

Batman didn't want to spook Feely again. If he wanted a quick capture, his best bet was stealth.

Silently, he climbed the rusted ladder that led to the top of the water tower. From this higher vantage point, he could study the warehouse. The roof was flat, with very little cover. The only possibilities for concealment were the large signs decorating each corner that proclaimed in huge letters that this was a RONALD MARSHALL CONSTRUCTION PROJECT, with demolition to begin this month. Beyond the warehouse, traffic rumbled steadily along the East Side Expressway. The derelict waterfront lay shrouded in darkness on the other side of the highway.

This close to the ocean, there was often a stiff breeze.

Batman waited for a particularly strong gust, activated the glider function in his cape, and felt himself lifted on the wind like a kite. Blocked from Feely's vision by one of Marshall's large signs, he sailed across the quiet avenue, above the chain-link fence and razor wire, and dropped into the shadows beneath the sign.

Batman flipped down his night-vision lenses and scanned the yard, looking for Feely. At first he didn't see him. But even dressed in black in the shadows, he ought to show up. Had he lost him?

A moment later, there was the faint sound of metal on metal in the farthest corner of the warehouse roof, beneath another large Marshall sign. Feely was crouching there, almost hidden, as he fumbled with a large roof-access hatch.

Batman frowned. *So Feely's been hiding on Marshall's property.* Unlikely as it seemed, maybe Ronald Marshall *had* hired the Man in Black to kill Teresa Williams. That bizarre possibility made it all the more essential that Batman bring him in now.

A gust of wind lifted the edge of Batman's cape and set it snapping in the breeze. Feely's head whipped around, looking toward the place where Batman was hiding. Too late, Batman hauled down his cape.

Feely jumped to his feet, leapt to the edge of the roof, and activated his jet pack. The motor choked and died.

Abandoning all further attempt at stealth, Batman raced toward him. He had almost reached Feely when the motor wheezed on, flame coughed from the engine, and, once again, the Man in Black shot out of Batman's reach.

Batman watched him fly above the eight lanes of high-speed traffic. No one seemed to notice the goggle-wearing *Flash Gordon* reject sputtering overhead.

This part of the highway was elevated and reached nearly as high as the roof of the warehouse. Beyond the far railings, it was a sheer drop of forty feet to the ground below. Cut off by the highway from the rest of Downtown, the waterfront was a narrow, blighted shoreline where homeless squatters

camped unmolested beneath the shelter of the overpass.
Gentrification was a long way from Kane's Quays.

Batman watched in growing frustration as the flame
from Feely's jet sank lower, and the engine's sputter faded
to a high-pitched whine. Slowly, inelegantly, Feely lurched
downward and out of sight.

There was no way he was letting Feely escape, not when
he'd come this close to nabbing him.

The wind was coming in, hard and stiff off the Atlantic.
The highway was wide, but Batman thought, if his luck
held, he could make it across. Once again he activated the
glider mechanism in his cape.

It stiffened, caught the wind. He pulled the grapple gun
from his belt and held it at the ready, just in case. He retracted the night-vision lenses.

A few quick steps, and Batman launched himself from
the warehouse roof, out over cars, trucks, and cabs that ignored the speed limit, cut one another off, and angled ruth-
lessly to be first off at the next exit. The streets of Downtown
might be empty of pedestrian traffic, but the expressway
was never quiet. The air was thick with the smell of diesel
exhaust and the blare of horns.

He had made it across six lanes when the wind died, and
he began to plummet like a falling kite.

Cars swerved below him. Horns blared. No one slowed.
In the distance, sirens wailed.

He landed jarringly in a crouch atop the semitrailer of
an eighteen-wheeler, toppled sideways, and nearly rolled
off the back of the semi into the fast-moving traffic. He
caught the edge of a vertical door bolt with the fingertips
of his left hand, and for an instant hung suspended. Almost
casually, Batman fired his grapple gun at a passing streetlight. The hook shot through the air and caught on an upper
crossbar. He squeezed the trigger, and the line retracted,
pulling him off the back of the semi and up over the roadway. He let his momentum carry him up, then out and over
the edge of the overpass. Then he lowered himself on the

end of his monofilament like a spider at the end of a thread of webbing.

Behind the semi in a BMW, Vivian Carpenter, on her way home from a long, long day at the office and a stopover at happy hour, swore she would never, ever touch a drop of liquor again before making the drive back to the 'burbs.

Batman dropped into the shadows and stood quietly, looking out over the water and listening, as his eyes adjusted to the relative darkness. The docks were alternately bathed in light and shrouded in shadow as the headlights overhead flashed past. The strobe effect made it difficult to make out more than the general outlines of things.

Traffic overhead was a constant rumble, interspersed with blaring horns and sounding sirens. Ahead of him, waves slapped against the crumbling remains of old wooden piers, made useless by the advent of the bright, new commercial docks plying their international trade at Port Adams and the Tricorner Yards. A wrecked car lay half submerged in the water, rusted and forgotten. The air stank of dead fish and seaweed, of urine and urban decay. Rats and feral cats slunk through the piles of refuse that accumulated on the shore.

Off to the right was the bridge that led to Blackgate Island, the state prison that housed the merely criminal.

Beyond Blackgate, he spotted a gleaming forty-foot yacht. He recognized the sleek lines of the *Amalfi*. It belonged to the old-line mobster, Sal Maroni, one of the combatants in the war for control of the departed Carmine Falcone's territory. A thug called "the Russian" and Maroni were working up to a bloody combat that could rip the city apart.

Preventing that war was a priority, but it was a problem for another day.

Batman turned and studied the thick footings that supported the massive overpass. With a sense of surprise, he realized that the ground beneath the great girders and massive supports for the expressway was empty, devoid of activity. On any given night, there were always a few homeless souls huddled around a campfire, sharing a bottle of forget-fulness. Tonight, there were no fires, no huddled forms, no life.

A loud roar sounded above him as two or three semis thundered past *en echelon*. His attention caught by the sound, Batman gazed upward at the massive iron girders that supported that amazing span of road, thinking how incredible it was that, even among the madness and corruption that Gotham sometimes seemed to embody, collaborative feats like this highway were somehow possible.

On the overpass, the sirens were getting louder. Cop cars, fire engines, *and* ambulances. Batman glanced up, momentarily distracted, as Kojak bars threw flashing lights onto the nearby water. Something big was happening. He thought about tuning in to the police emergency bands, then discarded the notion. One crisis at a time. And it sounded like the city had expended enough manpower to get the problem under control.

Something slammed into him with concussive force, blasting him back off his feet, engulfing him in flames. Another of Feely's firebombs. A big one. This was getting old.

Of course. The shadows directly beneath the overhanging highway. The perfect hiding place for a guy with a jet pack. Batman spun to his feet, fired his grapple gun, and, with a *whirr*, soared up into the I-beams. Another explosion erupted exactly where he had been standing only a moment before.

By its light, he saw Feely crouched on an I-beam above him, half hidden behind a support column. He was trying desperately to activate his jet pack. It coughed . . . and died.

Batman dropped onto an I-beam below and across from Feely, retracted his grapple, and stood for a moment, looking up at him. Then he began to walk across the girder, as Rā's al Ghūl had taught him, balance perfect, as casually as if he were strolling through the park on a summer's day. His cape flared out to his left. He knew that, in what was left of the firelight from the explosions, he looked like a demon from Hell.

Feely tried to scramble away from him but, overbal-anced by the weight of the jet pack, lost his equilibrium and fell sideways onto the beam. He tried to grab for the support but missed the handhold. In his slippery suit, he slid like a puck on ice. Feely grabbed the flange of the girder and hung there, dangling by his arms, forty feet above the ground, screaming for help.

Batman walked across the beam until he was right below.

Casually, he reached up, flicked open the latch that locked Feely's utility belt around his waist, and let it plummet to the ground. He didn't want to chance Feely's pulling out any more explosive pellets while he was trying to save his life.

He fired the grapple, lodged it in one of the upper rows of girders, and swung up beside Feely. He grabbed Feely around his waist, then lowered them both quickly to the ground before he could lose his grip on the slippery Man in Black.

As they reached the ground, Feely began to struggle in earnest, trying to worm his way free. Batman gave the back of Feely's head a short, sharp rap with his forearm. Feely dropped face forward onto the ground as though he'd been piked.

Batman knelt with one knee on the still-smoking jet pack, pinning the erstwhile criminal while he felt for the seam that attached Feely's mask to the body of his costume. He yanked at the seam. With a tear, the mask came loose. It had been held on by Velcro.

Batman tossed the mask aside. Beneath it, Jacob Feely's hair was lank and greasy, and his face was long, rodentlike, and pale.

"Why did you kill Teresa Williams?" Batman growled.

Feely looked at him for a long moment, then broke into a gale of laughter. "Who?" he said. "Ha! Never heard of her. You can't pin a single murder on me this time. I didn't kill *anybody*."

"Not for want of trying," Batman said. "Why the weird getup, Feely? I know you like explosions and blowing things up, but you didn't used to dress in black to do it." He found the seams on Feely's gloves and yanked them off as well. "Why do it this way? Why become the Man in Black?"

"Don't *you* know?" Feely said with a sly smile. His eyes didn't seem quite focused. "After all, *you* did it. You put on a mask and black suit and a utility belt and you hide in the night. You can fly. You throw bat-shaped knives and things that explode and make billows of smoke. That was a good one, by the way. You had me fooled, but I was distracted by the girl. And your suit is really armored. Nice touch. I'll be ready for that next time. But best of all, you scare the hell out of people! It's so cool!

"But I went one better, didn't I? My suit is slippery. I invented it. *My* design! Mine! I'm glad *you* caught me instead of some corrupt cop. You'll guard my suit. You won't steal it! You'll keep it safe . . . till I come back. And my jet pack, too. I got the idea from the old movie serials. It means I can fly anywhere . . . and do anything!"

Batman cuffed Feely's hands—those of a brilliantly inventive madman—behind his back, and sighed.

"Not anymore."

As he yanked Feely to his feet, Batman could hear Jim Gordon's measured tones in his head. Gordon had once told him that there was lots of weirdness out there, and that a violent and dramatic response could easily cause an answering escalation in drama and violence.

He sighed again. It looked like Gordon was right. But all he could do was help put the bad guys behind bars.

One at a time.

He didn't know how else to even begin to fix the problem . . .

8

Montoya and Allen's unmarked screamed up the East Side Highway, following a squad of black-and-whites with sirens wailing and beacons flashing. Montoya was at the wheel—her turn to drive. She swung into the right lane, cutting off a semi jockeying for the exit.

The trucker laid on his horn.

"Christ, Renee!" Allen yelped, as they turned onto the off-ramp on two wheels. "I know we're in a hurry, but we won't do much good in Little Roma if we're dead."

"Chicken!" Montoya swung left with authority and turned down a narrow street leading toward Infantino. She reached over and flipped the switch activating the Crown Victoria's flashing headlamps and its red beacons in the rear window. Allen glanced right as a light pole zipped past in a blur. He wondered briefly just how long it had been since he'd been to church.

The detectives had been doing follow-up interviews with potential witnesses in the Teresa Williams murder when the call came in that gangbangers were shooting up Little Roma. Two people were dead, and a uniform was down. Montoya and Allen were part of the cavalry, riding to the rescue.

"Might as well be of some use to someone," Allen muttered. "We sure weren't having much luck back there."

Montoya snorted in agreement. "Nobody saw anything. Nobody heard anything. Nobody's saying anything. Like the three wise monkeys. And they could all be lying. But I think, this time, they're telling the truth. It's like the gunman didn't exist . . ."

"Except imaginary gunmen don't blow people away."

They screeched to a halt behind a jumble of GCPD black-and-whites and Gotham General ambulances parked randomly across the pavement and halfway onto the sidewalks, blocking the narrow street.

As they leapt from the car, Detective Allen drew his SIG from his shoulder harness. His shirt was starched, his trousers were pressed, and his jacket fit impeccably. The lines of his suit improved slightly without the pistol in its shoulder holster.

Montoya pulled her Glock from the holster she wore at her waist. She was dressed for action, now, in jeans, a T-shirt, and a leather jacket. And—thankfully!—sensible cop shoes. Her ID badge hung from a chain around her neck, and her long, dark hair was pulled off her face and looped into a loose bun. She wasn't dressed up to Cris's high standards of sartorial splendor—he thought a detective should look the part as if that part were the lead role in *Law & Order*—but at least she could move without falling on her face.

There was a final barrage—*rat-a-tat-tat*—and the gunfire ceased. Other noises continued. The wail of sirens, the screech of car alarms, the shouts of cops, firemen, and EMTs. The cries of the injured. The frantic barking of dogs. The buzz of voices. And somewhere, of course, there was the distant sound of breaking glass. There was *always* breaking glass.

Allen and Montoya crept through the maze of cop cars and emergency-response vehicles, guns drawn, crouching low. When the weapons fire didn't start up again, they stood upright.

The air smelled of Italian food and baked goods, overlaid with the heavy scent of burning building. At the far end of the block, dense smoke billowed from a smashed storefront window.

EMTs rushed toward them. The detectives stepped aside to let the medics and their clattering gurneys roll past. They reholstered their weapons as they looked around.

Flashing their badges, the pair pushed through to the cordon cops had thrown up around Infantino Avenue to hold back news crews and gawkers, who seemed intent on becoming a part of the action.

The neighborhood was an old one. The street was lined with square prewar six-story apartment buildings and converted tenements. The buildings were shoved together, cheek by jowl, with an occasional narrow alley slicing between them. The ground floors housed the businesses—restaurants, cheese shops, and bakeries—for which Little Roma was justly famous.

Tables and chairs, set out on the sidewalks for alfresco dining, lay on their sides, overturned in the diners' mad rush to escape the hail of gunfire. Spilled food, broken glass, and shattered crockery littered the pavement.

"I ate there just last week. Best *pollo alla scarpariello* in Gotham," Allen said, nodding toward a building painted in horizontal stripes of green, white, and red, like the Italian flag. A sign read GIORDANO'S EST. 1915. Waitstaff huddled behind the white-haired owner, peering with scared faces through the remains of a shattered plate-glass window. The *patron* himself stood erect under a shock of white hair, not giving an inch before whatever disaster had befallen his beloved restaurant. "Old man Giordano's a decent guy. Why would anybody shoot up Giordano's?"

They stared down a street that looked like a war zone. Windows in restaurants and shops were smashed. Vehicles parked in metered slots were riddled with bullet holes. Car alarms screeched. Fire alarms wailed. Cops were fanning out through the area, and Allen could see a SWAT team in body armor disappearing down an alley at the far end of the block. Firemen muscled a thick hose toward a fireplug. The building pouring smoke was a bakery. EMTs were lifting a body onto a gurney. Allen couldn't tell if the person was dead or alive.

"Giordano's isn't the only casualty . . . and it's not the worst," Montoya said. "What I want to know is why would anybody be that stupid? Most of the mob may have moved their families to the suburbs, but they still have business interests here. Especially money laundering. The gangbangers who did this bought themselves a world of trouble."

She glanced at the upper floors above the shops. Fire escapes zigzagged down the front of the buildings in filigrees of steel. Mostly apartments, she thought, filled with mostly innocent tenants who, up until now, thought they lived in a very safe neighborhood. Up until now, they had been right. Now, they were behaving like big-city tenants everywhere—peering through opened windows and climbing out onto the small balcony-like landings, discussing the gunfight in hushed, shocked tones, heedless of the notion that the presence of the cops didn't necessarily mean the action was over. And that any ricochet might have their name on it.

As Montoya and Allen approached, they could hear above the wail of sirens a woman weeping.

EMTs rolled a gurney carrying an older, overweight cop with a bristling gray mustache toward an ambulance. The cop was pale and sweating, his shoulder bloody and roughly bandaged. His partner, a younger, fair-haired uniform, was trotting beside him, equally pale.

"What happened here?" Allen asked the partner.

The young uniform stopped for a moment. "Firefight broke out. We were in the neighborhood when the call came in. First on the scene. We heard the gunshots . . . Then we were in the middle of it. Frank—" He broke off, distracted, looking after his partner.

"Any idea who was doing the shooting? What the fight was about?"

"Several of the combatants are down. Guess you can ask them . . . if they're still alive." The young cop nodded down the street, where a medic was crouched beside a kid in his late teens wearing a red do-rag. "Gotta go." He turned and trotted after the gurney.

Allen and Montoya stepped over to the kid. Under the do-rag, his hair was dark and straight. His race appeared to be indeterminate, and his skin was gray with loss of blood. He wore a black sleeveless T-shirt, fatigues, and army boots. A tattoo of a spider covered his right biceps. His pistol lay on the asphalt beside him.

"He's an *Arana*—a Dominican gang. Call themselves the Spiders because they claim a large web of associates around New England. I ran across them once. Gun's a Makarov PMM semiautomatic—Russian-made."

"Over here," Montoya called.

She bent over another of the fallen gangbangers. Late teens, heavy-boned, very dark skin, head wrapped in a green do-rag. A wavy, snakelike raised scar wound around the knuckles of his right hand.

"This guy's one of the *Vipère*. Haitian gang." She looked at the weapon lying on the ground. "Cris, look at this! This guys packing a Stechkin."

"Another Russian pistol." He glanced at Montoya. "I know the *Aranas* and the *Vipère* have been going at it, but why here . . . ?"

Montoya and Allen got it at the same time.

"The Russian," Montoya said. "He and Sal Maroni are fighting it out for control of Downtown. The Russian's specialty is illegal-weapons trafficking."

Allen nodded. "Ten to one, he set this up—supplied both gangs with weapons and set them against each other here . . . in Little Roma . . ."

". . . Where Maroni has substantial legitimate business interests."

Allen snorted. "Guy's gotta launder all that drug money somewhere."

"So the Russian hits Maroni where it hurts . . . sends him a message he can understand."

"And intensifies their conflict." Allen grimaced. "If they keep this up, Gotham could go up in flames."

Montoya looked around, scanning the building tops. "Where's Batman? There's never a good vigilante around when you need him."

Hours later, Allen and Montoya climbed out of their Crown Vic in the private lot behind GCPD headquarters, designated for police vehicles.

"Almost midnight," Montoya said through a yawn.

"Get used to it. Between the Williams shooting and the Little Roma mess, we won't be catching up on our beauty sleep anytime soon."

"Still . . . no Batman."

They walked toward the brightly lit police entrance and slid their coded IDs through the lock slot. The electronically monitored doors slid open.

Allen and Montoya walked down the hall and punched the UP button. There was a creaking *whirr*, and the elevator doors slid open.

They stepped inside and rode up to the Major Crimes Unit.

The MCU squad room took up half a floor.

Even at this hour, it was bustling. Computers hummed. Telephones rang. Cops talked and listened. A TV sat on somebody's desk, loudly recounting the day's news. "Two dead, dozens injured as gang violence erupts in Little Roma . . ." Nobody seemed to be listening.

Detectives sat before the computers, keys clicking as they wrote up reports on the day's activities. It was vital that the day's facts be remembered clearly and presented precisely, since what they wrote down strongly influenced whether a case would go to trial or be dismissed. It was the most boring part of catching the bad guys and booting their sorry asses into jail, but it was also one of the most essential.

Detective Allen turned toward the door to Lieutenant Jim Gordon's office. Montoya was right behind him. The mess in Little Roma was worth a verbal debriefing in addition to a written one, considering what they'd found . . . and what they suspected.

Allen reached out to knock, then stopped abruptly. Over his shoulder, through the smoked-glass window set in the wooden door, Montoya could see Gordon's silhouette, gesturing as he sat at his desk. Then another figure slid silently across the room. Tall, dark. Flowing cape. Pointed ears.

"Speak of the devil," Allen said through gritted teeth. Instinctively, he reached for the doorknob.

"Cris." Montoya grabbed his arm. "No."

Inside the room, Gordon turned as Batman's silhouette rose behind him. There was the mumble of hushed voices.

"He's in there," Allen said, his voice flat. "Right now . . . he's in there. Again."

"I know. He probably came in through the window. You won't catch me doing that!" Montoya couldn't hide her grin as she stared through the frosted glass, trying to make out what was happening. "Just . . . back off for a few minutes, okay?"

She grabbed Allen's sleeve and started to drag him away from the door.

Beyond the glass, Batman's silhouette vanished.

Gordon opened his door. "Allen, Montoya. Inside."

"Yes, sir." Montoya said.

As Montoya entered Gordon's office, her eyes searched the room for any sign of Batman. A gentle breeze wafted into the room and ruffled the stack of papers on Gordon's black metal desk.

She glanced quickly toward the open window. She'd been right. Batman had come in through the window! How cool was that? For a moment she stared out into the sparkling night, ignoring its beauty, searching for movement of dark against the darkness.

Allen entered more slowly behind her.

"Who's that?" Allen's voice was flat and irritated.

Montoya glanced back into the room. Batman wasn't there any longer, but he had left a token of his night's activities.

A pale, thin man with limp, greasy hair down to his shoulders and a long, pointed face like a ferret sat in the wooden chair beside Gordon's desk. His hands were cuffed, and he wore an outfit that looked like a wet suit made of a black rubbery material. His slumped posture spoke of defeat and utter exhaustion.

Montoya raised an eyebrow.

"Jacob Feely," Gordon said. "Our self-proclaimed Man in Black."

Montoya grinned. "The high-tech psycho?"

Allen folded his arms. "Just dropped in, did he, sir?"

Gordon fixed Allen with a warning stare. "He's back in custody, Detective Allen. That's good enough for me. If his lawyers want to make a fuss about it, that's up to them. You and Detective Montoya are going to put Mr. Feely in some bar and leg cuffs and take him back across to the Narrows."

Montoya glanced at Allen. She could see he was ready to blow a gasket and figured it would be best if there weren't witnesses to the confrontation.

"Yes, sir." She looked at Gordon. "Detective Allen needs to update you on our evening's activities, sir. Something interesting has come up."

Montoya helped Feely to his feet. "This way, Mr. Feely." She led Feely from the room.

As she turned to shut the door, she shot Allen a cautioning glare. *Don't forget that's the lieutenant you're talking to! And don't say anything stupid!*

She closed the door softly behind her, leaving Allen behind in Gordon's office.

Gordon sat behind his desk, tapping the rubber eraser of his pencil on the desktop as Detective Allen made his report. He listened intently, lips pursed behind his bottle-brush mustache, eyes hooded.

"Montoya and I think it's significant, sir, that warring gangbangers—both sides wielding Russian weapons—shot up a street in Little Roma. The Russian's sending a message. He owns the streets of Gotham—even the streets in Little Roma. Now Maroni's guys will have to respond. Probably strike Little Odessa. Not that the two sides weren't taking chunks out of each other and Gotham already, but this escalates the conflict."

Gordon frowned as he nodded in agreement. His sandy hair, normally brushed back, had flopped forward onto his forehead. He waited for Allen to make his point.

"I'm just wondering if now's the time for us—any of us—to be acting courier for a vigilante, that's all, sir. We should be staking out Little Odessa—"

Ah. Batman. Gordon glanced up. His hazel eyes met Allen's dark ones. *The stick in Allen's craw. As if I couldn't guess.*

"Feely is still considered a possible suspect in the Williams shooting, Detective. That makes him your responsibility."

Allen raised an eyebrow.

"I admit it's unlikely." Beneath his mustache, Gordon's mouth quirked ironically. "Wrong MO. Preliminary report came through five minutes ago from CSI. Teresa Williams was killed with a 9mm round from a Russian-made VSS Vintorez sniper rifle. That's privileged information, Allen. Officially, we're keeping it from the press.

"So, as far as the media is concerned, Feely's all we have."

Allen opened his mouth but said nothing. Gordon could hear his unspoken *"But . . ."*

Gordon held Allen's eyes. "It's called trust, Detective, something this city's had in short supply until very recently."

"That's the point, Lieutenant!" Allen's temper was rising. "Batman's a vigilante. I *don't* trust him. Sir."

Gordon smiled. "You will."

His phone rang. He answered, listened for a minute, and leapt to his feet.

"I'll be right there," he said, and hung up the phone.

He rushed past Allen, out of the room.

9

Montoya drove the unmarked through deserted city streets, by the Superior Courthouse, and on past the Clock Tower.

Allen was riding shotgun, arms folded, scowling, his mind a million miles away.

Jacob Feely, slumped in the back behind the bulletproof suspect-transport enclosure, looked out the window forlornly. Wrist shackles connected to a bar twelve inches long bound his hands, and leg cuffs connected to a similar bar bound his ankles. This—such as it was—was his last taste of Gotham. He wasn't going anywhere except back to Arkham.

Montoya frowned. The streets really *were* deserted. This late on a summer night, you'd usually see Gotham's homeless camped out on church steps or sleeping in building entrances. Tonight, there was nobody. *Nada.* Not a soul to be seen anywhere.

"Does Downtown seem unusually empty to you?" she asked.

Allen looked up. "What . . . ?"

Montoya rolled her eyes. "You're like a dog with a bone, you know that, Cris?" She sighed. "The streets. Look at them. Nobody's home."

Allen glanced out the window. Montoya knew his eyes were looking at the streets, but his mind was seeing some inner landscape.

"He's a vigilante."

"So?" Montoya said. So much for rational conversation between adults.

"You're a cop, Renee. He's a *vigilante*."

"So far, he's doing a better job at some of this stuff than we are. And he hasn't lynched anybody, beat them up, or killed them. He turns them over to us. Which means a good lawyer could make a case that he *isn't* really a vigilante. Think of him as a concerned citizen making a series of citizen's arrests!"

There was a moment of silence as they drove past Cathedral Square.

Allen rolled his eyes. Montoya was a great partner, but she could be such a pain in the ass sometimes. "You're wrong about the streets, too. There's some homeless over there," he said, tilting his head in the direction of the church. "O'Fallon lets them sleep in the basement. The overflow usually sacks out on the church steps, so they'll be first in line for his soup-kitchen breakfast."

"Three guys, Cris. Count 'em. There are usually close to thirty."

The nearer they got to the Narrows, the worse the neighborhoods became. They passed boarded-up, crumbling brownstones. The occasional burned-out shell of a building. Empty lots strewn with used crack vials and discarded needles where structures once stood.

There were some signs of life. A drug deal going down on the corner that suddenly turned into two pedestrians walking rapidly in opposite directions as the car neared. A bum—another one—stumbling down the street pushing a stolen shopping cart that held all his worldly goods. A

flickering light in an upper room was most likely some lost
soul shooting smack or, more likely these days, chasing the
white dragon—taking meth.

There was worse ahead. Before they crossed the bridge
from the city into the Narrows, where Arkham Asylum lay,
they had to pass through Hob's Oven. It wasn't the official
name, but even the mayor used it. It was the strip of shoreline that fronted the Narrows Channel and looked across
the water directly at the asylum. It was a no-man's-land of
desolation and depravity, as if the contagion of Arkham
had reached out across the water to infect a corner of the
city itself. Hob's Oven—where the devil cooked his own.

Teresa Williams's lost cause, Montoya thought. She wondered if even Williams, had she lived, could have managed
to restore the area. Would anyone—even cops—have wanted
to live this close to Arkham Asylum?

No, thanks, she thought. *Not even if they gave me an
apartment rent free, with a Jacuzzi.* But then, she wasn't
trying to support a family on a cop's salary.

Montoya did a mental shake. *Snap out of it!* Maybe
brooding was contagious.

"What do you call him, then? Crime fighter?"

So they were back to that. Montoya shrugged. "Hell,
Cris, I don't know. I don't even know if he's human! All I
know is that this city's changing for the better, thanks to
Batman. You didn't grow up here. You don't see it. But I
did, and I *do*."

There was a manned checkpoint up ahead—a boxlike
concrete bunker rimmed with spotlights that washed the
surrounding area with brightness. Several other spotlights
shone on the drawbridge that straddled the narrow strip of
water between the Narrows and Downtown. The drawbridge
was in its raised position. No one would cross—in or out—
without permission.

Not that they couldn't swim to the Narrows easily enough, Montoya thought. The river here was hardly more than a canal. *Heck, they could practically jump across.*

As they closed the distance with the checkpoint, two more spotlights on either side of the post clicked on, picking out their cruiser and nearly blinding them.

A couple of uniforms in full tactical gear—Kevlar vests, helmets, pistols, rifles, Tasers—waited nervously at attention. No relaxing. No joke. No wonder!

Can't blame 'em for that, Montoya thought.

She pulled the unmarked to a stop before a red-striped drop bar across the road. One of the policemen approached the car cautiously, finger resting uneasily on the trigger of his shotgun . . . just in case.

Montoya rolled down the driver's-side window. A dead-fish smell wafted in off the channel. The water that flowed past the Narrows slapped lethargically against the concrete-lined embankment. In the distance, she could hear the *pop pop pop* of gunfire. Seeing uniforms stuck in posts like this enhanced her appreciation that she'd made detective.

Montoya held up the badge on the chain around her neck so the cop could see it.

"Major Crimes Unit, Detective Montoya and Detective Allen."

She saw the cop's shoulders relax slightly. "Dropping off or picking up?"

"Dropping off. Jacob Feely. The ex–Man in Black."

"You found him! We hadn't heard. Nice job."

Montoya shrugged. "We just looked, and there he was."

"You been across since the breakout?" the cop asked.

Montoya grimaced. "Haven't had the pleasure."

"Couple of things to keep in mind, then. The whole island's now Asylum grounds. Keep your doors locked and the windows up until you're at the administration building. *Do not stop.* Anyone you see on the streets is probably an inmate."

Montoya nodded. "Understood."

The cop backed away from the car toward the concrete

bunker. He unclipped the communicator from his belt and thumbed the ON button. "I'll let them know you're coming."

The two sides of the drawbridge creaked and groaned as they began to lower. They met with the solid *klang* of steel on steel.

Montoya rolled up her window.

Nerves jittered in her stomach. Cris obviously felt the same way. She heard him jack a shell into the firing chamber of the shotgun he'd pulled from the lockbox as they began to move forward.

The spots followed them. At least they'd driven past the lights so they no longer glared in their eyes. Montoya's eyes were still adjusting as she heard their tires hit the steel-grill flooring of the drawbridge.

"Arkham Asylum," she murmured. "Gotham's ultimate no-man's-land—here we come!"

The unmarked rolled across the bridge into the Narrows. Just ahead was a chain-link and steel-reinforced gate. And beyond that was Arkham—penitentiary and insane asylum—prison to the maddest, baddest, most dangerous criminals from Gotham City and beyond.

When Arkham Asylum was built during the early 1800s, it had been on a narrow, nameless island outside the city proper, a dumping ground established by the earlier city fathers for the city's human waste. Even then, Gotham seemed to have more than its fair share. But the city had grown to surround it, and, over the decades, Arkham had expanded its brief, growing from asylum to asylum/prison to legend. It had been maintained as a lockup, of one kind or another, for nearly two hundred years, and each generation had added its own repurposing . . . and its own distinctive architecture.

Approached from this angle—across the modern drawbridge—Arkham looked like a high-tech prison facility, enclosed by guard towers and twenty-foot-high fences topped with endless rolls of razor wire—well lit, well guarded, well run.

This was an illusion.

Arkham Asylum had been built on the foundations of earlier institutions. And its underlying structure was as mad as the inmates it housed.

Most recently, a madman had been put in charge of the institution—a psychiatrist named Jonathan Crane, who had used the inmates like lab animals, subjecting them to different forms of untested psychoactive drugs as he worked to perfect a fear toxin that would cause the ingestee to see the thing he or she feared most.

Jacob Feely—the Man in Black—the guy they were bringing back to this terrible prison, was probably one of Crane's many victims.

Crane might have experimented with his own drugs, or he might have been crazy to begin with. In any case, at some point he had pulled a burlap mask over his own head, renamed himself the Scarecrow, and become everyone's worst nightmare. It was a role he seemed to tackle with relish. When the mass breakout from Arkham occurred, the Scarecrow disappeared into Gotham proper.

Eventually, most of the escapees had been recaptured and returned to Arkham. But not all. Crane himself—the Scarecrow—was still out there somewhere.

Montoya suspected that the true number of inmates still at large would remain classified information. Wouldn't want to set off a panic or shake the public's confidence in their city's institutions.

As they drove off the bridge, six armed guards stepped forward, rifles at the ready. The steel-reinforced gate swung wide to admit them.

Montoya glanced over at Allen. His mouth was grim and set. He looked like a man who didn't want to be here.

Join the club.

In the backseat of the unmarked, Feely was slamming

his body rhythmically against the rear door and rattling his chains—*slap chink slap chink slap*. Definitely growing agitated. Trying to break free? she wondered. Or trying to knock himself silly, so he wouldn't have to be awake for what was coming next?

She drove the unmarked slowly through the gate and onto the floodlit grounds of the asylum/prison.

Guards pointed and gestured with sweeping hand signals that she should pull the Crown Vic over to an older building—now the admitting office—retained from an earlier era. Its sweeping stone steps led up to a sandstone building adorned with gables and a mansard roof, a building so old that maybe it was the original Arkham Asylum.

Another guard, at the foot of the stairs, held up his hand, signaling them to stop.

A doctor, a portly gray-haired man wearing a dark suit stretched tight across his middle, walked down the steps. Two large, burly orderlies dressed in green scrubs followed on his heels.

At the guard's signal, Montoya hit the button on the console that controlled the rear door locks.

The lock clicked open. The orderlies opened the door and hauled the cuffed and shackled Jacob Feely unceremoniously out of the backseat of the unmarked. When they bent over, Montoya could see the electronic stun guns clipped to their waistbands.

Feely's chains rattled as he stepped onto the ground. He didn't struggle. He didn't say anything. He stood in shackles before the doctor. His body was trembling but his eyes were glazed, as if, in his mind, he was somewhere far away.

The doctor smiled. Montoya noticed that he had lots of teeth. As the orderlies set Jacob Feely on his feet between them, the doctor's smile became even broader.

"Welcome back, Jacob," he said. "Welcome back to Arkham Asylum."

10

Batman watched as the cops pulled a second floater onto the shore of Gotham River.

He had just finished a fairly thorough examination of the interior of Ronald Marshall's warehouse, where Feely had his hideout, when the call about the floater came in over the police band.

His search had left him unsatisfied. He'd found a box filled with unexploded pellets and a weapon under construction—lacking armor-piercing ordinance. No Russian-made guns. No piles of cash. Nothing that further linked Feely to Marshall or marked Feely as Williams's assassin. Feely's use of Marshall's warehouse was probably coincidence. Marshall seemed to own half the derelict buildings in Gotham.

Still, he'd pass the hideout location on to Gordon. Maybe Gordon's forensics team would find something he'd missed. It was unlikely, but you never knew.

When the call came in, he had rushed toward the rocket-powered, high-speed Tumbler, which Alfred had taken to calling his Batmobile, parked out by the warehouse lot in the shadows.

The Tumbler looked like a cross between a Lamborghini

Countach and a tank, drove like a sports car, and maneuvered like a jet. It was built low to the ground with a rear exhaust port and a surface layered with aerodynamic flaps and ballistics-resistant windows. The front two tires were built on a swing arm, which allowed the vehicle to make extremely tight turns. The huge rear tires framed the exhaust. All the tires had off-road capability.

He juiced the right-side tires, spun the Batmobile ninety degrees to the left, and headed down the abandoned stretch of old Route 99 that ended just this side of the interstate.

Late night was the only time it was practical to drive the Batmobile in Gotham. Not that it wouldn't go up over the hoods of cars stalled in traffic. It was just that crushing a row of cars wouldn't do much to improve his image.

He grinned fleetingly. Good thing Batman was a creature of the night.

He stood in the shadows on the rooftop and looked down at the activity.

A couple of teenage boys—a fat kid called Porkchop and a tall, skinny one called B-Devil, who had found the body—looked on from the side. They were holding on to their skateboards for comfort, the way younger kids might hug teddy bears. They claimed they were practicing moves on the boardwalk now that most of the joggers and dog walkers had gone home, and that they had spotted the body as they wheeled past. One of them—Porkchop—had used his cell phone to call 911.

Perhaps not the total truth—Batman suspected pot might also have been involved. If so, the kids had been smart enough to ditch the contraband before the cops arrived.

For whatever reason the kids had been here, they were lucky to be alive. This wasn't a safe area this time of night. Usually there were lots of homeless and vermin who preyed on the weak.

Safe enough now, though, with floods illuminating the area and cops crowding the shore. No homeless in sight.

By the bright lights, Batman could see that the corpse had been mutilated like the first. This wasn't good.

The medical examiner arrived in her car, and a morgue van arrived soon after. Sheila Leiani took what appeared to be a cursory look at the scene and the body. Batman knew that, cursory though it may have appeared, she missed nothing. The flash from the police photographer's camera burned away the shadows every few seconds as he moved around the body, snapping photos, while Leiani was bent over the corpse, taking measurements. She straightened and nodded. The cops placed the corpse in a body bag.

Gordon arrived, walking from his car, parked half a block away at the police cordon. He was passing between the derelict factory building on his right and the failed loft cooperative on his left, moving into deep shadow when he heard an almost inaudible *thud* behind him. Gordon stopped walking, as if he were surveying the shore ahead of him, taking it all in before he entered the crime scene.

A whisper gave Gordon up-to-date information about Feely's hideout. Gordon replied that Feely was on his way to Arkham.

By the time Gordon turned to look over his shoulder, Batman was gone.

Once again, Arkham's gates swung wide. Montoya drove the unmarked back the way they had entered—through the gate, across the lowered drawbridge, past the block-house, back into Hob's Oven.

Allen picked up the handset from the two-way in the equipment console on the dashboard. "Dispatch, Victor Three-Two . . . drop-off complete. We are ten-twenty-four, en route to State."

The dispatcher radioed back, "Victor Three-Two, ten-four."

Montoya glanced in the rearview mirror. The Narrows and the Asylum were disappearing behind them, gradually blocked from her view by the ruined buildings of the Oven.

Somehow, even the desolation around her was more real, more *human*, than that terrible monument to madness they had just left. She could breathe again. She glanced at the road ahead, then back at the rearview, fascinated and repelled as the drawbridge swung into its upright position.

Allen replaced the radio handset on the dash.

"Place gives me the creeps," Montoya said. "It's horrible. Almost makes you feel sorry for Feely. A whole island . . . abandoned to madness."

"This whole *city* is abandoned to madness."

Montoya glanced at him, exasperated. "You are in a mood tonight, aren't you?"

"I am. I'm . . . thinking about transferring out of the MCU. Maybe going back to Vice."

"What? Cris! You can't!"

It was Allen's turn to roll his eyes. "Renee, we've been partnered six weeks. It's not like we're married."

"But . . . it's the Major Crimes Unit! Gordon picked you the same as he picked me. He picked all the detectives in the squad. You can't turn your back on that!"

"The MCU! Christ! If we focused on stopping major crimes, like the gang war that's been ripping this city into chunks for almost a month now, maybe I'd reconsider. But that's not what we do, is it? No, we run errands for a vigilante."

Montoya scowled.

Then, to Allen's surprise, she turned the wheel hard and swung right on State.

"This isn't the way back to headquarters."

Montoya shrugged. "We're not exactly enough for a full stakeout. Still, wouldn't hurt to drive by Little Odessa for a look-see. Just to check it out . . . get the vibes. It's not much out of our way."

Allen snorted. "Just on the other side of the city."

They cruised down Chaykin Avenue, the main drag through the area of Gotham known as Little Odessa. The road ran beneath elevated train tracks, held up by evenly spaced, towering steel pillars. At intervals, a series of steep, steel stairways led from the raised station platforms down to street level, narrowing the sidewalks where they debouched. Under the stairs, the detritus of the city gathered in the eddies. Old bags, both paper and plastic, the odd shopping cart, unidentifiable broken bits of stuff, the ubiquitous fifty-five-gallon drum, and the occasional human being, lost beyond recovery.

The avenue was lined with shops bearing signs in Cyrillic. There was very little English. Montoya spotted stores with purposes she recognized. A bookstore—the books in the window gave it away. *Duh!* A store displaying Russian stacking dolls and other tchotchkes, probably catering to tourists.

A series of posters plastered on a closed-down kiosk— maybe a Russian-language newsstand—showed a couple of macho-looking bare-knuckled boxers in team colors. The main tagline was "Russia vs. America." The rest of the poster was in Cyrillic.

"Older people here don't speak a lot of English," Allen said. "Young ones are mostly bilingual."

They drove past restaurants. Butchers. Bakeries. A large specialty market. *More* restaurants. All closed at this time of night. She rolled down the window, just a crack, hoping to get a whiff of the area.

"What is it with immigrant areas of the city—everywhere you look, there's food! Look at Little Roma. Look at Chinatown. And here *we* are . . . food central . . . and the shops are shut up tighter than a drum," she grumbled. "I'm *starving*. Where's an all-night Fat Boy Burger when you need one?"

Allen snorted. "You're a philistine, Renee. You should come here during the day, when Little Odessa's open for business. Borscht. Kebabs. Pierogis. Black breads. Caviar sold from sidewalk stands. Vodka. And the pastries!"

"Stop!" she groaned. "You're killing me."

She glanced overhead. The looming El made the area feel closed off and claustrophobic, not what she, personally,

would be looking for in a main drag. And Chaykin Avenue
definitely was that.

A late train rumbled overhead and stopped with a loud
hiss of its brakes. Footsteps clattered on the steel steps as
they cruised slowly past.

"Pretty late for people to be getting home," she said.
"Or leaving."

"Not really. Not in this part of Gotham," Allen said.
"We're about to hit what passes as the party district."

They cruised past bars and nightclubs that seemed to be
doing booming business. A group of college-age kids clustered outside a club. A girl with sharp cheekbones and red
hair pulled back in a ponytail was shouting into her cell
phone in a Russian/English mélange, trying to be heard over
the music pumping from the open door. Montoya could feel
the car vibrate slightly from the bass notes as they passed.

"Happening place," Montoya said. "See any wiseguys?"

"They'd be called *vory* here," Allen said.

Russian Jews fleeing religious persecution had settled
little Odessa in the late 1800s. Each generation brought a
new batch of émigrés, arriving for different reasons. The
newest wave sought not political or religious freedom, but
education and opportunity.

Though the immigrants were devoted to their new country, they felt comfortable with the trappings of the old. So
they brought the best with them . . . and the worst.

Little Odessa was, by reputation, a "Red Mafia" hotbed.
For years, the GCPD had been tracking people of interest—
mostly members of the *Vory v Zakonye*, or "Thieves in Law,"
crime group who resided there. Some had been arrested.
The wave of immigrants from the old country notwithstand-
ing, the charges were traditionally American. They ranged
from racketeering to narcotics trafficking, from extortion
and protection to illegal gambling and loan-sharking. Some
vory had been indicted. A few, mainly underlings, had been
convicted. The big fish had managed to slip through the net
so far, because the *vory* had a justified reputation for brutality, and most juries were terrified to cross them.

The unmarked reached a main cross street.

"Turn here," Allen said.

They drove down a narrow road lined with row houses and larger 1940s-era apartment buildings, with streets crossing at odd diagonals. A testament to the age of that part of Gotham, Little Odessa and the nearby Tricorner were neighborhoods with short blocks and meandering streets that didn't conform to Gotham's standard grid pattern.

Away from the main street and the clubs, this area seemed dark, ominous, and deserted. The streets were oddly empty. Few cars parked at curbside. Streetlamps flickering or broken. Shadows everywhere.

They passed a rubble-filled block, where buildings had been razed. A chain-link fence topped with razor wire surrounded the empty lot. A billboard read NEW HOME OF THE TRICORNER CONDOMINIUMS: A RONALD MARSHALL CONSTRUCTION PROJECT. IF YOU LIVED HERE, YOU'D BE HOME BY NOW.

But the word *Home* had been spray-painted over with the word *Dead*.

"Real encouraging. Kind of comforting and inviting," Montoya said. "I get any cash ahead, I'm investing in chain-link fences and razor wire. Does a booming business in Gotham."

"Standard operating equipment." Allen's lip quirked. "That's not a bad idea."

They cruised onto the next block. Steep sandstone stoops led past postage-stamp lawns to shabby three- and four-story duplexes. The alleys separating them were wide enough to park a couple of cars.

Across the street, a huge, sleek high-rise towered over the rest of the neighborhood.

Montoya snorted. "There goes the neighborhood."

"Pull over," Allen said.

They stopped in a pool of greenish light below a streetlamp, across from the entrance to the high-rise. It loomed, ominous and out of place, above the tattered row houses and bungalows of old Tricorner.

The claustrophobic, slightly creeped-out feeling Montoya had been ignoring for the past hour returned in spades. This time she couldn't blame it on the El.

It's just that it's been a hell of a couple of days, she told herself. Teresa Williams's murder. The shoot-out in Little Roma. Their trip to Arkham—a warehouse chock-full of crazed criminals. Enough to set anyone's nerves jangling.

The empty street didn't help—devoid of cars, except for a dark van parked toward the end of the block.

"There's your *vor*," Allen said, leaning forward to look up out the windshield at the roof of the towering high-rise. "Up there. The Russian lives on the top floor in a million-dollar penthouse condo. Doorman building. Amazing ocean and city views. He has an expensive lifestyle and no traceable means of sustaining it."

Allen worked Vice before he was picked for the MCU. Probably had the Russian under surveillance at one time or another, Montoya realized. *Must be how he came to know the neighborhood so well.* And here she'd been thinking her partner was just a sophisticated gourmand.

"He's importing weapons illegally, Renee. And he's not just raking in the profits. He's making deals and arming Gotham's gangs and laundering his profits through apparently legitimate businesses. I think what we saw in Little Roma was just the beginning. I think he's creating mercenaries for his own private army and plans to use them to break Maroni and take over Gotham's illegal trade."

"We'll get him, Cris," she said. "We'll get the Russian and Maroni both. Gordon's not going to sit on his hands while their goons rip Gotham apart. But he has to prioritize. There are the Arkham crazies running around, nuts far worse than the Man in Black. And Williams's murder—Gordon's under a lot of pressure there. And you heard the chatter on the radio—another mutilated corpse washed in on the tide. Looks like a serial killer. We're stretched too thin." She started to pull away from the curb.

Then she suddenly killed the engine and turned to face Allen. "Look, you can't walk away from the MCU, not when things are finally beginning to change. Not when the fact that you're an honest cop is an asset, not a liability."

Allen looked out the windshield and stiffened.

Montoya pressed her point. "Look. I know you don't want to hear this. I don't even know for sure that we can trust the Batman. But I know this—because of him, I'm not ashamed of being a cop anymore. If you want to give that up—"

"Shhhh!" Allen held up a hand to stop her.

Montoya scowled. "No, dammit, listen—"

"Renee, shut up!" he hissed, and pointed up the street.

Montoya looked where he was pointing. "Holy crap!"

While she had been distracted, the doors of the van parked down the street had slid open. Men, dressed in dark colors, slipped from the vehicle. Most were carrying submachine guns.

There was a loud *crack!* and the streetlight overhead went out. *Crack! Crack!* The streetlights at either end of the block went dark.

A final guy climbed from the van. He was hefting something much larger than an automatic—it looked like a portable surface-to-air missile.

He raised the weapon, aiming it toward the penthouse.

"Crap!" Montoya drew her Glock.

Allen drew his pistol almost simultaneously. "Maroni's taking the war to where the Russian lives. *Literally.*"

Headlights shone in the road ahead; other headlights flashed in their rearview mirror as two cars pulled onto the street, coming toward them from opposite ends of the block.

Montoya glanced ahead, then turned in her seat to look behind them. The cars—she thought they were Hummers—stopped in the middle of the road, one in front, one behind, effectively trapping the van between them. The bad news was that the unmarked was caught in the same trap.

"Looks like the Russian was expecting company and sent a welcoming committee," Renee muttered through gritted teeth.

"I hear you," Allen said. "We're going to need backup. A *lot* of backup."

Large men dressed in jogging suits and expensive sneakers—the preferred uniform of the *vory* "bulls"—jumped from the Hummers. Their hair was cropped short—a bull didn't want to give an opponent something to grab on to.

A red-haired young giant shouted something in Russian, and they raised their automatic weapons.

One of the wiseguys from the van yelled, "Is that you, Anton? We told you Ivans to stay the hell off our turf!" The guy with the rocket launcher was raising it onto his shoulder, preparing to take out the Russian's penthouse.

One of the Russian *vory*—Anton?—shouted back in accented English, "Tell your *capo* he has no turf. Just as he has no power. *Nyet*. Never mind! Your corpses will send the message more effectively."

The *vory* opened fire.

Maroni's men dove toward the sidewalk and crouched behind the van, trying to shield themselves from the *vory* gunmen as they fired back.

Several stray rounds tore through the unmarked.

Montoya and Allen ducked low in the seats, still holding their drawn weapons, trying to shield themselves from the withering crossfire as all hell broke loose around them. As she slid down, Montoya had a glimpse of several of the Russian gunsels racing down the street, diving for cover behind the cop car itself.

"Okay," whispered Montoya. "So coming here wasn't my brightest idea."

Maroni's men, caught in an ambush between the Russian's thugs, dove for the sidewalk beside their van, firing back. The enforcer with the rocket launcher had joined them, crouching low, still trying to wrestle the large weapon into position.

Allen grabbed the two-way from the equipment console and shouted into the handset, trying to make his voice heard above the rattle of gunfire. "Ten-thirty-four! Ten-thirty-four! Tricorner. Southwest Bogdanove and Milgrom!"

Several rounds smashed into the windows of the unmarked, showering the cringing detectives with broken glass.

The dispatcher's voice crackled over the radio. "Officers in need of assistance, southwest Bogdanove and Milgrom. Be advised, backup ETA three minutes."

Allen shouted at the dispatcher, "Screw that! In three minutes, we're gonna be dead!"

Montoya raised her head and peered through the shattered window, needing to see what was happening.

Lights blinked on in a few windows up and down the street. Most of the area's occupants had enough sense to keep their lights off and their heads down.

Automatic weapons fire, coming from directly behind the unmarked, ripped into Maroni's mobsters, perforating the guy with the rocket launcher.

He dropped the weapon and pitched onto the sidewalk, literally cut in half by the barrage of bullets. Another mobster snatched up the rocket launcher and swung its barrel toward the parked car . . . planning to take out the Russian's thugs, who were using the sturdy body of the Crown Vic as shelter.

"Cris! *Out!*" Montoya shouted. "Incoming!"

She kicked open the driver's-side door and dove out of the car. Bad as it was out there, they'd have a better chance of surviving on the street than in the unmarked.

Allen shoved open his door, leapt onto the curb . . . and crashed into the pole of the decommissioned streetlight. Stunned, he sprawled onto the sidewalk.

Maroni's mobster sighted the rocket launcher on the unmarked, his finger tightening on the trigger.

11

Batman crouched on the roof of a four-story duplex across from the high-rise co-op where the Russian had his penthouse. He had arrived thirty seconds too late to stop the firefight that had erupted below.

Several hours ago, he had driven the Batmobile to the edge of Little Odessa and parked it in a little-used alley-way, in the dense shadow of a derelict building. From there, he patrolled the area on foot, leaping from rooftop to rooftop, needing to be everywhere at once. He knew Maroni would retaliate against the Russian. He just wasn't sure what form the mobster's revenge might take.

This—the attempted destruction of the Russian's penthouse—was a bolder move than he had expected. Too bad for Maroni's wiseguys that it had been a setup for an ambush. Maybe the Russian had known Maroni better than Batman had. More likely, the Russian had thugs stationed around Little Odessa, on the lookout for trouble.

As *he* had been.

And, like the cops in the unmarked who'd driven into the middle of a firefight, he'd found it in spades. If it were

not for the imperiled police, and the fact that the buildings
on both sides of the street were occupied with innocent people who could be downed by stray bullets—he might have
been tempted to let the thugs annihilate each other. There
wouldn't be many tears shed for the loss of any of the combatants on the street below him.

The *vory* were using the unmarked as cover as they tried
to cut down Maroni's enforcers . . . and they had been partially successful.

Except for the rocket launcher Maroni's goon had
pointed at them.

The cops realized their danger and tried to abandon the
unmarked. One of them—it looked like Montoya—had
leapt from the driver's side and rolled onto the street. Her
partner had tried a similar move, but had hit the pole of the
streetlight and gone down.

Normally *down* would have been good—in their situation, above or below the line of fire was the safest place to
be. Unfortunately, when the car blew, it would leave a big
crater in the pavement . . . and would take anyone nearby
with it.

He had five seconds to get the fallen cop—it had to be
Allen—away before the car became a fireball.

The Russian's thugs sprayed bullets at Maroni's wiseguys. The goon with the rocket launcher flinched back out
of the line of fire.

Now!

Batman fired a grapple down at the top of the streetlight.
Even as the segmented hook was latching on to the light's
curved top, he threw a half dozen smoke pellets all around
the Crown Vic. As they exploded in a blinding white flare
and formed obscuring black clouds, he leapt down from
the roof toward the street. His sense of direction was unerr-
ing. In the midst of the roiling darkness, he reached low,
grabbed Allen by the collar of his jacket, and retracted the
monofilament at top speed. All around him he heard curses
in both Russian and Ukrainian. He shot to the curved top

of the light pole, a few bullets bouncing off his armor, as
the distracted Russian mobsters transferred their attention
and weapons fire to Batman. Most of the shots went wild.

The guy with the rocket launcher wasn't similarly distracted.

Batman pulled Allen up and over his shoulders, shielding the detective with his own armored body, as the unmarked exploded in a roar of billowing flame and shrapnel.
The streetlight shuddered but remained upright. The force
of the explosion blew away the black smoke of Batman's
pellets.

When the flames died down, Batman dropped toward
the ground. He set Allen on what was left of the sidewalk,
away from the burning unmarked.

He yelled, "Stay down!" as he swept toward the goons
crouched beside Maroni's van.

From the bottom steps of a duplex, Detective Allen
watched openmouthed as Batman raced away from him in
a swirl of cape and shadows. Allen had been grabbed,
jerked from the ground, and protected from shrapnel, and
he'd hardly gotten a good look at the man who'd just saved
him. If he really *was* a man.

What was the Batman doing here, anyway?

Dumb question.

Shadows flickered wildly across the building facades and
down the street as the police car was consumed in a blazing
fire. Maroni's thugs, those who had survived the earlier hail
of Russian bullets, were busy reloading. Between the initial
flares, the black smoke, and the exploding car, nobody had
gotten a clear look at what had just happened. But they were
certain that the Russians were toast.

As one of the thugs snapped his clip into place, he looked
up and screamed. A horned devil seemed to be coming at
them right out of the flames, reaching out to take them to
Hell.

Batman was on them before Maroni's thug could reload

the rocket launcher. Two of the others had gotten their pistols reloaded and raised. Bullets from their automatic weapons pounded at the demon, but they didn't seem to faze him. The rest of the survivors had apparently decided that enough was enough and were running like hell the opposite way down the street.

Allen glanced at the unmarked. His head ached; his ears were still ringing. The Russian's thugs who'd crouched behind it were history. Pieces of them were scattered on the sidewalk. He felt his gorge rise. If Renee hadn't seen the—

Renee!

He bolted off the sidewalk, moving low. He had to find her.

Montoya lay on her back in the middle of the street. He crouched next to her, keeping low. Her nose was bloody, and blood spattered the front of her shirt and the badge on its chain, resting on her chest.

"Renee!"

She opened her eyes and frowned at him like she was having trouble focusing. But she'd made it out alive and, apparently, in one piece.

"How?" she asked.

"The Batman."

"Batman?"

She tried to sit, but he pushed her back. "Stay down!"

It wasn't over.

A bullet whizzed past them. He heard an engine gun. He looked toward the Hummer parked at the end of the block beyond the burning unmarked. The Russian's goons, the ones who were left, were running for the vehicle, making a break for it. Several had already climbed inside.

He heard sirens, cop cars coming fast. But they wouldn't get here soon enough to catch these goons unless—

Allen found that he still had his SIG in his hand. All that had happened, and he hadn't dropped his weapon. That was a cop for you!

He threw himself flat on the ground, bracing his elbows to steady his aim, and fired—*Bam! Bam! Bam! Bam!*

The 9mm slugs ripped through the tires of the Hummer.

One of the *vory* piling into the car—he thought it was the red-haired boss goon, the one Maroni's thug had called Anton—snarled a curse in Russian. He swung around and raised his pistol, ready to blast the interfering cop to smithereens. Allen thought it was a Makarov PMM, but he couldn't be sure. It flashed through his mind that the PMM could carry armor-piercing rounds, but he wasn't wearing any body armor anyway. He rolled in front of Montoya.

Something flew through the air—Allen caught the glint of metal. The goon yelped and jerked, and his bullets slammed into the asphalt. A knife blade protruded from the thug's arm.

Allen rolled onto his side, sighted the other Hummer, and pumped several rounds into its wheels for good measure.

The Russians goons weren't going anywhere.

GCPD backup finally raced onto the street, sirens screaming. Police cars slammed to a stop behind both Hummers, blocking the road.

The *vory* broke and raced for the alleys.

Allen leapt to his feet and gave chase. He launched himself into the air and caught one of them in a flying tackle, slamming the *vor* to the ground. A pistol flew through the air and bounced off the wall beside them. It was a PMM.

The backup cops ran past him after the others. One of them pulled up short next to Allen, took out his cuffs, and yanked the *vor's* arms behind his back.

Allen held his SIG against Anton's forehead and read him his rights.

Montoya struggled to her feet.

The street was flooded with cops.

She walked—more like staggered, she thought—to the van, gun held in front of her. Maroni's men—the ones who hadn't been shot during the firefight, anyway—had been cuffed hand and foot. Most of them were unconscious.

Batman! Cris had said it was the Batman.

She glanced skyward. She thought she saw the tip of a

cape as it disappeared over the edge of a rooftop. But she couldn't be sure.

Can he really fly? Montoya wondered blearily. *That's so* cool. *He was here . . . and I missed him!*

Lieutenant Gordon arrived in Tricorner half an hour later, looking disheveled.

"What is it, sir?" one of the cops joked. "We get you out of bed?"

"Hard to get my beauty sleep with all this noise going on," Gordon joked back.

Beauty sleep. *Any* kind of sleep.

He wished.

On his way home, he'd stopped by Smuggler's Point, where a third mangled floater had washed onto the shore. Then he'd gotten the call about the firefight in Little Odessa and had to turn around and speed to the other end of the city. At this rate, his wife and kids were going to forget what he looked like.

Cops were shoving cuffed suspects into transport enclosures. Gotham General Hospital ambulances were carrying off injured thugs and the few neighborhood residents who'd caught stray rounds or been cut by shattered glass. Crime-scene investigators were taking pictures and gathering evidence, making official records in the aftermath of the shoot-out.

He walked past the medical examiner. She was bent over, studying a body sprawled on the sidewalk beside a van. The body had been nearly cut in half by automatic weapons fire. Gordon glanced at the top half. It was Vito Margolisi. If it had to be somebody, it might as well be Vito. Or was that too cynical? He thought he heard a bell tolling in the distance. Was it Sunday already?

As he approached the burned-out skeleton of the un-marked car, firemen finished spraying foam on its remnants and began to pack up their equipment, ready to head back to their station house. They, too, had had a long night's journey into day. Neighborhood residents, braver now that the excitement was over, had emerged to watch from their windows and front stoops.

Detectives Allen and Montoya were directing the operation. Gordon saw that Allen's left calf was wrapped in a rough bandage below his cutoff trouser leg.

Montoya had blood spattered down her shirtfront. Gordon knew she'd been nearest the blast. He figured her ears were still ringing, and she probably had a devil of a headache. He also knew both detectives had refused transport to a hospital until all the suspects were in custody.

Gordon stopped beside them. "How's the leg, Detective?"

"I'll live." Allen had been nicked by a piece of shrapnel and, in the excitement, hadn't realized he was hurt until one of the EMTs had pulled him aside to dress his wound.

"Lucky you two just happened by," Gordon said.

Allen grimaced, coughed slightly. "After we dropped Feely, we took a . . . uh . . . roundabout route back to the station, sir. Stumbled into the middle of this mess."

"So I heard."

Allen hesitated. "Batman was here. He saved my life. Twice."

He reached into his pocket and pulled out an oblong of dark cloth—probably the remnant of fabric from Allen's trouser leg, Gordon thought. Allen flipped it open. Inside was the small bat-shaped blade, sharp as a razor, that had sliced into Anton's arm and spoiled his aim.

Gordon looked from the blade to Allen's face. He raised his eyebrows. "Evidence?"

"Your call, sir. It was lying on the ground. I . . . picked it up after we got Anton into the van. Probably shouldn't have. But I did. I thought . . . when you saw Batman again, you might want to give it back to him."

It was five thirty in the morning. The sky over Gotham had begun to lighten. For the most part, the city was quiet.

Inside Gotham General Hospital, however, the emergency room was a madhouse. Aside from the gun battle in Little Odessa, there had been several gang-related shootings in the area of Uptown known as Crime Alley. And a multiple-car collision had pretty much shut down the Midtown Bridge as early commuters sped through a morning fog.

Ambulances wailed. EMTs hauled gurneys down the corridor toward the triage workstations, past the crowded waiting room, where Detectives Allen and Montoya were slouching on orange plastic chairs, waiting for their turn to see a doctor. It occurred to Allen that somebody must have spent a lot of time deciding just which plastic chairs were the most uncomfortable. Probably public money and a commission.

Would-be patients sat with varying degrees of patience. Several sick children had fallen asleep slumped across chairs, half-lying in their parents' laps. Harried doctors and nurses rushed up and down the corridor, ignoring the waiting multitude. To give the triage nurses credit, anyone with a life-threatening injury or condition got shunted to the front of the line. Everyone else waited his or her turn.

The TV in the corner was turned to the Wayne Media news channel. A perky blonde was talking about the successful launch of the new I-Brite 7 communications satellite. The screen showed a hexagonal satellite sprouting antennas like a hypersensitive bug.

"Looks like a giant water bug," Allen muttered, and went back to reading a months-old sports magazine. He obviously had the wrong job. The shortstop for the Gotham Grizzlies had just signed a contract worth better than $200 million over the next ten years. With additional bonuses built in. He flipped to the article on synchronized swimming. The girls were pretty. The pages were pretty well thumbed.

Detectives Montoya and Allen had been waiting for an hour when Lieutenant Gordon slouched into the room, looking exhausted. The lines on his forehead and around his eyes seemed etched deeper than usual beneath the harsh fluorescent lights.

Montoya figured they all looked tired. None of them had had a lot of sleep in the last couple of days.

Gordon slumped down in the empty chair next to Allen. "I returned that item to our masked friend with your thanks," he said. "He told me how you shot out the tires on those Hummers. He said cops like you and Montoya were Gotham's best chance of cleaning up the city. Told me I was a good judge of character." He smiled ruefully. "Need someone to wait here with you?"

"We're fine," Allen said. He looked around the crowded waiting room. "They'll get to us eventually."

"Go on home, sir," Montoya said. "We'll catch you later."

The sky was lightening in the east as Batman turned the Tumbler down a narrow road toward the rail yard and the secret entrance to the bunker. He hit the brakes, pulled the vehicle into a tight 180-degree spin, and brought her to a complete stop with her rear exhaust ports six inches from the back of the garage. Practice apparently did make perfect. He switched off the ignition, hit the switch that opened the hatch, and climbed from the cockpit.

Alfred looked up from the computer console he had been studying. "You should be careful about showing off, sir. Pride goeth before the fall. However, I understand that you've had a busy—and rather successful—evening of it, and there should be *some* room for youthful exuberance."

Batman smiled as he pulled off his cowl and swiped at a smear of blood that trickled from a deep gouge on his cheek.

Alfred frowned. "You've been hit, sir?"

Bruce shrugged. "Piece of flying shrapnel . . . or maybe a ricochet. It's just a scratch. I didn't realize I'd been nicked till the fight was over."

"It will need stitches," Alfred said, looking at it closely. "Or it will leave a telltale scar. Perhaps you can tell the curious that you cut yourself shaving. With a straight razor."

* * *

Gotham City law required that, in the case of a serious felony, a preliminary hearing be held before a grand jury within a week of the arrest of the accused.

One by one, Maroni's and the Russian's mobsters came before the grand jury. As was usual, only the prosecutor presented evidence. This was a practical measure, since this preliminary hearing was meant only to confirm that there was adequate reason to believe that the accused had committed the crime he was charged with and that there was sufficient evidence to go to trial.

It was a busy week for Detectives Allen and Montoya, who testified in all the pretrial hearings. The forensics team presented their evidence. The DA asked for an indictment.

The grand jury indicted several of Maroni's men on counts of first-degree murder and first-degree homicide.

They refused to indict the Russian's thugs, despite overwhelming evidence against them.

"I can't believe it!" Montoya unbent from her dejected slouch and reached across the aisle to snag a sugar donut from the box lying open on Allen's desk. They were at MCU headquarters, drowning their anger and resentment in bad coffee and good donuts from Nocenti's Bakery down the street.

Half the box was gone, but neither cop felt any better.

"What can they be thinking?" Montoya railed. "Not that Maroni's mobsters are on the side of the angels. But the Russian makes Maroni look like a Boy Scout. At least Maroni's goons were targeting the thug in charge. In Little Roma, the Russian sent gunmen against a batch of *civilians*.

"Not that we can prove that," she added. She bit into her donut glumly.

"Which may explain the verdict." Allen grabbed a chocolate-coconut donut from the box. "Several of the jurors in favor of indicting the *vory*—or people in their families—received threats. The jurors got scared and caved. Who can blame them?"

Montoya sighed.

So much for the antidepressant effect of fried dough and sugar. She washed her mouthful down with black coffee and tossed the rest of her half-eaten donut in the trash.

Allen sighed as well but held on to his donut.

"We'll get them," she said. "The big fish. Maroni and the Russian. They *have* to be our targets."

They both glanced toward Gordon's office. Behind the frosted-glass window, a large, dark shadow moved.

"Maybe Gotham can use a vigilante after all," Allen said.

Lieutenant Gordon shoved back the hair that had flopped in his face and scowled at Batman. "If we can't get an indictment against the little guys, we surely won't be able to get one against the Russian. Or Maroni, for that matter."

Batman folded his arms across his chest. "I never really expected we would. I'm going to convince those thugs to cut back on the violence while we work to get proof of their involvement in gunrunning and drug trafficking."

"How? By becoming a mediator between the Italian mob and Russian mob?"

Batman grinned slightly. "Something like that."

"It all comes down to the money," Gordon muttered. "Somehow, the *vory* are laundering Russian mob money here in Gotham. I'll have people work that angle as well."

12

The headline in the *Gotham Times* the next day read: "Ronald Marshall Scours Hob's Oven."

Bruce Wayne tossed the evening edition of the paper on his desk with a snort of disgust. Somebody actually got paid to write those headlines. And somebody probably got paid to write the puff piece praising Ronald Marshall. So much for the city's independent media. Where the hell was the liberal press when you needed them? Or the conservative press for that matter.

He shoved his hands in the pockets of his suit jacket and stalked toward the window of his Midtown penthouse office. Daylight was waning. Bruce Wayne's time in Gotham had almost ended. Batman's was about to begin.

He looked south toward the Narrows. The low clouds were already opalescent with the reflected light that marked the location of Arkham Asylum. As twilight advanced, the Asylum's yard lights, spots, and sweeping searchlights had been switched on, converting that particular corner of Hell into a radiant pool of white fire.

Arkham and its escapees were a seemingly intransigent problem. But they were a problem for another day.

Beyond Arkham lay Ronald Marshall's newest reclamation project, Hob's Oven—that lost area where Teresa
Williams had hoped to build a community that would benefit both Gotham's neediest and its most deserving. Until
someone had murdered her.

And with that thought, Bruce's mind returned to Ronald
Marshall.

With Teresa Williams out of the picture, the city council
had unanimously accepted Marshall's plan for the "gentrification" of Hob's Oven. That was what the papers and the
local news programs were calling it. In fact, it meant the
wholesale destruction of the Oven down to the ground and
the displacement of all those unfortunate souls who still
lived there. Even now, Marshall's wrecking balls and bull-
dozers were plowing through the area, razing whole blocks
of derelict buildings. The *Times* had printed architectural
renderings of the high-end co-ops and lavish entertainment
center that would cater to the wealthy—complete with tennis courts, driving range, and putting greens—that Marshall planned for the area. But even the *Times* wasn't
showing any pictures of the few dilapidated architectural
gems still left in Hob's Oven that were now being ground
to dust. No national landmark status there.

Bruce wondered for a moment if one of the factors at
work here was some sort of collective guilt over the failure
of the city or the state or even the Feds to restore the blight
that was the Oven to some sort of decency. Best to sweep it
aside and forget it ever existed.

The paper had printed, almost as an aside, a smaller picture of the homeless shelter that would be constructed on
the far edge of Hob's Oven. This would be built using
money raised through the newly formed Ronald Marshall
First Invitational Celebrity Golf Tournament to Aid the
Homeless, a benefit scheduled to take place during the
upcoming weekend at a country club across the Gotham
River.

Marshall's whole plan seemed ill conceived. Who would
pay top dollar to live across the river from Arkham Asy-

lum? Thrill seekers, Bruce decided. People who were going to need opaque curtains at night. People who got off on the illusion of danger. People who failed to understand that the illusion could turn very real and very ugly at a moment's notice. As Bruce was all too aware.

But there had to be some kind of sense to it all. Playing devil's advocate, Bruce considered Gotham City, built on a patchwork of islands. The land was finite. The way property values had been climbing, even lesser real estate was gaining value. And Hob's Oven *was* part of Downtown— Gotham's center for governance and the arts. Maybe Marshall was just a smart developer. Maybe he understood the Gotham real estate market better than Bruce did.

But the shadow of the Asylum was long and dark.

No, Bruce decided. Something was off there. Marshall apparently owned a lot of property in Gotham. Most of it, from what Batman had seen as he roamed the city, was posted with signs announcing various construction projects, all scheduled to begin soon. But nothing actually seemed to be under construction. So what was going on? How was Marshall financing his many acquisitions?

Most damning of all, he couldn't forget that flash of triumph on Marshall's face as Teresa Williams's corpse crumpled to the floor.

Buildings, construction, bureaucracy. Maybe this was a job for Bruce Wayne, after all.

Bruce took the private elevator from his penthouse of-fice to the applied sciences division, housed in the subbasement of Wayne Enterprises. He smiled, thinking how it might please or horrify his different ancestors if they could see how he was using the company's resources.

His family had owned the company since its founding in the seventeenth century.

The original Wayne Company was a merchant house with holdings in the fledgling Americas. Thomas Wayne, the family patriarch, had foreseen the upcoming war between

England and its colonies, and had moved his family to the Americas, where they settled in the area that eventually became Gotham City. He continued to run his merchant company from the family's new home, where the Waynes had been essential to the supply chain that kept the newly emerging country going throughout the Revolutionary War era. For a time, he'd cornered the market on lead and was the principal supplier of shot to the Colonial army. There were even rumors, never substantiated, that he'd resupplied local British troops as well.

Whatever the case, through luck, innovative management, and the occasional bit of piracy, their business grew over the centuries to become Wayne Enterprises, a large, family-owned multinational conglomerate with special interests in shipping, media, and applied science, including communications and aerospace technologies.

Despite a recent effort by an ex-CEO to take the company public while Bruce was out of the country and presumed missing, Bruce had managed to buy up the majority of the stock. He continued to own the controlling shares in Wayne Enterprises, which had given him a great deal of leeway when it came to remodeling the corporate headquarters.

The Wayne Enterprises building took up an entire city block. It rose in art-deco splendor into the skies of Gotham, just as splendid, in its way, as the taller Aparo Tower. It was one of Gotham's indispensable hubs of financial power and a vital center for public transportation. Half of its first floor and basement level was a nexus for subway, monorail, and commuter train lines.

The building had been badly damaged during the violence that followed the recent outbreak at Arkham. Wayne had used the excuse of much-needed repairs to install a private elevator that ran from his office, through the basement, and into the subbasement level that housed the newly refurbished Applied Sciences Division.

He stepped from the elevator into a long hall. It was after

eight, and most of the scientists who worked for this division had gone home for the night.

Stopping outside a plain metal door that led to Lucius Fox's private lab, Bruce swiped his keycard through an ID monitor, then put his eye to the retinal scanner. There was a click. A heavy fire door slid into the wall, and he stepped through the doorway into a filtered air lock.

Beyond that was a second metal door.

He stood quietly within the air lock, allowing hidden scanners to verify his identity. At the confirming beep, he swiped his card through a second ID card slot, and the door that led into the lab slid open.

He stepped into a large, well-lit main lab area, and the door slid shut behind him. The room was filled with gadgets and spec projects, some of which only Bruce and Lucius Fox, Wayne Enterprises' new CEO, knew existed.

Fox was bent over, studying a computer monitor. He turned his head and smiled.

Bruce looked around. "A far cry from the dark and shabby lab you'd been relegated to when I first returned home," he said.

"I like the new digs. More room for innovation here."

Fox was a wiry African-American man in his fifties, gray-haired and of medium height. The suits he wore now were better cut and more expensive than they'd been when Bruce had first met him—the CEO of Wayne Enterprises had to maintain an image—but Fox's round, wire-frame glasses were the same. As was the intelligence of the eyes that looked out of them. He still wore his signature bright red bow tie.

Right now, Fox's expensive Italian-made suit jacket was tossed carelessly over the back of a chair, and the sleeves of his hand-tailored shirt were rolled up to his elbows.

"You come to take a look at those boats we've been tracking?" Fox asked.

"Among other things," Bruce said.

Bruce had dropped out of college and spent his youth

traveling around the world. He knew now that he'd been
looking for answers, trying to make sense out of things that
had happened. There had been a lot to deal with. At the age
of ten, he had witnessed the murder of his parents. The
smell of the blood from that night, even its metallic taste,
was with him always. He had been looking for a way to put
it into context . . . to give it all meaning.

Thanks to Alfred and, oddly, to Rā's al Ghūl—he had
found his answers.

On his return home and resumption of his role as head
of Wayne Enterprises, he had wondered how Fox, the man
his father had called "the best hire he ever made," would
receive him. After all, he was a college dropout, and Fox
had doctorates in engineering, chemistry, and physics.

Bruce hadn't had to worry. With his usual perceptive-
ness, Fox had accepted him. And he had understood, more
than Bruce had at the time, the needs that drove the younger
man. Fox had become a mentor, and something more.

Fox had given Bruce the means to accomplish his goals.
As part of the old, and nearly defunct, Wayne Enterprises
Research Division, Fox had invented a number of military
prototypes. And when Bruce had decided to walk the dark
nights of the city as Batman, Fox was there. During a series
of visits, he had handed Bruce the creations that had become his armor, his cape, his grapple, and his Batmobile.

In return for his loyalty, and in appreciation of Fox's
brilliance, when Bruce retook control of Wayne Enterprises,
he promoted Fox to CEO. A more intelligent, capable, and
honest leader couldn't be found anywhere.

The only real drawback was that the time Fox spent as
CEO managing Wayne Enterprises was time spent away
from his beloved laboratories. He'd complained to Bruce
more than once, but always with a wry good humor beneath the complaints. And Bruce knew that he could not
have chosen more wisely for the good of the old family
firm.

As CEO, Fox encouraged innovation. He was responsible for expanding Wayne Enterprises' communications and

computer surveillance system. The recently launched Wayne satellite, the I-Brite 7, was one of his—and Bruce's—favorite projects. Its virtual electromagnetic lenses could bring the smallest detail on the surface of the Earth into sharp focus. Its extensive filter arrays could neutralize the effects of a cloudy day, to say nothing of Gotham smog. It had infrared sensors, full-spectrum capability coupled with broadband real-time analysis, and more gigahertz and memory than nearly any computer on the planet.

Bruce sat on the edge of Fox's desk and peered over at the monitor. "I wanted to ask if I could fill in for you at that charity golf tournament Ronald Marshall is holding. You mentioned he'd sent you an invitation. He's someone I'd like to get to know a bit better."

"The invitation is over on my desk there. I thought you might ask. I was going to pass on that one, myself," Fox said. "Mr. Marshall's reputation is a little too shady for me. But . . ."

Bruce smiled. "I like shady."

Fox's eyes twinkled. "About those boats . . ." He sat at the computer and began typing into the keyboard.

A picture appeared on the monitor screen. The curvature of the Earth. A few clicks of the keys and the image enlarged, becoming the United States. *Click. Click.* Another enlargement, and the focus was on the East Coast. Fox hit a few more keys, and the focus tightened onto greater Gotham.

"This what you were looking for?"

"Nice to have an eye in the sky," Bruce said. "Let's see what's happening at the Rogers Yacht Basin and a bit farther out at sea"

"You looking for anything in particular?"

"I want to check the position of those boats we're monitoring—the forty-foot yacht *Amalfi.* And the fifty-footer, a 'go-fast' boat called the *Сокровище.*"

"Russian for 'treasure.'"

"Show-off." Bruce grinned. Of course, Fox would speak Russian. "Probably named for the contraband it's brought into the country. It's a cigarette . . . a long, narrow racing boat, the modern-day smuggler's choice."

Fox smiled. "I'm assuming both are up for sale, and you're just trying to see which one looks better from space?"

Bruce raised an eyebrow. "What else would you use a satellite for?"

Fox studied him shrewdly. "That little cut you got shaving is healing up nicely."

Bruce shrugged. "Playboy klutz, that's me!"

"I may have discovered something that means you'll never have to use a straight razor again. Come with me."

13

The two men walked through a small door to the left of the far wall of Fox's main lab. The door was heavily shielded, and the inner surface was gunmetal, polished to a satin finish. Bruce raised an eyebrow. "The inner sanctum of doom?"

Fox looked back at Wayne. There was a little starch in his voice. "I'll have you know, *Mr.* Wayne, that—"

Bruce cut him off with a laugh. "Relax, Lucius. There's a rumor floating around Wayne Enterprises that Fox has got a safe room that could contain a small nuclear explosion. I don't know half of what goes on inside your inner sanctum here, but considering some of the avenues of research you've pursued in the past that I'm aware of, I sleep better at night remembering that this room is here. What have you got?"

"Something odd," Fox said as he walked over to a large workbench against the wall. "Remember that research satellite we recovered, I-Brite 7's predecessor? We put out word to the press that it had taken meteor damage."

"Were we lying?"

"Since all of us are made up of star stuff if you go far

enough back, I imagine that one could find at least a tad of an ancient meteor in the materials that made up the satellite. But . . . yes, we were lying. The satellite had been crushed from the inside. In fact, it imploded. And then seems to have blown much of itself apart."

Bruce's eyes traveled across the workbench. The shell of the dismantled satellite case lay to one side. Thousands of bits of wire, circuit boards, various other electronic components, fragments of unidentifiable detritus—all of it neatly arranged in serried ranks—lay across the surface of the bench.

"Isn't that . . . unusual?" he said.

"Unique in my experience," replied Fox. "So is this."

He handed Bruce a pair of blast goggles and put on a pair himself. As Bruce slipped them on, Fox gave him the leads to a set of jumper cables. "Get ready to hook these into Batbaby when I say the word. And then step behind it and watch from cover."

Batbaby was a large ungainly vehicle, stripped now of its ten wheels and sitting on cinder blocks in one corner of the inner sanctum. Never completed, it was a first prototype for what had eventually become the Batmobile. The sophisticated miniaturization that made the Batmobile possible had only been in its infancy during the Batbaby's construction. The thing was the size of an Abrams main battle tank. But Fox always hated wasting resources. He'd improvised, and now, among other things, Batbaby served as a powerful generator for the laboratory. On more than one occasion, she'd kept the entire Wayne complex up and running during citywide blackouts.

As he opened up a rear hatch to reveal a large bank of batteries, Bruce wondered if Fox had ever removed any of the more exotic weaponry with which the prototype had been outfitted. Only if he'd needed it elsewhere, he decided.

Meanwhile, Fox was soldering several delicate leads from the other end of the jumper cables to a small box on the workbench. "Haven't worked up the finished connections yet," he said in answer to Bruce's unspoken question. "But this'll do." The smell of hot metal permeated the air of the room. "Done. Hook 'er up."

Bruce snapped the alligator clips to the battery terminals on either side of the vast array nestled in the depths of Batbaby's open rear compartment. As he stepped behind the protective bulk of the armored vehicle, Fox climbed into the driver's compartment and fired up the ignition. The exhaust of the big diesel engines was vented out through a special system of ducts, but Bruce still caught a bit of the acrid smell. He'd have to see about reventing the sanctum.

Then Fox flipped the switch that sent a charge from Batbaby down the jumper cables and into the little black object on his workbench.

There was a high-pitched whine followed by a sharp crack and a flash of light.

Simultaneously, nearly every metal object in the room, including Fox's pen, loose change, and Bruce's watch, was sucked toward the black box. A split second later, they were hurled all over the room. Bruce dove to the ground as a set of socket wrenches, still in their case, whistled past his head and bounced off the wall behind him. The racket throughout the entire room was terrific.

Bruce reached cautiously over the back of Batbaby, took a firm hold on one of the jumper cables, and yanked. Hard. There was a snap, a spark, and a moment later, the entire room was silent, as every flying bit of metal fell to the ground.

"Well," he said as he stood up and dusted off his trousers, "that was interesting."

"A thousand apologies, Bruce," said Fox, climbing out of the cab. "I had no idea the results were going to be quite so . . . spectacular!"

"But you had some idea of what might happen," said Bruce.

"In kind. Not in scope," said Fox ruefully.

Wayne felt something and looked down to see that the

back of his left hand had been slightly abraded when his watch was ripped from his wrist at the summons of the black box.

"There may be a little less in your Christmas bonus this year, pal," said Bruce as he sucked for a moment on his skinned knuckles.

Fox picked up what was left of Bruce's watch and held it out to him. "I guess you won't be boating with this anymore."

Bruce looked at the pieces in the palm of Fox's hand. "My Yacht-Master II Rolex," he said in mock horror. He looked up at Fox, his eyes dancing. "Ronald Marshall has a Rolex, for Pete's sake. How can I be Bruce Wayne without a Rolex?"

Fox looked at him unsympathetically. His own wrist had been sporting a Timex, now lying in bits scattered all over the room. "Bruce Wayne is a shallow, self-centered, wealthy playboy who consumes the bounty of the world. Treat yourself. Buy a new one."

Bruce looked at him for a moment, then burst into laughter. "Touché!" he said. He walked over to the black box lying on the workbench and picked it up, carefully. "The Wayne-6 satellite used a gyroscopic electromagnetic navigation system to orient itself. Isn't this—?"

"Yes. It's what's left of the gyro. Some of the prototypes developed capacitance—magnetic anomalies that interfered with their navigational capabilities. Nothing this strong, of course, but we thought we'd solved the problem. Apparently that wasn't the case. But this one is demonstrating an anomaly field light-years beyond anything we saw in the experimental models. In fact, I wonder if . . ."

His voice trailed off as his eyes ran across the chaos that was now his special workshop.

"Go fund a charity or buy a small country or something. And come back in six hours. I've got an idea." Fox was already turning away from him toward the workbench, and Bruce recognized the signs of inspired illumination at work. He left quietly.

* * *

Six hours later, on the dot, he walked back through the entrance into Fox's inner sanctum.

He saw that the workshop, though still in disarray, had now been restored to a series of local disorders instead of one great monument to chaos. And what he could see of Fox's vast array of implements related to electronic tinkering were once again neatly arranged across the back of and on the wall above the workbench.

"Don't tell me," said Bruce. "You've fixed your watch!"

On Fox's left wrist was his ever-present Timex.

Fox shoved the goggles back on his forehead and smiled, shaking his head. "Some things are beyond even *my* genius," he said. "I keep a couple of dozen spares in my desk in the next room."

"I'll never trust a genius again," said Bruce. "What's up?"

"Get us a gun out of the armory," said Fox. "Something heavy. The Desert Eagle Mark XIX will do. And bring a full magazine."

Bruce raised an eyebrow.

Fox grinned at him. "It's fine, Bruce," he said. "It's for science."

"Well," Bruce replied, "if it's for science . . ." He walked out of the room.

A few moments later he returned carrying the Desert Eagle, just as Fox was fastening shut a small, dark plastic cylinder. "Are we doing whatever we're doing *here*?" he asked.

Fox smiled wryly. "I think we've learned our lesson. We'll adjourn to the shooting range for our next experiment."

The two men took the elevator to the final subbasement, several levels below Fox's lab. The intervening levels were filled mostly with maintenance equipment, cold storage space, and, at the last level but one, the curious and inventive prototypes of a variety of projects from Lucius Fox's fertile mind. Several of them had already made their way into Batman's personal armament.

The shooting range itself was heavily shielded from the rest of the underground complex and could be entered only through the high-security elevator that was now carrying both men. The maximum range was two hundred yards, but a series of setbacks, secure booths, bulletproof shielding, and moveable partitions gave the range complete flexibility. And very secure protection for the shooter, no matter what he was firing.

Fox walked to an elaborate control panel and ran his fingers across the sensors there. Downrange, a transparent but completely enclosed cage slid out of the back wall and came to rest at the range's far end. Inside the cage was a life-sized mannequin. In a fit of mordant amusement, Bruce had painted a pair of x's on the mannequin's eyes.

Bruce watched as Fox hooked a spare utility belt around the dummy's waist and fastened the plastic cylinder to the back of it. There were several small metal patches around the circumference of the cylinder, and a couple of small leads.

"Constant-scanning motion sensors," said Fox, catching his glance. "They'll enclose Ralph here in a sphere of detection about ten feet in diameter." He carefully fastened the leads to a battery pack hooked to the belt next to the cylinder.

"I'm still not sure what we've got here. I'm guessing that the satellite's containment shielding was breached at some point, maybe by a micrometeorite. Maybe it was contamination introduced before launch. But there's been some alteration in the circuitry I don't recognize. It's even possible we're looking at the first magnetic monopoles in captivity. And that *would* be something to write home about."

"I thought monopoles were only theoretical. That even in theory, they'd be hugely massive. Prohibitively so."

"Yeeeees," Fox said as he finished connecting the ground to another part of the belt. "That's what makes this so interesting, don't you think? But I'm game to go with the em-

pirical evidence. And we're about to get that. By hooking
the gyro up to an alternating power source, we can reverse
the polarities, just like in every bad science-fiction film
ever made.

"Small-arms fire, at the level Batman generally works,
is one of his greatest hazards. This may reduce that hazard
to extremely small dimensions.

"There's a bit of rogue iron, even in the finest steel. The
monopoles sense it, amplify the connection as the metal
closes range, then repel the iron molecules magnetically,
carrying the entire bullet—or whatever—along with it.

"Naturally, I've modulated the frequencies with smart
chips. We don't want to be throwing police cars through the
nearest store window. But in theory, you'll be wearing a
bulletproof screen."

"And if this doesn't work?"

"Well, you've still got your body armor." Fox grinned.

They walked back to the far end of the range and stood
behind the transparent shielding. Fox handed Bruce a pair
of Caldwell Electronic earmuffs and put on a pair himself.

"Would you like to do the honors? Or shall I?" said Fox.

Bruce handed him the Eagle. "It's your show," he said.
"Be my guest."

Holding the Eagle with both hands in a pistol-shooter's
stance, Fox took aim at Ralph's body mass through a small
opening in the shield. He squeezed off a round. Even
through the ear protectors, the noise seemed deafening.

To their left, there was a wranging sound as the round
veered away from Ralph and hit the angled wall of the
shooting range, raising a small puff of dust as it dropped
into the sand-filled trough that ran all around the perimeter
of the range. They looked at each other for a moment, and
Bruce nodded. Fox fired off six more rounds as rapidly as
he could. Small puffs of sand chuffed up from various
points at the range's other end.

Ralph was undamaged.

Bruce Wayne closed his mouth.

"Incredible," he said. "And with a .45 round!"

"I'll do a bit more testing, but it should work against all small-arms fire. Even at close range. But if somebody pulls out an assault rifle with high-velocity armor-piercing ammunition, you'd better be prepared to duck."

Bruce cocked an eyebrow as he and Fox walked down the range to Ralph. "Now why would anyone want to shoot *me*, Mr. Fox?"

Fox disconnected the wires and unclipped the cylinder from the belt. "Let's just say your good looks and boyish charm might not work with everyone, Mr. Wayne. Come by before your golf game with Marshall tomorrow. I should have the gyro ready by then."

Bruce's face became serious. "Lucius," he said, "you know this is incredible. If what you've got here really are captive monopoles, this is the stuff Nobel Prizes are made of!"

Fox looked back at the range, but his eyes seemed to be seeing something else.

"Bruce," he said, "I know better than anyone that you can't keep the genie in the bottle forever. Now, I could get the best minds in the country together, and we could take this thing apart and maybe figure out, finally, how it works. And what it says about the very structure of the universe. We could publish our findings, but after that?

"That knowledge could be used to wreak untold havoc if it were used improperly. Without even working up a sweat, I can think of a dozen different ways this cylinder could be engineered to kill hundreds of people. Maybe thousands. Terrorists would sell their firstborn for a crack at this device. Whereas here and now, it may help Batman save lives.

"Not everything is about Nobel Prizes, Bruce."

For a moment, Bruce's eyes seemed hooded, impersonal, without depth or even humanity. Fox almost stepped back, and he thought that for a moment, he was seeing what criminals saw when they were confronted by the implacable demon who seemed to pursue them to the very edge of Hell.

"I know," said the Batman.

14

The eighteen-hole golf course at the Bill Finger Country Club was generally regarded as a first-class assortment of sprawling fairways and close-cropped greens, approaching, but not quite reaching, the standards of elite PGA Tour stops. This wasn't for the management's lack of trying. The course had recently undergone a multimillion-dollar overhaul supervised by a famous—and famously well-compensated—course designer, and was becoming known for its enticing playability. The complex array of doglegs, islands, and hazards on the back nine in particular rewarded strategy over pure power, but it played fair for pros and duffers alike. Membership was by invitation only, and the fees were astronomical, but Bruce could see where the money had been spent.

Anyone who was *anyone* in Gotham was a member.

The club had been delighted to host the Ronald Marshall First Invitational Celebrity Golf Tournament to Aid the Homeless. Given its high-profile attendees and celebrity guest list, it was guaranteed to fill the coffers of the city's charities and aid in their efforts to do good works.

Mayor Hill was there, along with the more influential

members of the city council, and a number of Gotham's wealthiest businessmen, all of them eager to see and be seen as donors to a worthy cause. It didn't hurt that they also got to play alongside—and in the case of the highest donors, be partnered with—the movie, television, and sports celebrities who had donated their time to aid Gotham's neediest.

Bruce had maneuvered effectively to guarantee being in the same foursome as Ronald Marshall—not difficult when everyone else was vying for a celebrity partner.

An army of golf carts, driven by a squadron of neatly dressed caddies, chauffeured the golfers between strokes. In the twin interests of atmosphere and photo ops, the drivers and caddies were dressed in seventeenth-century Scottish golfing wear modeled after that worn at St. Andrews Links in Fife. The press and a throng worthy of a major packed into the roped-off spectator galleries along the fairways and greens, eagerly watching the action, their excited cheers and groans adding to the carnival atmosphere.

The tournament was a stroke-play event, where all players competed against one another, and whoever notched the lowest total score for the round would be the winner.

The late-morning summer sun beat down relentlessly as the last competitors teed off at the first green. Despite the heat, the course looked lush and well watered. Each green, seeded with the traditional Bermuda grass, had been meticulously manicured—undulating fields of green bordered by breaks and bunkers.

Bruce's putt veered just wide of the hole on the twelfth green.

Of course, he had had to work at missing it. His eye had seen the lie, his hands had settled comfortably onto the putter's grip, and his mind had understood the exact stroke and angle that would send the dimpled white sphere rolling into the waiting cup. But his will had overridden his instinct. Wayne was himself a fierce competitor. But this day, the game he was playing had little to do with golf and everything to do with sizing up an opponent. With luck, his opponent would never know he was even there, a tiger in the smoke. A slight tightening of his wrist altered his swing just a fraction, and his tap sent the ball rolling toward the cup. As Bruce had foreseen, the ball lipped the rim, then drifted past toward the edge of the green. He knew that if he played his best, he would win the game of golf but would chance losing the bigger prize. His interest was in a tactical defeat but a strategic triumph.

He knew how competitive Ronald Marshall was, and he needed to lull the older man into a sense of superiority and false security. He had to make sure Marshall dismissed him as a playboy nonentity, that Marshall didn't see him as a threat. A few inane remarks about the spectacular view of the blond starlet's posterior in the party ahead of them, a politically naïve observation about the price of gas, and he was off and running. He was aiming to establish the Wayne persona as entertaining but completely harmless, and perhaps a little dim.

It worked. The crowd of press and spectators that lined the field groaned as the ball rolled six feet past the cup, clearly hit too hard by an amateur. Out of the corner of his eye, he saw Marshall's smirk. Bruce's peripheral vision was excellent.

"Up too late last night to make it to the practice green this morning." Bruce grinned sheepishly. "You're away," he noted, prompting Marshall to take his turn.

As Marshall strode toward his ball, Bruce continued an earlier conversation. "I understand the sports center will be finished even before the co-ops are begun," he said.

Marshall grunted as he squatted to examine his lie. "We'll break ground next summer."

Bruce raised an eyebrow. "I really admire a man who vows to rebuild a neighborhood and starts by putting in an elite sports and recreation center."

Marshall's bulldog jaw jutted forward. "It's all about setting a tone, isn't it?"

Bruce shrugged. "That area needs tone more than anything. I just hope there'll be some decent tennis courts there when you're done. There isn't a decent one anywhere in the entire city!"

Marshall looked assessingly at Wayne, who was flirting with the pretty young tournament volunteer who stood nearby holding the flag she removed when each party approached the green. Marshall ducked his head to hide a wolfish grin and lined up his shot. A visor pulled on over his greased-back hair shaded his eyes from the bright sunlight. Thick gold chains gleamed amid the chest hair that billowed from the open collar of his blue-and-white-striped golf shirt. His chinos were cinched tightly below an incipient potbelly. He had clearly been a strong man in his youth and, just as clearly, was beginning to soften around the edges. Since he was a left-handed player, he wore a glove on his right hand. His spiked shoes, like his clubs and gloves, were the best money could buy.

He putted and sank a twenty-four-footer.

The audience cheered.

Satisfied, Bruce two-putted in to finish.

Marshall's caddy pulled the golf cart over at the thir-teenth tee.

"When can we expect construction on the Hob's Oven co-ops to begin?" Bruce asked.

"Why?" Marshall asked. "Are you considering moving there? It will be a self-enclosed gated community . . . everything anyone could need—shops, recreation, the best of everything—right in Downtown Gotham. Everything will be top-of-the-line."

"I don't know, Ron," Bruce said. "It all sounds pretty amazing. But I was there when Teresa Williams was gunned down. It was . . . frightening. You know, I don't believe in ghosts or anything, but to have it happen at such a

crucial time in the city's redevelopment . . . And right there
where the Marshall Mansions project is going up. I just
think it would be bad for my feng shui. Or maybe I mean
karma."

Marshall's long upper lip curled into a sneer as he
climbed from his seat in the back of the golf cart.

"Teresa Williams was a thorn in my side, Bruce. I admit
that. But our differences weren't personal. We just had con-
flicting visions for improving a run-down part of the city.
These little contretemps between people of goodwill happen all the time when you're working to make the world a
better place. But she was an admirable person. The irony is
that she died from a bullet fired by one of the very punks
she defended and whose life she hoped to improve."

"Did she really?" Bruce asked, all innocence. "The police have found the person who shot her?"

Marshall ignored Bruce's questions. "By the way, I'm
naming the shelter I'll be building the Teresa Williams
Shelter for the Homeless in her honor. It seems like the
least I can do. Maybe that'll help your feng shui." In the
distance, the party with the attractive starlet had cleared
the green and was moving off to the fourteenth. "We're
up," said Marshall.

Hypocrite. The shelter you'll *be building—if you even
get around to it—will be constructed using the money we
contributed at this fund-raiser,* Bruce thought. Marshall
might have lacked ethics, but he definitely had brass balls.
Bruce had found that the two often went hand in hand. He
was going to enjoy creating his small diversion.

While he waited for Marshall to begin, Bruce casually
put his hand in his pocket. His fingers closed around a
small plastic cylinder and felt for a toggle switch. Fox had
indeed been busy the previous night.

Marshall's caddy stood next to him, looking a little ill at
ease as Marshall checked for messages on his BlackBerry,
then slipped the device back into his golf bag. The caddy

carried the bag back behind the tee and a moment later was standing next to Wayne.

As the player in his foursome who had the lowest score on the previous hole, Marshall had honors on this hole and would play first. He pushed a tee into the ground, leaning it a bit forward, setting up for a lower trajectory. It was a long hole, almost 550 yards, much of that distance directly in front of him, and he wanted a line drive for maximum fairway distance. His caddy passed him his titanium driver.

Marshall's form was good—spine straight, bent forward slightly at the hip. He bent his knees a fraction, maintaining his balance, feet shoulder width apart, driver positioned just inside his front foot.

"One thing I've learned in life, Bruce. You're only as good as your drive."

He cocked his wrists and eased into his backswing.

Bruce pressed a button on the side of the gyro. There was a nearly inaudible *bleep!*

Marshall's club flew out of his hands and right over Bruce's head. It arced high into the air . . . and landed in the lower branches of one of the maples that grew behind the tee.

Onlookers laughed. Marshall's face turned red and apoplectic as he sent his caddy to retrieve the driver.

Bruce fumbled with his own bag as he looked around. All eyes—all cameras—were on Marshall as he yelled at his caddy to get a move on. The caddy dashed for the trees, and Bruce caught Marshall's golf bag before it could tip over and compound the disaster. Without seeming to, he reached into Marshall's golf bag and slipped out Marshall's BlackBerry. Fortuitously, the caddy was having trouble reaching the errant club, and Marshall was stalking over to him, looking like a corked volcano about to let go.

Without seeming to hurry but still moving quickly, Bruce palmed the BlackBerry in one hand and pulled the end of a small cord out of his left front pocket with the other. Inside the pocket, the other end of the cord was plugged into a small but powerful hard drive accessorized with a miniature

decrypting device that would have been the envy of the CIA.
He plugged the connector into Marshall's BlackBerry. The
decrypting and downloading of the BlackBerry's contents
began automatically as Bruce stood looking a little vacantly
in the direction of the commotion under the maples.

Just as the caddy, now in the lower branches of the tree,
finally hauled in the club to the slightly sarcastic cheers of
the crowd, Bruce felt a small buzz from the hard drive in
his pocket. The download was finished.

Quickly, he unplugged the cord and shoved it back in
his pocket.

A very self-contained Marshall strode past him, forcefully heading for the tee, aware that any public display of
anger would be a viral video on YouTube in a matter of
minutes. And probably on the evening news if anyone still
watched that.

Bruce smiled at the caddy and politely handed him the
golf bag he'd rescued, the BlackBerry safely restored to its
original pocket in the bag. The caddy thanked him grate-
fully, suddenly aware that Mr. Wayne had probably saved
him another tongue-lashing.

The clubhouse, a modern building with rustic overtones,
was first-class all the way. The walls were redwood and
cedar, with soaring ceilings that were almost half skylights.
The bar and restaurant boasted floor-to-ceiling windows
that looked out on the beautiful fairway. The pro shop
faced the driving range.

Bruce sat on a bench between the rows of lockers in the
locker room. He'd deliberately dawdled, studying the items
in the pro shop, letting the others clear out ahead of him. A
few moments earlier, a small buzz in his pocket had told
him that his own rather special hard drive had completed
its task. He pulled it out of his pocket and looked at the
small screen. Phone numbers, e-mails, a whole host of information was flashing in front of him. He thumbed it off
and put it back in his pocket. *Gotcha,* he thought.

Now the room was empty. He dug into his duffel bag and pulled out his shoes.

He'd gotten the information he needed from Marshall's BlackBerry—phone calls, contacts, appointments—enough to get started on, anyway. Now it was on to the next phase of the project.

He was pulling his jacket zipper shut when he heard footsteps. Marshall turned down the aisle between the lockers and stalked toward him. Some of the day's steam seemed to have been released in his easy victory over Bruce Wayne, but clearly, he had had some new ideas about releasing the rest of it.

"Got any interest in a friendly game of poker tonight?" he asked.

Maybe I did too good a job of portraying a guy with "sucker" stamped across my forehead, Bruce thought wryly. He shook his head. "Sorry. I have some business to attend to."

Marshall leered. "Oh yeah? Blonde or brunette?"

Bruce flashed a wicked grin and winked. "Half-Russian, half-Italian."

Marshall whistled and looked at Bruce as if he had gone up a couple of points in Marshall's estimation. "Wow! Now *that's* a handful."

15

Batman crouched like a gargoyle, balanced on the railing of the pedestrian walkway that ran along the outer edge of the Robert Kane Memorial Bridge. Ignoring the traffic that rumbled behind him across the six-lane span from Uptown to the mainland, he looked east, out toward the Atlantic. He was watching for a glimpse of Sal Maroni's *Amalfi*. Behind him on the roadway, several cars veered around a Ford Escort as it suddenly slowed to a crawl. The driver had caught sight of the great cape flapping in the wind and was fumbling madly for his point-and-shoot. The other drivers just shook their heads. Out-of-towner.

Through the I-Brite 7 satellite, he had been tracking the movements of the Mafioso's motor yacht. He knew that it was inching its way through the dense smog shrouding the Gotham City harbor, heading into the channel that would carry it beneath the bridge and into its berth in the Rogers Yacht Basin. He knew this was a route that would almost certainly lead to a direct confrontation between Maroni and his rival mobster, the Russian.

The bridge lights bounced off the fog that had shrouded the Gotham coast for hours, making travel treacherous and

slowing traffic in spots to a near standstill. Rush hour had
been a bear. Not every driver had had the good judgment to
slow down, and the city had been gridlocked by a series of
chain collisions. Even now, at two in the morning, the
roads had a lot of traffic, but most of it was delivery trucks
driven by professional drivers, who were moving much
more slowly than usual.

Moisture beaded on Batman's cape, and his costume felt
clammy against his skin. The scent of diesel fuels, trapped
in the dense fog, burned his nostrils, so that he was half
tempted to engage the air filters in his cowl.

A sharp wind gust brought a break in the fog. Far below,
he could see choppy waves reflecting the lights of the bridge
in sharp spikes of brightness. A hurricane was sweeping up
the Atlantic coast, and the coastal seas would soon surge
dangerously high. His ears listened for the thrum of the
Amalfi's motor as he searched for lights and movement in
the water below.

Sal Maroni, head of the Maroni crime family, was on
that yacht. He had been out at sea for several weeks, hoping his goons would take out the Russian while he established a solid and plausible alibi. But while the Russian's
bulls had been unable to find Maroni, Maroni's soldiers
had been unable to find the Russian. It had been a stale-
mate . . . until now.

Even without his ability to track the yacht, Batman would
have known the approaching storm would send Maroni
scurrying back to land. It was all in his files. Maroni was
prone to seasickness—it was well-known that the mobster,
so tough and pragmatic in many ways, was a terrible sailor.
In fact, it was a notorious Maroni family trait. In the early
1900s, it was rumored that the reason members of the Maroni family had never returned to Italy was that it meant
travel by boat. Exactly why Maroni had a boat in the first
place was something of a mystery, and even Batman's files
didn't hold the answer.

But if Batman knew Maroni's weakness, the Russian
would know it, too. The storm rushing up the coast would

drive Maroni back to port. And the Russian would be waiting, like a wolf, to bring him down.

The contest that had become an outright war between Maroni and the Russian had begun as a fight for control of the void left by the removal of Carmine Falcone. Underworld chatter said that once Maroni had targeted the Russian's penthouse, the contest between the men had become a personal vendetta. The Russian had put killing Maroni at the top of his private to-do list.

The wind blowing in off the ocean began to clear the fog surrounding the bridge, though the haze still lay dense on the water. In the distance, Batman heard the quiet chug of a motor and saw the fog lit by a boat's running lights. Finally, through a hole in the shroud, he spotted Maroni's motor yacht, a Little Harbor Whisper Jet, moving cautiously toward the bridge.

From his research, Batman knew the *Amalfi* was a fortyfoot powerboat, touted to combine quiet, comfortable accommodations with high-speed performance. It had a shallow draft, necessary for navigating coastal harbors and bays, state-of-the-art construction, and the standard JetStick control, making the *Amalfi* easy to drive.

Which was just as well, since the four thugs crewing for Maroni were inexperienced sailors. The Russian might still come out ahead, Batman thought, if the *Amalfi* came to grief simply trying to get into the harbor.

The *Amalfi*'s floor plan included a small but elegant master suite, where Maroni probably slept, and a tiny guest room with twin bunk berths that would house his soldiers. Though the yacht had recently been refurbished with luxury upgrades, Batman knew it must be feeling crowded to the five men who had been sharing its tight spaces . . . and had been doing so for a while.

As the yacht drew nearer, he activated the high-gain microphones that allowed him to eavesdrop on distant conversations.

He was right. It *was* Maroni's boat.

He listened as Sal Maroni, heir to the Maroni crime

family and self-appointed successor to head Gotham's
Mafia and its underworld activities, vomited over the railing into the water.

Then, through another break in the fog, Batman got his
first good look at the boat. Maroni was on the side deck,
making gagging sounds as he leaned wearily over the railing. Three of his soldiers were standing back against the
cabin. The fourth man would be inside the upper cabin, pi-
loting the boat through the fog and choppy waters.

"You all right, boss?" one of the thugs asked. Batman
thought he was trying to sound solicitous but noticed that
the man was keeping far back from the railing, away from
his boss and what he was spewing.

"What's it look like to you?" Maroni swung around and
scowled at his men, big chin with its deep cleft thrust out
belligerently. He was of average height and weight. His
Windbreaker was zipped up to his neck, and his trousers
looked rumpled. His thick shock of light brown hair, which
was usually combed neatly back, whipped in the wind.
"Someone want to tell me why everyone's standing around
here when you should be out there putting the Russian in
his grave?"

"I can't kill what our guys can't find," Guido Caliolo
said calmly, knowing that the question was addressed to
him. Caliolo, tall, stooped, and nearly gaunt, didn't look
like your typical *Cosa Nostra* thug. His specialty was sharp-
shooting, and it would likely be his bullet that would put
down the Russian. If and when they ever found him.

"We gotta look harder," Maroni snarled. He glared at
the three men. "Now that we're back, all of you make it
your top priority. Long as that piece of garbage breathes
air, I'm stuck keeping out of the way—out here, puking my
guts out off the side of this boat, or hiding out somewhere
else. I want that Ivan found, and I want him dead—"

Caliolo raised his fist to his mouth, and Batman heard
crunching sounds coming through the microphone, loud and
clear. Caliolo had popped a mouthful of beer nuts. He was almost as known for his beer nut habit as Maroni was for his

seasickness. Of the three men watching Maroni, only Caliolo seemed unfazed by his boss's retching or his ill humor. One on one, Caliolo was the most dangerous man on the boat.

The water got rougher in the channel that passed beneath the bridge. The slow-moving boat lurched up on a high swell, then dropped abruptly. With a groan, Maroni leaned over the side of the boat again.

Batman smiled grimly.

Salvatore "Sal" Maroni had grown up as the privileged only son in the Maroni crime family, headed by his father, Luigi "Big Lou" Maroni. Big Lou had been Gotham City boss Carmine Falcone's biggest rival. When Big Lou died, Sal, as heir apparent, had taken over the family business. Now, with Falcone out of the picture, Sal Maroni wanted Falcone's job as Gotham's Boss of Bosses. Unfortunately for Sal, the Russian also had designs on Falcone's territory. The other Mafia families had decided to back off and wait to see how Maroni handled the situation before involving themselves in the conflict. Even if Maroni went down, he might take the Russian with him, or damage his organization so badly that someone else could move in. They were all circling like sharks waiting for the chum.

As the *Amalfi* chugged closer toward the bridge, another sound caught Batman's attention—the smooth roar of a racing boat. He'd been waiting for it. The Russian and his crew were coming fast.

Batman had had his satellite tracking the movements of the Russian's "go-fast" boat as well as Maroni's motor yacht. He knew when the Russian had boarded the vessel. Now, as the Russian's go-fast roared closer, Batman was able to make out their conversation as well.

The Russian was berating Anton, the young red-haired *vor* bull who had led the attack against Maroni's thugs, and whom Allen had arrested during the groups' confrontation on the outskirts of Little Odessa.

"You're too reckless," the Russian said. "You started

that firefight and drew the attention of Batman and the police against us. It is *your* fault my men were jailed. Your ineptitude caused me problems, Anton, and I don't like problems. This is why I am forced to step in and deal with this crisis personally, instead of leaving it to you. I fear you are not dependable enough. Nor have you the strength or brains—"

Up on the bridge, Batman shook his head in disgust. The truth was that the Russian was volatile and impatient. He so feared losing control that he micromanaged every detail of the movements of every man in his crews. Then, when something went wrong, as something inevitably did, he flew into a blind rage and blamed his underlings for not carrying out his vision properly. It was their fault alone when a plan failed. The Russian had already gone through more than one lieutenant.

Batman could see that Anton was headed for the high jump. He wondered if Anton could see it, too.

He wondered fleetingly if the Russian had begun to use some of the drugs his group distributed along with their Russian-made weapons.

The Russian hadn't always been so unstable. Batman knew this because he had done a lot of research on Yuri Dimitrov, the criminal who, in this country, called himself the Russian.

Dimitrov hailed from the Ukraine. He was a sophisticated and well-educated member of a family with deep roots in the Russian military, where he was a recognized demolitions expert. While stationed in Afghanistan, he had made useful connections with those involved in the heroin trade.

After he was wounded in Afghanistan and sent home, he became an officer in the FSB, Russia's combined security, secret police, and intelligence agency. He developed a taste for fast cars and fast women and was soon living well above his means. Obviously, he was corrupt, but his honesty was never challenged, possibly because so many of his peers were also lining their pockets at the nation's expense. His position allowed him to create a black-market heroin network, building on his Afghan connections. He also made useful connections with less-than-reputable foreign businessmen.

By the time he lost his post with the FSB, in the reduction of forces that followed the end of the Cold War, Dimitrov was in a good position to exploit the collapse of security in Russia. Through his army connections, he began a highly profitable and exceptionally illegal venture in the theft and sale of military arms and equipment.

Motivated by greed and a burning desire for power, as well as a return to the good life he had lost, Dimitrov clawed his way to the top as one of the best of Russia's new class of violence entrepreneurs. When he immigrated to America, he settled in Gotham City, bringing his criminal contacts and organization with him. Now, in his pursuit of the American Dream, he was bent on extending his entrepreneurial empire in new and equally profitable directions.

The Russian's long, slim Cigarette 50 Marauder was set on a direct course for Maroni's slower *Amalfi*. With a starting price of over a million dollars, the Marauder had more cabin and cockpit space than a normal "go-fast" boat, and, with its triple Mercury 850 SCi engine, more speed. It was, in fact, the perfect drug-running craft and, not surprisingly, Dimitrov's choice for a little Gotham Bay piracy.

It was also overkill. The longer go-fast could run rings around Maroni's *Amalfi*, particularly as the yacht crept warily toward its berth through the fog and choppy water. But the Russian could be counted on to equate faster with better.

Startled, Maroni and his crew looked up as the Marauder roared up on their right, cut its engines, and slammed into the *Amalfi* with a glancing blow that knocked it toward one of the huge steel-and-concrete slabs that held up the long span of the bridge.

The yacht rocked violently under the impact, sending

Maroni and his men sprawling onto the deck. A startled cry from the wheelhouse suggested that the thug driving the boat had been equally taken by surprise.

The *Amalfi* slammed against the massive footing. A loud grinding sound came from its fiberglass hull. The yacht wallowed in the water. Then, slowly, it began to sink.

A voice shouted to the *vory*, telling them in Russian to hold their fire. Then the same voice shouted over the sound of the motors in accented English.

"You are dead, Maroni. I personally will blow your little yacht to splinters and feed your mutilated body to the fishes. The shattered remains of your corpse will wash in on the tide to tell Gotham that it is now *mine*."

Batman looked down from his perch on the edge of the bridge. For a moment, he was tempted to let the two sides fight it out. They were relatively isolated, it was unlikely that any civilians would be hurt in the cross fire, and they just might kill each other, saving the GCPD and city taxpayers a great deal of trouble and expense.

But this battle for supremacy had erupted when Falcone was taken out of commission. There were other Mafia families waiting to see how Maroni handled things. If he failed to win out over the Russian, they would step in to try to gain control of Falcone's old territory. And other groups would fight them for the franchise. The present struggle for supremacy was bad enough. Gotham didn't need a wider war and more casualties.

And he couldn't have anyone setting off a C-4 charge near the footings of the Kane Memorial Bridge.

Besides, this intervention would make for an interesting field test of Lucius Fox's new bullet-bouncing gizmo.

Batman engaged a grapnel and leapt from the walkway railing. Only a thin thread of monofilament kept him from falling toward the water like a stone.

16

Dimitrov, the "brigadier," medium height, broad-shouldered, with a beak of a nose jutting above his brush mustache and dapper goatee, was the first to leap from the racing boat onto the deck of the *Amalfi*. He was wearing a silk sport shirt unbuttoned halfway down his chest. His boat shoes were leather and top-of-the-line. Gold chains flashed from around his neck. Among them, a cross reflected the light from the bridge. Rings glittered on his fingers, and a gold Rolex shone from his wrist. His only concession to his ethnicity was the square, fez-like cap worn on his clean-shaven head, which had earned him the nickname "the Russian." He was brandishing an RPK-201 automatic.

Red-haired Anton and his other bulls, wearing the jogging suits and sneakers that seemed to be the uniform of their profession, followed.

Maroni and his men stumbled to their feet, pulling pistols from the shoulder holsters they wore beneath their Windbreakers.

"It's the Russian!" Maroni shouted. "Kill him!"

Dimitrov shouted in Russian, "Shoot out the eyes of the others! But Maroni is mine!"

As both sides opened fire, Batman dropped through the eerily lit fog, his cape billowing. He landed on the deck of the *Amalfi* in a crouch, a living barrier between the opposing sides.

Everyone fired at once.

The gizmo, attached to his utility belt, flashed as it registered the hail of incoming bullets. It emitted a series of nearly inaudible high-pitched *bleeps* that signaled the erection of an electromagnetic field surrounding him.

He braced himself for multiple impacts. But as each round hit the field, it bounced off, sending a hail of bullets flying in all directions.

Several goons screamed as ricocheting rounds plowed into arms and legs. The rest of the thugs hit the deck as bullets sheared off everywhere, slamming through the wheelhouse of the *Amalfi* and the hulls of both boats, sounding like a drum solo.

Batman frowned, evaluating the effect of the bullet-bouncer gizmo.

He was completely unscathed, not a scratch on him. Not even the usual bruising that came from close-range impacts. But the effect of the gizmo was too unpredictable, he decided. Bullets flew off in a random pattern. If there had been innocent civilians around, the ricochets could have hurt or killed them. Which was one reason the *Amalfi* was the perfect place for a field test.

The Russian struggled to his feet. He was holding his right shoulder where a ricochet had ripped a shallow furrow across his deltoid. Blood was trickling down his arm and onto the gun he still clutched in his right hand.

"Shoot him!" Dimitrov shouted in Russian. "Anton, you gutless coward! What are you waiting for? Kill him!"

As the red-haired young *vor* raised his pistol with practiced smoothness, Batman lashed out with a roundhouse kick. The heel of his foot connected with Anton's jaw, and the *Vor* went careening backward. The gun flew from his hand as he crashed into the two other *vory* who had been struggling to stand. The three thugs went down in a tangle of jogging suits, flailing sneakers, and waving weapons. A couple of wild shots tore off into the sky. The fourth *vor* was rolling on the deck, holding his leg where a bullet had ripped a chunk from his thigh.

Behind Batman's back, Maroni's hit man, Caliolo, calmly raised his Glock and pointed it at Batman's head. Maroni grabbed his arm.

"Wait!"

Behind Maroni, two of his men were clutching flesh wounds. The fourth, the boat's driver, leaned down from the wheelhouse deck, leveled his weapon, and fired at the back of Batman's cowled head. The bullet bounced off the Kevlar armor and whizzed half an inch above Maroni's head.

Batman whirled on the shooter, looking like a horned demon silhouetted eerily against the glowing mist. The gunman gaped, speechless, as Batman hurled a spinning projectile. The Batarang lodged in the driver's shoulder and, with a cry, he stumbled backward.

Ignoring his painful flesh wound, the Russian raised his automatic. Every man on the boat dove for cover as he pumped round after round into the center of Batman's back. The next moment, bullets were whistling through the air in every direction.

There was a soft *fzzt!* that only Batman could hear, followed by the faint smell of burned insulation. The next instant, Dimitrov's bullets were shredding his cape, pounding his back. The force of the impacts slammed him forward. For a second, he was almost knocked over the side of the boat and into the river.

Then he found his balance.

The gizmo had failed. *So much for a Nobel Prize,* he thought. Maybe the hail of bullets had overloaded the circuits of the gizmo, or maybe the feedback was too much for it to handle. Whatever the reason, he was glad he was wearing his body armor.

The Russian kept his finger on the trigger, pumping out round after round that slammed into Batman's body as he turned. Through his armor, Batman felt the punch of each bullet as it struck—on his back, his shoulder, his chest.

He faced Dimitrov, noting that the Russian's eyes were wide and wild. Lit by the glowing fog, his pupils were pinpoints of darkness. "Demon!" he yelled in Russian.

He's been sampling his own goods, Batman realized. *Wired on something. Mad, bad, and dangerous as a wounded rhino.*

As Batman took a step toward Dimitrov, the Russian swung his weapon away from Batman and pointed it right at Anton.

"*You* did this!" Dimitrov screamed in Russian. "Your ineptitude brought this demon down upon our heads! You will die for your treachery."

Anton screamed and jerked as bullets ripped through his shoulder and the side of his chest.

With a smoothly flowing motion, Batman launched himself into the air, right leg and foot extended. The automatic flew in an arc from the Russian's hand, over the railing of the yacht, onto the sleek hull of the racing boat, and slid into the river beyond.

The two uninjured *vory*, deciding that their guns were useless, charged Batman. He kicked one thug overboard, then ducked and used the momentum of the other to fling him onto the curved front hull of the Russian's go-fast boat, where he landed and lay still.

Batman grabbed Dimitrov by the collar of his silk shirt and threw him against the steps that led up to the wheelhouse. Dimitrov hit the steps hard and stayed there, teeth bared in a snarl, eyes glistening with unconcealed rage. "I will kill you with my bare hands," Dimitrov snarled in Russian.

"Then both of your hands will be broken," Batman said, in equally good Russian.

He glanced around. The *Amalfi* was riding low in the rough seas as water continued to pour into the boat through the holes ripped in its hull. The pumps wouldn't be able to keep her afloat much longer.

Batman glanced at Maroni, who calmly held up his hands to show that they were free of weapons. Caliolo and the two injured thugs raised their hands, too, following their boss's lead.

Maroni raised an eyebrow quizzically.

Batman looked from the Mafia thugs to the injured *vor* bull to Anton, who was lying in a pool of his own blood. "Take your guns—all your guns—along with your other weapons, and throw them overboard."

Moving slowly, the goons disarmed, removing guns from shoulder, side, and ankle holsters, and pulling out knives from sheaths. One by one, they moved to the side of the boat and dropped their weapons into the bay.

"You and your men are free to kill each other with my blessing, if you so choose," Batman said, looking from Maroni to Dimitrov. "But you are not free to endanger innocent lives or destroy the property of noncombatants in my city. Your private war on the streets of Gotham ends *tonight*."

Batman grabbed the Russian by his collar and yanked him to his feet. "You get the docks."

He grabbed Maroni by the front of his Windbreaker. "You operate in the slums."

He yanked on both hard, glaring down from the brown-haired wiseguy to the bald *vor*. "That's the arrangement until I get something on you both that you can't worm or threaten your way out of. When that day comes, you can fight over who gets the top bunk in Blackgate Prison. Understand?"

Calmly, Maroni nodded to Batman.

He glanced over to the Russian. "The docks are yours."

The Russian glared, saying nothing.

Batman let go of his collar and slapped him hard twice across the face, palm and backhand. The Russian stumbled back a step. "Do you understand?" the demon said. He spoke in Russian.

Dimitrov's eyes burned with hate, but even he understood the fury that confronted him. *"Da,"* he hissed between clenched teeth.

"For now, I'm playing this by the book," Batman continued. "But if a single innocent person gets caught in your cross fire, I'm going to forget the book and give you the justice you deserve . . ."

He flung the gangsters back toward their men. The Russian tripped over Anton, nearly falling. With a muttered curse, he kicked the fallen young bull viciously in the side.

Anton groaned. He lay in a rapidly spreading pool of blood, his face pale and frightened. "Help me!" he whispered in Russian.

"Weakling! Fool!" The Russian kicked him again. Anton's eyes closed. His breathing was shallow. This time he didn't move or groan.

A quick glance told Batman that Dimitrov's bullet must have nicked the brachial artery on the inside of his upper arm. A small tear, he thought—the artery wasn't completely severed, or Anton would already be dead. Even so, his life was in grave danger. Bruce Wayne had seen similar wounds during his travels in Africa as a young man. He knew that Anton was bleeding out. Without intervention, he'd be dead in another fifteen minutes.

Batman glanced at the Russian. The second he was able, Dimitrov would summon a doctor for himself and his other men. But Anton would get no help from him.

Batman grabbed Anton by the front collar of his jogging suit, hoisted him up, and encircled his waist. He withdrew his grapple gun, glanced overhead, then fired a grapnel straight up at the high railing that separated the lanes of traffic from the walkway. Trailing its monofilament, the grapnel rose high into the air and caught on a cross wire. He didn't look back, and no one made a move to stop him.

Batman squeezed the trigger, and the monofilament retracted, pulling up the Dark Knight and the injured *vor* with him. Once he was safely on the span, he released the grapnel and dropped onto the walkway with his unconscious burden.

He put Anton down and tore a strip from his shredded cape to make a tourniquet, grateful once again for the skills he'd acquired as a young man helping out in a field hospital in Africa. A gold baptismal cross on Anton's chest caught the light from the bridge. He saw that the *vor* was wearing a *bratskie smertnik*, an ID bracelet favored by members of the Russian mob, designating the wearer's blood type. A useful accessory if one were in a profession where getting shot was an occupational hazard. Practical jewelry as much a part of the *vory* bull's uniform as the sneakers or baptismal cross.

Far below in the water, Batman saw Dimitrov drag the other injured *vor* into the racing boat. He left smears of blood everywhere he touched. Dimitrov yelled in Russian, "Into the go-fast! We go after them! We must kill Anton! Do I have to think of everything?"

Obediently, one uninjured *vor* inched gingerly up the front hull, climbed over the windshield, and slid onto the deck. The *vor* in the water swam toward a ladder Dimitrov had tossed over the side of the craft.

Batman glanced down past the walkway at the two boats resting against the footing of the bridge.

Maroni was standing in the middle of the deck of the *Amalfi*, ankle deep in water, swearing into a cell phone, his seasickness ignored in this moment of crisis. The water was almost up to the *Amalfi*'s railing. Pretty soon, Maroni and his crew would be grabbing for life vests and kicking off for shore.

Briefly, Batman wondered who the mobster was calling. Probably not the shore patrol. The spent shell casings on the deck and bullet holes in the hull might be difficult to explain.

The Russian was at the helm of the racing boat, gunning its engine as the waterlogged *vor* clambered up the ladder. He looked up and caught Batman's eye. Out of arm's reach, his courage had returned to fuel his fury. The Russian kicked open a small box on deck and pulled out another automatic pistol. The uninjured *vor* was running for the helm.

Batman smiled grimly.

He reached into his utility belt and changed the grapnel

in his grappling gun. Then he pointed it down at the go-fast and fired. The unopened grapnel smashed through the upper hull of the go-fast and down, lodging itself firmly.

Batman watched for a moment from the bridge. Then he wrapped the monofilament cable attached to the grapnel around his knuckles and held up his fist so Dimitrov could see it. The cable pulled tight as the go-fast slid into a shallow wave trough.

The Russian got it. "Jump!" he yelled.

Batman yanked hard on the cable. The grapnel—fitted with a shaped charge—exploded, destroying the hull of the Russian's million-dollar cigarette.

The go-fast wallowed in the choppy surf and began to roll on its side as water poured into the cabin.

Batman lifted Anton across his shoulders and raced down the walkway toward the Batmobile.

17

The Batmobile was parked in the shadows, on a small off-ramp generally reserved for bridge-maintenance vehicles. If anybody had seen it, nobody had come close.

As Batman approached, he pressed a control built into his glove. With a soft *chirp*, the car unlocked. Batman keyed another control, and the cockpit of the Batmobile flipped opened.

He heaved the unconscious Anton into the passenger seat, strapped him in, and leapt into the driver's seat. At another signal, the cockpit window slid shut and locked. He hit the gas, and the Batmobile roared off the maintenance ramp and onto the bridge, heading for Gotham General Hospital.

In the seat beside him, Anton groaned and opened his eyes. "Who . . . ? Where . . . ?" He groaned. "Batman."

"I'm taking you to Gotham General," Batman said in Russian.

"Doesn't matter," Anton said through teeth gritted against the pain. "Dimitrov failed to kill me once. And he will try again. My life . . . it's worth nothing."

Batman glanced at him. "Turn state's evidence. Give testimony against Dimitrov. I'll see you get put in the Witness Protection Program. You can disappear. Begin a new life."

"Can't. Family." Anton groaned. "Wife. Mother. Infant son. Dimitrov will take his revenge on them if he can't have me. Maybe . . . he will kill them, anyway. Maybe . . . they, too, are as good as dead."

"Tell me where the members of your family are, and I'll see they're hidden where the Russian will never find them," Batman said. "Give up your evidence, and I give my word that they'll be protected."

"*Da*," Anton said. "Yes. I will do it. Only way . . . to save them. Go to them . . . hide them . . . quickly . . ."

Anton's family lived in Little Odessa. They would be easy enough to find, Batman thought. By anybody. And if the police wouldn't hide them, Bruce Wayne had the connections to secret them away safely.

As he raced the Batmobile toward the hospital, Anton lapsed into near unconsciousness. Glancing at his passenger, the Dark Knight thought he'd probably make it. The flow of blood had been staunched. Looking back at the road, he frowned, deep in thought.

Maroni was playing by old-time Mafia rules, where women and children and innocent noncombatants would be spared—if at all possible. And he had been losing to the Russian's terrorist tactics.

Until now.

His most recent actions had driven Anton into the waiting arms of the law. If the young *vor* stayed alive through the next several days, his input would be invaluable.

Anton would be safe once he was in the Witness Protection Program, as long as he kept his head down and maintained his bland new identity. Batman wouldn't have given long odds on that. For a *vor* bull used to action and violence, keeping his head down and working at some low-level, and probably dull, job wasn't very likely.

For two organizations that made their fortunes by exploiting human weakness, the structures of the *Cosa Nostra* and *Vory v Zakonye* were very different.

Legend had it that the Mafia had originated in Sicily in the ninth century as a secret society created to stand against Arab and Norman invaders. Supposedly, its original goals were to create a sense of family and to foster the belief that a man shouldn't look to his government for protection but should take care of his own.

Whatever its origin, by the 1700s, the Mafia "Black Hand" was running protection rackets and extorting money from Italy's wealthy.

The members of the *Cosa Nostra* who came to America were criminals, but they brought with them the traditions of an earlier time. The American Mafia remained disciplined and hierarchical. There were rules that everyone knew and at least pretended to follow. Their traditions involved a certain romanticism, even if the realities of their existence were very different.

There was nothing, nor had there ever been anything, romantic associated with the Russian mob. Its organizations—including the *Vory v Zakonye*—weren't hierarchical, but were instead relatively unstructured confederacies of smaller, loosely linked criminal cells.

Leadership was won through brains and brutality, not conferred by right of birth.

Nor did the *vory* have a tradition of honor, like that that supposedly existed in the *Cosa Nostra*—even if that tradition, too, was now more legend than fact.

The *vory* appeared to have no scruples. There was no sparing the innocent. Underlings were kept in their places by fear of retaliation. Punishment was swift, brutal, and deadly. A *vor* and his whole family could be painfully slaughtered as penalty for an infraction.

Among the *Vory v Zakonye*, it was every man for himself and play the others for suckers. Betrayal was the order of the day.

If it came to a choice of which crime lord would continue

to operate in Gotham, Batman would take Maroni over
Dimitrov any day. He definitely didn't want the Russian
running organized crime in Gotham. Sometimes, your choice
was only between the lesser of two evils.

Gotham General Hospital took up an entire block of
Midtown. It was thirty stories tall and built of tan sandstone that eighty years of smog had turned a smudged
blackish brown. It had first been built during the 1930s,
renovated during the 1960s, and was badly in need of further modernization. In other ways, however, it was a first-
rate facility, a teaching hospital that had acquired, thanks
in part to the generosity of the Wayne Foundation, the modern equipment it needed to provide Gotham's citizens with
excellent medical care.

Batman turned off Clark, drove half a block past a red
and white sign proclaiming EMERGENCY, and swung the
Batmobile onto a wide drive that ran beneath the second
floor of the hospital, bisecting the first floor of the building.
This arrangement sheltered the entrance from inclement
weather and provided a large area where emergency vehicles could unload their patients out of the weather and
without blocking Gotham's streets. It also meant that the
area was well lit and easily policed.

Batman pulled his vehicle to the curb in a smooth, gliding
motion, stopping behind an ambulance disembarking an eld-
erly woman on a rolling gurney. He was struck by the sights
and sounds of business as usual for the big-city hospital.

An EMT shouted "myocardial infarction" to a waiting
doctor—"heart attack" to the layman—as they rushed their
patient through the swinging doors that would take them to
critical care.

Beyond the ambulance, a cop car had its back door
open. A couple of uniforms were hauling out of the suspect
transfer enclosure a cuffed, drunken man with blood running from a cut on his forehead.

A ragged younger man was helping on older one stagger

down the sidewalk toward the entrance. The older man was doubled over and groaning with pain.

A young Asian woman climbed from a cab carrying a crying infant in her arms.

Another ambulance pulled in behind the Batmobile, flashers whirling.

Batman popped open the cockpit hatch of the Batmobile and climbed out. For a long moment, everyone not involved in a life-or-death situation—cops, EMTs, nurses, doctors, the staggering bums, the young woman, even the cuffed drunk with the cut on his head—stopped and stared, open-mouthed.

"It's Batman!" a doctor said.

"Holy cow! I don't believe it," an EMT muttered.

A nurse gasped, "Omigosh! He's real!"

Another grumbled, "What's *he* doing here?"

The policemen's hands crept toward the guns in their holsters.

Batman knew that, in his dark armor, black cowl, and shredded cape, his appearance was uncanny. But he had designed his armor to strike fear into the hearts of criminals. The last thing he wanted to do was distract these people from the important service they were providing Gotham's sick and injured.

He unfastened Anton's seat belt and lifted him from the passenger seat. Over his shoulder, he said to the nearest doctor—a young man who was gaping at him—"I have a man here who's been shot. Bullet nicked his left brachial artery. I've applied a tourniquet, but he's in bad shape . . ."

All eyes turned to the blood-soaked man in Batman's arms.

Several emergency workers—real professionals, Batman thought—closed their mouths and rushed a gurney forward. Batman placed the unconscious Anton on it, and the EMTs strapped him on for transport.

"He's wearing a bracelet that says, in Russian, that his blood is type A," Batman told the doctor.

"Th-thanks. We've got him, sir." With a jerk of his head, the doctor snapped out of his daze. "Get that man into an OR, stat!"

The emergency workers rushed the gurney into the trauma entrance and the doctor raced after them, the situation too critical for the usual stop at triage to answer questions and fill out forms.

Batman turned to the cops and their gaping prisoner. "Please notify Lieutenant James Gordon of the MCU that that man has arrived here. He needs to be under police guard. He's a *vor* willing to turn, and the Russian is going to want to kill him very badly as quickly as possible. Is that clear?"

The cop blinked. "Yeah. Right. I'll . . . tell him."

Batman leapt into the cockpit of the Batmobile and closed the canopy. He pulled the car out past the ambulance and around the cop car, and roared out the exit ramp, onto the street beyond.

At the first opportunity, he pulled into an alley and called Lieutenant Gordon's private number. Anton was too valuable, and his safety was too important, to trust to GCPD hierarchical channels and the vagaries of cop politics.

He needed to go straight to the top.

The phone rang shrilly, jerking Lieutenant Jim Gordon from the first good night's sleep he'd had in a week. He grabbed groggily for the phone on his bedside table and fumbled for his glasses. What time was it?

Beside him, his wife groaned and buried her head deeper in her pillow.

He glanced at the window. Still dark. He slid his glasses onto his nose. A definite improvement. He could think better when he could see clearly.

He glanced at the clock: 3:55 in the morning. Calls at this time never meant anything good. He pushed himself upright and sat on the side of the bed. The caller ID had come up as UNKNOWN CALLER. At this time of night, he had an idea what that meant.

"Gordon here. What's up?"

A deep voice said, "I've caught you a Russian canary. You'll have to move fast. Right now, he's in an operating room at Gotham General. His name is Anton. Last name unknown. He ran afoul of his boss, who shot him. Now he's ready to sing for us. I've promised him and his family protection. His boss, Yuri Dimitrov, is a very bad guy."

"The Russian," Gordon said. "Definitely a bad guy. Thanks for the heads-up. I'll have Anton in a private room with armed uniforms stationed outside his door, twenty-four/seven. I'll do what I can to protect him and his family."

"Our canary Anton is the *vor* Detective Allen captured a few weeks back."

Gordon smiled. "Thanks. I'll give the detective a call. He and Montoya have earned the right to be there when he wakes up and to conduct the initial interview. And I'll notify our friends in the ATF. This may be just the break we were hoping for. What about his family?"

"Little Odessa. I'm on it."

It was closing in on four in the morning, and Batman still had to seek out Anton's family, tell them what had happened, and see that they were transported to a safe house before Dimitrov could get to them.

As he drove the Batmobile through Midtown's deserted streets toward Little Odessa, he thought about what Gordon had told him. Gordon had made the Feds aware of Gotham's situation. The Bureau of Alcohol, Tobacco, Firearms and Explosives was cooperating in the acquisition of evidence, especially concerning Dimitrov's illegal-weapons ring and money-laundering activities.

Batman knew the state grand jury had been frightened

out of indicting the lower-level *vory*. He hoped Anton's revelations might give the ATF the evidence they needed to arrest the Russian on federal charges and make it stick.

In the meantime, Batman needed to keep a lid on the violence so more innocent people—including Anton's wife and child—didn't end up as cannon fodder.

Once again, Bruce Wayne took the private elevator from his penthouse office to the Applied Sciences Division in the subbasement of the Wayne Enterprises building.

So far, Anton had survived his injuries, his family was hidden, and things were quiet in gangland Gotham. That plate was spinning. Time to move on.

Yet another mutilated body had washed in on the tide. Maybe he'd put the serial killer next on his to-do list.

Forty stories later, he stepped into the long hall that led to Lucius Fox's lab.

Again, the hall was nearly deserted. But then it was Saturday, an entire week since the golf tournament and his temporary and useful partnership with Ronald Marshall.

Outside the metal door, Bruce swiped his keycard through the ID monitor, got scanned, and stepped through the second sliding door into Fox's lab.

Once again, Fox was bent over, studying a computer monitor. He was dressed casually, for Fox—chinos and a sweater over his button-down shirt. And a slightly different bow tie.

"Don't you ever go home?" Bruce asked. "Or do you sleep like that, bent over a computer standing up, a flamingo among inventors?"

Fox turned his head and smiled.

"I caught you on the news last week, missing that putt on the twelfth. Looked like a five-footer. Embarrassing. But probably not as humiliating as having your club mysteriously launched into a tree. Wonder how that happened."

Bruce *tsk*ed. "And after Marshall had just finished telling me how a man is only as good as his drive."

Bruce put the gizmo down on Fox's desk. "It works . . . too well. Protects its target amazingly, while flinging incoming at everyone else."

"Too unpredictable?"

Bruce grinned. "It would be great if the idea was to mow down the maximum number of casualties with a minimum number of flying projectiles. And, what might be worse, it fried during the fight. It may need to draw too much power during operation for a belt battery to handle. Fortunately, I was wearing body armor."

Fox smiled wryly. "I'll look into it. Wonder if there's a way to reduce the kinetic energy of the bullets after they're deflected so that they drop to the ground instead of flying off helter-skelter."

"If you get it up and running again, and we pursue this avenue of research, let's make sure we don't reduce the outgoing force so much that the bullets continue on their original trajectory." Bruce frowned. "I don't think we should test this one in the field again until we've had a number of stationary trials!"

Fox picked up the gizmo and studied it thoughtfully. Bruce could practically see the wheels turning in Fox's mind as he considered the myriad possibilities.

"Still, I'd like to keep that prototype in reserve, if you can put the pieces back together again," Bruce continued. "A situation may arise where its present properties would come in handy."

"For creating a diversion?"

"That's one possibility. It *was* amazingly protective, and it was nice to avoid the impacts. I've got bruises on my bruises right now." He sighed with some regret. "I guess I'm willing to put my life on the line to do what I have to, Lucius. But it has to be mine. No one else's."

"I hear you." Fox opened his desk drawer and tossed the gizmo inside. "I'll check into it, let you know how it turns out."

Bruce spotted a new device Fox had sitting on a worktable. "Anything good?"

Fox shrugged. "Don't know yet. Preliminary stage. About to start some tests. See what it can do."

Bruce grinned. "Well, if it's something that can help me with my putt, let me know."

Fox raised an eyebrow. "Oh, we already have something for that."

Bruce raised his brows in silent question.

"You simply have to play a straight game, Mr. Wayne. With honest people."

Bruce was smiling as he left through the metal sliding door.

18

For two days, Anton lay in the intensive care unit at Gotham General Hospital, amid a tangle of drips and bags, tubes, drains, and wires, hovering between life and death. During this time, he was under constant guard.

The second night, after he was moved to a private recovery room, his doctor gave the okay for Allen and Montoya to speak with the young *vor.*

"But only for fifteen minutes," the prematurely balding surgeon with the bushy eyebrows said as he walked the two detectives down the hall toward Anton's room. "He was in bad shape when he came in, and he's still weak. If . . . Batman hadn't moved fast, this young man would be dead." He shook his head wryly. "Batman. I never thought I'd be saying his name. I wasn't sure he actually existed."

"Did you see him?" Montoya asked eagerly.

"I wish," the doctor said. "I could've dined out on that for a month. But some of the guys in the ER did. They're telling the story to everybody who'll listen. They say he was a real hero. He saved that guy's life. And he was very polite."

"Polite." Montoya raised her eyebrows.

The doctor grinned. "That's what my friend Melissa said. She's an EMT. He was tall, masked, had a very hot car . . . and he was polite."

At the door to Anton's room, Allen and Montoya flipped their badges, confirming their IDs for the cops who were guarding the *vor*. They walked into the hospital room.

The Venetian blinds were closed, blocking out the remnants of the hurricane that was, even now, moving out over the northern Atlantic, sending driving wind and rain in Gotham's direction.

Anton lay in the bed with an IV dripping nutrients, pain meds, and antibiotics into his arm. Tubes ran up under his blanket. Monitors flashed and beeped. The *vor's* skin was still pale, but not the ashen color it had been when he was first admitted. And, as he looked over at them, his eyes were clear.

"You're better," Montoya said. "We've been checking on you for the past few days. It's good to see you no longer look like a corpse."

"Who?" Anton's voice was a froglike croak.

Montoya and Allen stood beside the bed so Anton could see them easily and introduced themselves.

"Do you feel well enough to talk to us?" Montoya asked.

Anton swallowed. "Yes. That is . . . my wife and son. And my mother?"

"Safe. In the federal Witness Protection Program. They know you were shot and that you'll recover and will eventually be able to join them."

"How . . . can I be sure that you are cops—honest cops?"

Allen reached into his pocket and brought out a small gold chain from which depended a locket in the form of a Cyrillic character. It resembled an upside-down *U*. Allen held it out and laid it in Anton's palm.

"Luda," he said. "I gave it to her when we were married. How did you—?"

"She gave it to Batman when he took your family to safety. She thought you might need a guarantee."

Anton smiled slightly, almost shyly. For a moment, he

looked younger, more vulnerable. "She is smart, my Luda. And he is good, this Batman. Almost as good as *vor*. But he is not hard enough. He will pay for that one day."

Montoya's eyes widened.

"Now . . . I will tell you what I know," Anton said. "You will not be able to protect me. My life is forfeit. But you will protect them? That's how it is done here?"

Montoya frowned, but she nodded. "Of course. And we'll protect you, as well.'

He looked at Allen. "No matter what happens to me, you'll protect them?"

Allen nodded.

Anton sighed. "What is it you wish to know?"

Anton gasped out the basics in very abbreviated form— fifteen minutes wasn't much time for an interview. Much of what he told them they already knew or had guessed.

The Russian's activities ranged from arms smuggling to drug dealing to extortion and money laundering. He also had contacts in the Gotham business community. Anton promised them details.

A nurse—dark-skinned, buxom, and pretty—came in to say their interview time was up for this evening. "Anton needs his beauty rest." But if they wanted, the doctor said they could have another fifteen minutes with Anton in the morning. She was talking to Allen as she said this, giving him a flirtatious smile.

Montoya and Allen looked at each other. They didn't like it—they were eager to find out all that Anton knew— but they would have to leave for now.

"We'll be back tomorrow morning," Allen told Anton.

The *vor* nodded wearily.

As the detectives walked past the uniforms who were guarding the door, the nurse began to fuss with the blinds, talking cheerfully to Anton about what he might like to have

for breakfast the next morning, when he would be allowed
solid food for the first time since entering the hospital.

As they walked down the hall toward the elevators, Montoya's eyes were shining. "This is it! The break we've been
waiting for. He knows names, dates, contacts. He's going
to blow this case wide open!"

"Maybe," Allen said, more cautious. "If we ever get the
chance to interview him for more than a few minutes at a
time, we can—"

A loud *pop* sounded behind them, followed almost instantly by the sound of shattering glass. A woman screamed.

Allen and Montoya looked at each other in horror, turned
on their heels, and sprinted back toward Anton's room.

The uniforms stood at the door, staring into the room
with dumbfounded expressions. The nurse was standing by
the window, staring down at Anton in horrified shock. There
was a cut on her cheek. The floor was littered with shards
of glass

Anton lay on the bed. At first, it looked like he was
asleep.

It was only when Allen and Montoya moved around to
the other side of the bed that they saw the hole where the
bullet had entered in his temple.

The Gotham City Hotel Suites was right across the street
from Gotham General, a convenient place for out-of-town
visitors and medical dignitaries alike to stay.

Montoya and Allen stood looking out the window of
room 1053, staring across the street at the shattered window of Anton's private hospital room. Behind them, the
GCPD forensics team did their thing, testing for fingerprints, looking for DNA evidence, and finding nothing to
suggest the shooter had ever been there. Not a fingerprint,
not a hair, not even a flake of skin. Certainly not the spent
cartridge.

"Ten to one our only evidence will be the recovered bullet. And, of course, Anton's body," Allen said bitterly. "So far, no one we've talked to saw or heard anything. It's like the Teresa Williams shooting all over again."

"The nurse opens the blinds," Montoya said. "Doesn't roll them up. Just . . . adjusting the angle of the slats a bit, curious to get a look outside at the storm, since she gets off work in a few hours. And our assassin fires through the rain and wind, through the glass, through the opened slats of the blinds, right past the nurse and into Anton's temple. And we're back at square one."

Allen frowned. "Not . . . exactly."

"It's the same guy, Cris," Montoya ranted. "The same MO as the person who killed Teresa Williams. It has to be. The man that wasn't there . . ."

"I agree," Allen said. "So let's stop and think this thing through. Anton was killed because he was going to spill beans on the Russian, right?"

"Had to be," Montoya said. "So the Russian hired an assassin . . . or possibly already had one in his employ."

Allen nodded. "And, whoever it is, it's the same shooter who hit Teresa Williams . . ."

Montoya frowned. "You're right. But why would the Russian have wanted to blow away Teresa Williams? She was a writer and community activist. All she wanted to do was to turn Hob's Oven into a viable community. Why would Dimitrov care?"

Allen nodded. "Good point. The way I see it, the one who seemed to profit from her death the most was the developer Ronald Marshall. With her out of the way, he was able to buy Hob's Oven from the city for next to nothing . . ."

Montoya raised her eyebrows. "And, just the other day, we were wondering where he was getting his financing to make so many purchases."

"So maybe the Russian is laundering his dirty money through Ronald Marshall."

Whipped by winds from the storm that had stalled off the coast of Gotham, Batman watched and listened from his perch atop Gotham General Hospital as the cops gathered their evidence. His thoughts had been running along the same lines as Allen's and Montoya's.

Whoever had used the same hit man to murder Williams and Anton had made a grave mistake. The assassin was too good, his MO—or lack of one—too obvious. Batman was certain that Allen and Montoya were on the right path, and that they would lead the Feds there also.

Ronald Marshall was the weak link in the chain, a place to start. Batman had the downloaded information from Marshall's PDA ready for analysis. It was time to go over Marshall's finances with a fine-tooth comb. Analyze for monies received and payments made.

Forensic accounting, not physical action, would probably be what finally brought the Russian down. For now, he would let the police follow the money. That was something that the cops, and the ATF, were really good at. They could handle that as well as he could.

It was time he did something about the monster who was preying on Gotham's homeless.

19

"I know that, on the surface, the connection seems tenuous," Detective Renee Montoya argued into the telephone. "But this isn't a fishing expedition. The same hit man who took out Teresa Williams also hit Anton Solonik." She paused. "Yeah, he was the guy who was one of the Russian's bulls." She looked over at Detective Crispus Allen, who was sitting across the aisle, listening and drumming his pencil on his desk. She rolled her eyes.

It was dark outside, and raindrops hammered on the windows of the old GCPD headquarters. A sharp burst of wind rattled the loose panes so loudly that Montoya looked up from her phone conversation with Assistant DA Anderson, startled.

"All right, we can't prove it was the same guy—he switched weapons. But the MO's the same. No . . . follow me here. The person who profited from Williams's death is the developer Ronald Marshall. We think Marshall's laundering—"

Montoya glanced over at Allen, who had slumped in his chair. He was staring morosely out the windows, where the

lights of Downtown were caught and refracted in the drops
and rivulets that ran down the windowpanes.

Around them, the MCU squad room was humming. Telephones rang, computers hummed, cops' voices rose and fell
in lively discussion. This was the storm's last gasp if the
weatherman could be believed. A good night for catching
up on paperwork. A good night to harass the DA's office for
some cooperation.

Montoya did a thumbs-down at Allen. *What is it with
the DA's office, anyway? Does Ronald Marshall have them
in his pocket, too?*

She made a talking gesture with her hand as the ADA
explained ad nauseam about probable cause and search
warrants. As if she didn't know.

She wished they'd been given Rachel Dawes. She was
known to be honest. She, at least, wasn't in Ronald Marshall's pocket. But she wasn't the ADA who had been as-
signed to their case.

Finally, Montoya hung up.

"We're 'going to need more than suspicion,'" she
quoted, "to get a warrant to comb through Marshall's finances. 'Marshall's a respected businessman, a friend of
Mayor Hill,' *blah, blah*. They want friggin' proof before
they'll okay a look at Marshall's finances! Talking to Anderson is like hammering my head against a brick wall."

Montoya cut her eyes to Gordon's closed door, where a
black shadow flickered across the frosted glass. "I'll bet *he*
could get something on Marshall," she muttered.

"Yeah," Allen said. "Except—"

"I know." Montoya's mouth quirked into a wry smile.
"He's an upright guy. And he saved our lives. But he's still
a vigilante."

Batman stood beside the open window in Lieutenant
Jim Gordon's office. Water dripped from his cloak and
pooled on the floor around his feet. Fortunately, the wind

was blowing from the east, or Gordon's floor would have been even wetter from rain blowing in through the window.

I'm lucky, Gordon thought fleetingly. *Unlike Batman, I don't have to go out in that mess unless I get a call.* Not that Batman had to go out, either, he supposed. He wondered fleetingly what pain drove a man to put on a cape and cowl and stalk the dark streets of Gotham, looking for criminals to capture on a night like this one. Whatever the reason, Batman should have a quiet night of it. In weather like this, even the crooks stayed home.

"Autopsies on the floaters suggest the introduction of a systemic poison before they drowned," Gordon said. "Maybe some kind of hallucinogen. Hard to tell when the other injuries were introduced."

"Crane?"

"He's still out there." Gordon sighed. "He's been at large since the night Arkham's prisoners were released."

Jonathan Crane had been fascinated by—and proficient at inventing—fear-inducing hallucinogens. For years, as a doctor, he had secretly terrorized and dominated the Arkham inmates—not the most stable bunch to begin with. He was brilliant and mad and, in the end, had pulled a burlap mask over his head, called himself the Scarecrow, and joined the inmates in their escape from Arkham Asylum.

Batman shook his head. "Crane may be insane—and involved—but so far as we know, cannibalism isn't his thing."

Gordon grimaced. "Those corpses looked more like they'd been mauled by a beast than eaten by a man. Too bad they were in the water for so long. A lot of evidence was destroyed or washed away. But not everything. Some of the bones of the recovered bodies appear to have been damaged, as though they'd been gnawed on by an animal."

"No one on the list I have of Arkham escapees suggests any prisoner who was a cannibal." Batman looked at Gordon quizzically.

Gordon shrugged. "Mine, either."

"Of course, it's possible that we're missing some files. Jacob Feely said we didn't know everything about what went on at Arkham. What if Crane hid or destroyed a batch of the files before he left? We may not have a complete list of inmates."

"Or know how many escapees we still have to recapture," Gordon said. "We've been relying on the files we recovered to tell us who was in Arkham. I, too, have become increasingly concerned that they aren't complete. I'll assign a couple of officers to double-check our list against the court records to see who should have been in Arkham when the breakout occurred. We need to know if we have an accurate register of the prisoners who are still at large."

"I'll speak to a few people. See if I can learn anything." Batman took a step toward the open window. Then he turned back to Gordon. While he was in Gordon's office, he had had his high-gain microphone trained on the squad room outside. He had heard Montoya's frustration with the DA's office over their uncooperative attitude.

He had analyzed the data in Marshall's BlackBerry and found a pop mail account linked to an encrypted wire transmission of a great deal of money exactly one week before Teresa Williams's assassination. Following the activity on that account, he had discovered another transmission for the same amount on the morning the *vor* bull Anton Solonik went into the hospital.

That tangible information—from an anonymous but reliable police informer—might help the police obtain a warrant to check further into Marshall's finances.

Batman suspected that Marshall was not the most loyal business associate. That, if he was linked to the Russian mob, with charges of murder and racketeering hanging over his head, he would turn state's evidence without a single scruple if it would save his own hide. Assuming, of course, that he believed that the cops would be able to keep him alive against the Russian's best effort to have him zipped.

Batman pulled a computer disk from a pouch in his utility belt and handed it to Gordon.

"For Detectives Allen and Montoya. From a concerned citizen. It may contain some information they'll find useful in the Teresa Williams and Anton Solonik investigations."

The R-44 Raven helicopter rotored through dense fog, heading across Midtown toward the Narrows.

Batman leaned from the open cockpit and looked down, but Arkham Asylum was hidden in the roiling mist. A beam from one of the prison's many searchlights swept past the chopper, refracting off the shrouding fog and nearly blinding the chopper's occupants.

"At least the rain's stopped," Batman muttered.

Alfred chuckled. "And the spotlights make the place easy to find, even in this fog. It's like following the yellow-brick road to the Emerald City."

"I want to avoid the asylum itself, for now," Batman said. "I'll have to time my entrance carefully to miss the spotlights and perimeter patrols."

A second spotlight swept past them, lighting the fog.

Batman unsnapped his seat belt.

"Mind the razor wire," Alfred said. "Your suit can take the punishment, but it would be a shame to destroy another cape unnecessarily."

Batman grinned. "Takes more than a needle and thread to mend it. I know."

He launched himself from the opening in the cockpit into the clinging mist. For a moment he was in free fall. Then he pressed the switch in his glove that sent an electrical current through his cape. With a sharp crack, the molecules realigned, reshaping the cape into its predetermined glider configuration. It caught the breeze coming in off the ocean, and he rose, then glided over the canal and above the twenty-foot-high fence that had been hastily erected to enclose the island.

Another floodlight swept toward him, and he dropped

quickly toward the shadowy buildings, a blur of darkness in the light-soaked fog. He pressed another switch to deactivate the glide function in his cape and dropped several feet onto the cracked pavement that had once been a city street.

He landed in a crouch, then darted for the shadows. Off in the distance, he heard someone shout—a guard from one of the squads who patrolled the perimeter island. "This way! I saw something moving in the fog."

This patrol was late, Batman realized with disgust. Or maybe they were early. Apparently the fog had thrown their tour off schedule.

"Over there," the guard shouted.

Batman could hear the clatter of their footsteps. A troop of cops, hyped on adrenaline, burst onto the street, weapons drawn. They'd be popping caps at the first thing that moved. Someone was bound to get hurt.

Time for a diversion.

He activated the hypersonic sounder hidden in the heel of his boot.

Responding to the summons, a huge colony of bats swarmed from the broken windows of a nearby building, where they had been quick to take up residence when it was abandoned. They rose, darting in the light-diffusing fog, straight toward the fast-approaching guards.

The troop skidded to a startled halt, weapons raised, gaping at the roiling mass of tiny bodies coming straight at them.

Several of the guards fired into the swarming colony.

"Bats!" He heard the disgust in a guard's voice. "Rodriguez, that swarm is what you saw. Something must have disturbed them."

"Let's get back to the perimeter," another voice said. "This place creeps me out."

Batman knelt motionless in the shadows as he watched them leave. He heard the troop leader checking in with the office, confirming that shots had been fired—at a swarm of bats. Batman could practically see the cop rolling his eyes. He smiled.

So far so good.

He looked around at the tenement buildings looming ghostlike in the fog, a hazy mix of ominous light and even more ominous shadow. The guard had a point. Anyone—anything—could be lying in wait, hidden by that glowing mist.

The slum properties that shared the Narrows with Arkham Asylum had been sinister even before the escape of the inmates prompted the evacuation of the island. Deserted, the place was even eerier. The inability to see more than thirty feet in any direction just made it worse. Now remnants of Arkham's criminally insane lurked in the abandoned buildings, brutally preying on those weaker than themselves. The more rational among them would be plotting their next move into Gotham City.

The streets were devoid of traffic. A few burned-out shells of cars littered the curbs. Firelight flickered in a high window. He could feel eyes assessing him from alleys and shattered windows as he strode down the middle of the street.

He turned down a side street, trying to get clear of the bright lights and the perimeter path, and into the shadows. He knew patrols swept past the area every half hour. He was setting a trap, using himself as bait, and the last thing he wanted was for some well-meaning police guards to spoil his plan.

Behind him.

The rustle of cloth.

The patter of feet.

The whisper of voices.

The bait had already attracted predators.

Seven of them leapt from an alley, surrounding Batman like a pack of ravening wolves. They were a stinking, scraggly lot, shaggy-haired, bearded, dressed in the ragged remnants of orange Arkham Asylum jumpsuits.

Two of them had guns they had probably found in the abandoned ruins. Neither gunman had fired. Either they were conserving their ammunition or were afraid the sound of gunshots would bring a perimeter patrol running. That would imply a certain degree of rational cunning.

Or maybe the guns were out of ammo and the weapons were for show.

Three others had pipes. Two had knives.

But they were clearly united by their murderous intent.

A thick-jawed thug came at Batman from behind, the heavy pipe in his hand raised to deliver a killing blow. Batman pivoted and kicked straight into man's stomach. The tattooed thug flew backward, and the pipe dropped from his hand.

Batman moved like a living shadow. A roundhouse kick took out one of the gun-toting inmates. Caution forgotten, the second gunman, a hulking thug covered with tattoos, was raising a Beretta 96 when Batman's palm strike to his chin knocked him into the skinny knife-man behind him. They sprawled together onto the asphalt.

A kick dropped a fat goon with a knife. An elbow to the throat sent another heavily muscled thug with a pipe to the ground. The black shadow ducked effortlessly under the raised hand of the final pipe wielder and brought the stiff edge of a gauntleted palm down sharply on the bridge of his nose. The man dropped like a stone.

Seven former inmates were now sprawled on the ground around Batman. The entire confrontation had taken less than thirty seconds.

The tattooed gunman struggled to his knees, pointing his Beretta at Batman. "I have a gun," he said. "You got any matches in that belt? You got a lighter?"

A skinny knife-man squinted up at the dark figure looming over them. "Dude—you know who this is? It's Batman. He's like this . . . robot monster. He'll crush you—"

"Shut up! I don't care," the tattooed thug said. His eyes glittered, and his hand shook as he pointed the weapon at Batman. The barrel of the gun wobbled. "He's gotta have matches. They all got matches."

Batman stepped toward him. Generally, the Arkham inmates weren't the most rational bunch. Batman had been hoping that better weapons denoted leadership and that the ability to think and speak with relative coherence was a requisite for higher status. Now he wasn't sure.

The tattooed goon squeezed the trigger.

Pop pop pop pop pop.

Bullets slammed into Batman's chest and ricocheted off his armor.

Batman reached down, grabbed the gun, and wrenched it from the gunman's hand.

His tattooed face was frozen into a rictus of terror. "Demon!" he muttered. "Not a robot. A demon! Bullets don't stop him. Need fire. Demon needs to *burn*."

Batman dragged the man upright by the collar of his jumpsuit. "Your name," he demanded.

"J-Josephus Quigona."

Batman nodded. An arsonist. Wanted for setting fire to a series of buildings to destroy the "demons" that were living there. Six people had died in his blazes, including a fireman, before Quigona was caught. The arsonist was probably responsible for at least some of the fires that had recently ripped through the abandoned tenements in the Narrows.

"Were you ever treated by a doctor called Jonathan Crane?" Batman asked.

"They couldn't see the demons. So they came for me one night. They put me in white hell. Said I'm crazy!" Quigona's voice lost its anger and became aggrieved. "But Crane . . . Crane was the one who was crazy." His voice fell to a confidential whisper. "But really, he's smart. Only pretends to be crazy. Crane's a demon. Crane needs to burn."

"Where did Crane take you . . . to treat you?"

"Treatment room. Above. But one time . . . I tried to burn him—burn them all!—and he took me to the Pit. Demons made the Pit . . . back a long time ago. Pit's filled with demons. Horrible demons. And monsters."

"The Pit?" Batman asked.

"Oldest part of Arkham, dude," the skinny knife-man said. "Brick. Basement. Crane called it Hell's Anteroom.

That's where he brought the worst of us . . . the most promising of his devils, he said . . . for . . . for 'behavior modification.'

"Kept us prisoner down there, that's what Crane did," Quigona mumbled. "Ever seen a dental pick go into a man's nose and come out with his brains? I have! Ugly. Crazy. Mad. Evil. Dangerous. Crane! *Hee! Hee!* He's the evilest of all of us! He was makin' demons!

"An' once, when I was screamin' and cryin' and damnin' him to Hell strapped in his chair, he laughed. Said he was already there. An' he opened a door and summoned up a demon from the Pit somewheres! Showed me the monster. Scales like a snake. Teeth like razors. Eyes like marbles. Said I tell anybody the demons wuz down there, he'd feed me to the crocodile. An' he would've, too." The mad thug gave Batman a sly look. "Crane's gone now. Can't feed me to nobody. Can't stop me. I can free the demons . . . all they gotta do is burn!"

20

Batman left the seven escapees cuffed in the shadows.
He had listened in on the police band and knew the gunshots had indeed drawn official interest. A beefed-up police
patrol was on its way.

He had gotten lucky. The first rats in his trap had given
him the information that he needed. Maybe any inmate
would have done. Possibly all of Arkham's inmates had
been subjected to Crane's tortures at one time or another.
Maybe it was just a matter of asking the right questions.

Within the next ten minutes, these seven, at least, would
be in official custody. Their retrieval would distract the
guards nicely from what he planned to do next.

With any luck, sneaking into the oldest part of Arkham
Asylum was going to be relatively easy. Bruce Wayne had
been born with an eidetic memory—perfect recall of every
word he heard or read and every image he saw. It was a
useful facility in his chosen avocation.

Before he entered the Narrows, he had studied a series
of blueprints and maps of Arkham and the surrounding

area—from the time of the asylum's earliest inception to its modern layout. Municipal Web sites were a gold mine of useful information if one took the time to search through them. He had located an old steam tunnel that ran from the old power plant in Downtown under Gotham River beneath the Narrows itself. It housed the pipes that had been used to heat the Narrows' ancient municipal buildings. Most of the buildings had long been abandoned. But the tunnel remained open since the steam pipes were still used to heat Arkham during the winter. The same steam drove the Asylum's huge air-conditioning turbines during the summer.

Following his mental map, Batman entered the derelict Social Services building through the shattered glass of the front door. He activated the tiny xenon-powered spotlights that were built into the drop-down lenses within his mask and looked around.

Eyes gleamed at him from the darkness. There were scurrying sounds as disturbed rodents dove for their bolt-holes. Thick dust decorated with rodent droppings and thousands of tiny footprints covered every surface, and the air within the neglected lobby was musty and stale.

Batman wound through a maze of corridors until he found the service door that led to the basement levels. At the bottom of two flights of dusty metal steps, he followed a narrow corridor to a subbasement storage room. Embedded in its cement floor was a manhole cover. The sounds of tiny scurrying feet whispered all around him behind the walls. He hefted the heavy metal disk, shifted it aside, then clambered down a metal ladder into a narrow arched brick-work corridor. A series of pipes carrying steam and electric cables were bolted to the ceiling and walls of the tunnel.

The air was stale. As he stood a moment to get his bearings, Batman became aware of something else. It was completely silent.

Batman followed the steam tunnel beneath the streets and buildings of the Narrows. He knew from his research that the steam tunnel had been part of a public works project created during the Great Depression. The workers had done their jobs well. Despite the geologic forces affecting it, the tunnel still appeared to be in good shape.

Occasionally smaller pipes split off from the larger ones. Sometimes manhole covers and ladders appeared. Batman ignored them and walked on.

The tunnel surfaces were thick with dust, but scuffs on the tunnel floor told him he wasn't the only one who had discovered this hidden passage. He wondered if Crane had found and used the underground corridor for his own purposes. Crane was insane, but no one had ever suggested that he was stupid.

The roof of the tunnel grew lower. For a time, Batman walked bent over in a crouch. He was glad it was summer and that the heat had been turned down. He was warm, but in winter, high-pressure steam boiling through the pipes would heat the corridor, leaving it unbearably hot. Still, by the time the passage opened up, and he was again able to stand, sweat was pouring down his body beneath his armor.

Maybe I will talk to Lucius about installing a cooling system in the armor, he thought. *In winter, an ability to traverse the steam tunnels might make the difference in the success or failure of a mission.*

He popped a salt pill.

A hundred yards farther on, he spotted a junction with branching pipes and a ladder that led to an overhead hatch. His internal map told him this one led into Arkham Asylum.

He climbed the ladder, pushed open the manhole cover, and slipped quietly into the whitewashed brick subbasement of the oldest part of the institution. From the inmates' description, he thought that this must be the level where Jonathan Crane, aka the Scarecrow, carried out the worst of his nightmare experiments. At least, it was a place to begin.

The level was deserted. Except for the faint scuff marks on the dusty floor, there were no signs that anyone ever came here. But the trail led out into the corridor and away into the darkness.

Batman shined the xenon-powered beams downward. He followed the trail through a crumbling corridor to an old wooden door. There the tracks ended abruptly. The door was closed with a large metal padlock.

In less than ten seconds, Batman had unlocked it.

He pushed the door, and it swung open so silently that he knew it had been recently oiled. *A good sign,* he thought. He was on the right trail.

Beyond the door was yet another corridor. Here, the brick had once been overlaid with plaster. Now the walls were scabrous, crumbling, and covered with mold. Several wooden doors opened off the hallway.

He opened doors as he walked past, shining his spotlight into ancient, dust-covered treatment rooms.

To the left was a tiled space filled with large tubs. He knew that, during the mid–seventeenth century, doctors had prescribed that icy water be dumped over the heads of those deemed lunatic, to cure them of madness.

A door to the right led to a large, long-abandoned operating room. Judging by the charts on the wall, as well as the more modern equipment, prefrontal lobotomies had been performed there. During the mid–twentieth century, doctors had believed that severing the nerves that connected the prefrontal cortex to the rest of the brain would cure a patient of violent tendencies. Generally, it did. It also "cured" them of much of their intelligence. Batman's face tightened slightly.

The trail in the dust led to a third room. It, too, was tiled. At the center of the room was a thronelike wooden chair with leather belts attached to its arms, front legs, and back. The restraints would have been used to bind the patient's forearms, torso, and legs to the chair. Against the wall, a dark box had been discarded, the metal clamp attached to it half-buried in the dust. The clamp would have gone around a patient's head, Batman knew, and would have been used to send an electric current coursing through a patient's body. That had been another mid-twentieth-century treatment, when many doctors believed that electroconvulsive shock treatment could cure a person of depression. The patients who received the treatment, however, historically hated and feared the procedure.

Batman studied the chair. Its surfaces gleamed in the glare of the spotlight. Clearly, it had been used more recently than fifty years ago.

He swiveled his spotlight toward a table in a corner. Light glinted off a modern blood-pressure and EEG machine. It appeared that Crane had adapted this old treatment room for his own torturous experiments, shackling his patients to the chair while he tested his noxious gases on them. The walls were thick. The basement was deep. No one would hear them scream.

To the left of the door was a light switch. He flicked it, and the room was bathed in harsh light from a single overhead bulb hanging from a wire. He stepped inside.

A dented black file cabinet stood in the near corner. He slid open the top drawer. Inside was a stack of folded straitjackets. A second drawer held drugs, needles, and atomizers.

He opened a third drawer. It held ten files.

Batman flipped through them rapidly. Crane had kept meticulous records of his experiments over the last five years, the time in which he had been in charge of the asylum. The inmates in his special files were his chosen masterpieces.

Three of these inmates, confronted with hallucinogenic images of the things they feared most, had died: two from heart attacks; a third had had an allergic reaction to the hallucinogenic gas Crane had used. Two more inmates had been driven into catatonia.

His "successes" included five inmates whom he believed to be completely under his sway. Those he abused and would soon use. They would be the seed crystal for the Scarecrow's nightmare army.

Batman read the files quickly and carefully, committing the information to memory.

He left the tiled room and strode down the corridor, taking the files with him. At the end of the hall was another padlocked door. Centered in the door at eye height was a shuttered peephole. A glance told Batman the room inside was empty. A moment later, he was looking at the interior of an eight-by-eight windowless, cell-like room. There was a dry water bowl overturned in one corner and some filthy straw on the floor. Batman's eyes studied the steel sheathing that lined the floor, walls, and ceiling. It was dented but unbroken.

There was something partially covered by the straw. Batman knelt and brushed the straw away. He found himself looking at a long bone, broken off just short of one end. It was a human femur, a thighbone. There were grooves on two sides, striations that were clearly teeth marks. Batman looked around the cell again. This must be where the Scarecrow kept his demon, Quigona's "crocodile," the monster who was clearly no nightmare illusion.

Batman knew now who had been killing the homeless of Gotham. What he didn't know was where Crane, his chosen lunatics, and his demon croc had gone. He stood up. That was a problem for another day. For now, he had to get this information to Lieutenant Gordon.

Batman left Arkham through the steam tunnel, climbed the steps into the derelict Social Services building, and continued upward, taking the service stairs to the roof. He knew that the old building was one of the tallest in the Narrows.

While he had been inside Arkham, the rain had stopped, at least temporarily. The new moon shone, pale and thin, through a break in the scudding clouds. The wind whipped his cloak, making it snap like an unfurled flag, as he circled the roof, studying the area around him. He would need to time his departure to avoid the sweeping spotlights and the perimeter patrols.

He stopped, looking toward Uptown. He waited as a

spotlight swept overhead, then stiffened his cape into its glider pattern and launched himself off the roof.

He caught a thermal, rising over the hastily constructed steel fence topped with razor wire that edged the perimeter of the Narrows. He sailed unseen over the river and into the shadowed desolation that was Hob's Oven.

Detective Montoya sat at her desk, munching on a chocolate cigar as she stared across the aisle at Detective Allen while he spoke with the DA's office, ignoring the party going on around her. Detective Jessup's wife had just presented him with triplets: two boys and a girl. Prompted by his five-year-old daughter, in lieu of the tobacco, he had handed out candy cigars to everyone in the squad room. A couple of virulent antismokers had looked at him sourly, but for the most part, the gesture was taken in the spirit of bonhomie by the other members of the MCU.

Montoya had peeled back the pink aluminum wrapping and was chewing slowly on the end of her cigar as she watched Allen talk and gesture. It was his turn—she had made the last call to the DA's office—and they both had raised hopes for this one. For one thing, their case had miraculously been reassigned to the honest young ADA Rachel Dawes.

Allen's candy lay unwrapped in front of him while he talked and listened. Finally, he gave Montoya a thumbs-up. Dawes felt sure she would be able to get a judge to okay a warrant that would allow them to look into Marshall's finances.

Allen hung up, and he and Montoya high-fived. Then they went over to pound Jessup on the back and tell him what a mighty stud he was. After that, they would go in and give Lieutenant Gordon the good news.

Montoya glanced at Gordon's office. The door was closed, but she could see a large dark shape move against the frosted-glass window.

Batman! She had yet to see him, except through frosted

glass. She squelched the mad impulse to break in on them with the good news about the warrant. She was curious . . . but she wasn't suicidal.

For a moment, she wondered if Batman had had anything to do with Dawes's reassignment to their case. With a roll of the eyes, she dismissed the notion. Batman was a vigilante, for Pete's sake, not a high roller with political clout. Maybe Lieutenant Gordon had called in a marker . . .

Well, once Gordon's office was clear, she and Allen would give him the good news. After that, she'd make the call to forensic accounting and get that ball rolling. She couldn't wait to begin to follow the money trail. Not to jump to conclusions, but she was damn sure it would lead them right to the Russian's front door.

21

The demon pushed through the calf-deep water that flowed sluggishly through the storm drain toward its egress into the Gotham River. Yesterday, the flood had been up to his waist, forming rapids as runoff poured from the streets through the storm drains into the pipes that snaked beneath the city streets. But today the skies had been relatively clear, and the waters had abated some, making travel easier.

It was now dark, too—in the tunnels and in the streets above. He loved the darkness. It allowed him to reach his full potential. In darkness, he could almost imagine he was not a monster at all.

After that terrible time of confinement in Arkham Asylum, he reveled in his freedom. He had existed in his tiny subbasement cell for so long that his eyes and other senses had adapted. He could literally sense his way through darkness, steered by a mélange of visual, olfactory, tactile, and auditory cues.

The roar of the water as it swept past him or slapped sluggishly at his ankles. The rustle of wings and the scurry and splash of tiny feet. Fresh air wafting through a grate.

Mold. The rotten-egg stench of hydrogen sulfide. The sweet
decay of corpses. The roughness of brick. The knobs of
cobblestones. Smooth concrete. Satiny wood. A ray of light
slanting through a grate. A bare bulb glinting on subway
tracks.

These were the signposts that guided him toward his
quarry.

Once people had tormented him. Now he knew he was
better than any of them—tall and strong, his hard, scaled
body impervious to mold, damp, and the diseases carried
by the large cockroaches and even larger rats that called the
Gotham sewers home. They hardly seemed to notice as he
passed among them—another denizen slithering through
the night.

Even the constant pain in his cracked and scaling skin
seemed bearable when he was on the hunt. He would drag
another human down into his world. One less man to plague
him. Dead meat. Dinner. A midnight snack.

Amused by his own cleverness, he gave a rasping chor-
tle.

This time, though, there would be no killing. Not right
away. He was to find the human who had thwarted his master and given sanctuary to those who refused service in his
master's army. He would punish and break the human, and
then fetch him to his master, still alive. This time, he was
not to feed until his master gave the word.

But he was growing hungry. He wanted to disobey. To
pounce. To rend. To sink his pointed teeth into pink flesh
and tear and—

The demons that were always with him began their
admonitory clamor—clogging his ears and disturbing his
mind, so he could hardly hear the flow of water above their
shouts and whispers.

In the last five years, the world had grown full of demons.
He gave a deep guttural roar and slammed his fist into the
ancient bricks beside him. They cracked and powdered, but
the voices diminished. Pain helped.

He found the ladder. It was old and rusted, and part of it

crumbled away beneath his clawed hands. Overhead was a
square stone, set into the brickwork. He reached up and
pushed hard. Despite his years of confinement, he was
strong, as if his muscles, like his skin, had turned to rock.

The marble slab lifted, and he shoved it aside. Rock
rasped on rock.

He pulled himself up out of the hole and into the ancient
crypt beneath Gotham Cathedral. He reached into the
pocket of his ragged trousers and fingered the stoppered
glass globe he carried there. His master said it was a demon bomb—he was to throw it on the ground, to break it
and loose the fiends of Hell into the human world and
teach the holdouts what they had to fear. Theology was not
his strong suit, but at the thought of dozens of screaming
humans running in abject terror, his face cracked slightly in
what might have been a smile.

Batman crouched among the decorative figures that
covered the ornate facade of Gotham Cathedral, gazing
down on the organized turmoil below. From the vantage
point of anyone on the street, he would be just one more
fantastic figure among the lineup of stone saints and angels
that adorned the front of the magnificent old church. If
anyone noticed the pointed ears on his cowl, they might
think he was a particularly demonic-looking gargoyle.

Not that anyone seemed to be looking up. There was too
much of interest happening below—in Cathedral Square,
on the steps of the church, and in the church itself.

GCPD patrol cars, CSI trucks, ambulances, and news
vans blocked the roads surrounding the cathedral. Across
O'Reilly Avenue, reporters, gawkers, and concerned family
members crowded the open square, edging in beside its
spouting fountain and trampling the small decorative gar-
dens that edged the plaza. Tourists stood on park benches,
snapping pictures and babbling with excitement.

Umbrellas sprouted like mushrooms above the crowd as
it began to rain. Again.

Camera strobes flashed as another victim strapped to a gurney was wheeled out the church door and down the wide steps. This one, a man, was conscious—alive, awake, and screaming.

Batman switched on his high-gain microphone.

"Monster!" the man shouted. "Teeth. Claws. *Noooo!*"

Batman didn't know if the man was talking about what he had seen in reality, or what he thought he was seeing now. Maybe both. He knew that the EMT first responders had been felled by the same potent hallucinogen that had affected the congregants attending the special evening service for the indigent and the volunteers who aided them.

Batman noted that, as the victims were carried out, the volunteers appeared to outnumber the homeless. An unusual situation in Gotham . . . until recently. He thought again of the vanishing street people, of the bodies washed up on Gotham's shores, and the discovery he had made in the subbasement of Arkham Asylum.

He had a bad feeling about how tonight's investigation might end.

Lieutenant Jim Gordon hunched under a small, retractable black umbrella as the wind kicked up, blowing the driving rain sideways. His pant legs were already soaked. He had turned up his collar, but somehow drops still trickled down his neck.

"Talk to me," he said.

Detectives Allen and Montoya, huddling under their own umbrellas, glanced up at Gotham Cathedral. It was a Gothic masterpiece with magnificent soaring spires, arched doors, and elaborate stained-glass windows, laid out in the requisite cruciform shape. Construction on the church had begun in 1842. The main part of the exterior took nearly thirty years to complete, though its magnificent spires, immense bronze doors, and great rose window were added later.

As was usual at night, the front of the cathedral was

washed in light. That was where the usual ended, and the truly bizarre began.

"Reports are contradictory," Allen said. "From what we can tell, Cardinal O'Fallon was midway through a special service for a congregation that included the homeless he shelters at night in the church basement, the soup-kitchen volunteers, and others who provide health and social services when all hell broke loose."

Behind Gordon, a woman babbled unintelligibly as she struggled against the grip of a duo of GCPD uniforms. She was trying to rip out her own throat. They half led, half carried her from the church vestibule and down the steps toward a waiting ambulance.

Allen didn't even blink. "Whole congregation went bug-eyed. Began hallucinating. Some became violent."

Several had rushed from the church out into traffic, screaming and incoherent. Luckily, a beat cop had been outside and had called in the incident before rushing inside with other volunteers to aid the injured. The cop and other would-be rescuers had then fallen victim to the same hallucinogen that had attacked the others—a gas that, apparently, lingered in the air.

Gordon, Allen, and Montoya exchanged significant looks.

The ambulance that held the screaming woman left for Gotham General Hospital. Another pulled forward to take its place. There had been so many victims that the trucklike GCPD armored offender vehicles had been pressed into service to transport those who were less severely affected.

Several EMTs rolled a man out past them on a gurney—one of O'Fallon's homeless, from the look of him. He lay still and quiet. It looked like he was barely breathing.

"That's the last of the victims, sir," a fresh-faced young uniform said to Gordon. "We'll take their statements, sir, in greater detail when they come around."

"Thanks, Officer Franklin," Lieutenant Gordon said. "Seal the place off, will you?"

The young policeman practically saluted, obviously thrilled that the legendary Lieutenant Gordon remembered his name. "Yes, sir. Right away, sir."

Allen glanced after him in wry amusement as he, Gordon, and Montoya walked up the steps toward the main door. "Were we ever that young?"

They furled their umbrellas and stepped through the high-arched open doorway, through the vestibule, and into the nave beyond.

The interior of the cathedral was a soaring, graceful space lit by massive hanging lamps. As the three police officers walked down the center aisle, their eyes rose, following the series of carved stone pillars up to the vaulting arches that supported a ceiling laced with decorative filigree. These columns also lined the ambulatory at the front of the church and rose to a domed cupola over the sanctuary and its magnificent high altar. The upper part of the space—the clerestory—was decorated with a series of large windows depicting the life of Christ, lit intermittently from the outside by a news-van floodlight. The walls below were lined with a series of apses—little chapels enclosing lesser altars. Above these, the walls were pierced with smaller stained-glass windows, illustrating the lives of the saints to whom the altars were dedicated.

Some of these smaller windows had been smashed during the madness. Oak pews had been flipped over on their backs. Smashed statues lay in chunks on the marble floor. The table before the high altar had been overturned.

Montoya frowned. "My mom used to bring me here sometimes when I was a kid . . . you know, for the blessing of the animals. Kid-friendly ceremonies like that. Now the place looks like a war zone."

"Most of the victims . . . even the more coherent . . . say they saw a monster," Allen said.

"A monster?" Gordon raised an eyebrow.

Montoya checked her notepad. "That's what they said, sir. A 'lizard man.' Eight feet tall, covered in scales. Big, shiny teeth. They said he attacked Cardinal O'Fallon and carried him off . . . down into the crypt."

"This way, sir," Allen said.

Gordon, Allen, and Montoya followed the ambulatory—the aisle that led around the high altar—toward the back of the altar, where steps led downward.

"Wait a second." Gordon stopped and crouched. Montoya and Allen stooped. All of them studied a half-smashed glass globe.

Gordon rocked back on his heels as the world began to shift around him. "Whoa!" He stood rapidly and stepped away from it quickly, taking a few quick breaths.

Montoya and Allen stood, trying to clear their heads.

"Guess we found the source of the hallucinogen," Allen muttered. "I'll have the CSI team bag it—carefully. Be interesting to see what monster fingerprints look like."

The detectives led Gordon down a flight of marble stairs past several smaller rooms—sacristies, where the priests kept their vestments and holy relics—and down another flight of stone steps toward the crypt.

"You'll need your flashlight, sir," Montoya said. "For some reason the lights are out down here. The caretaker got zapped like the others. They've sent for his assistant to try to find the problem."

They switched on their flashlights and shined them around.

"Might not hurt to keep your other hand on your gun," Allen muttered.

The crypt was a simple, spare space, much less elaborately decorated than the grand and soaring nave. They had to duck occasionally as they passed beneath the plain, load-bearing stone arches that supported the ceiling and the floor above.

The flashlight beams threw strange, slanting shadows on the floors and walls. They walked past a line of carved sarcophagi—marble coffins decorated and inscribed with the names of the former archbishops and cardinals who

had served at Gotham Cathedral and who were interred in
the crypt beneath it. Several stones embedded in the floor
had inscriptions indicating that other individuals had been
laid to rest there.

"Creepy," Montoya muttered. The weight of the huge
stone cathedral that rose above seemed to press down on
her. "Claustrophobic."

Intellectually, she knew that was absurd, that every time
she entered police headquarters, she had thirty stories over
her head, and she never gave it a second's thought. She
supposed the darkness and the stone were getting to her.
That . . . and the graves. And, maybe, the talk of monsters.

They split up, moving slowly, searching for any sign of
O'Fallon or the monster that had supposedly taken him.

"Like everything else in Gotham, this cathedral was
built on the bones of the dead," Allen said, making Montoya jump. "I read somewhere that this site was reconse-
crated when the church that was here before burned down.
They built part of the cathedral over an old graveyard.
Many of the markers in the floor are actually tombstones
from an earlier era."

Montoya swept her flashlight over the floor, momentarily distracted by the names and dates carved there. JERE-
MIAH KAN 1754–1803. RUTH ALEXANDER 1696–1716.

She swung the flashlight to the right . . . and encoun-
tered a black hole.

She frowned and stepped closer. It looked like a marker
had been pushed up and shoved aside. She could hear water running down below. She shined her flashlight downward. Was that a sewer? And what was—

"Sir! Cris!" she called out. "Over here!"

Gordon and Allen stood at her side, staring at the hole
that opened onto the sewer main. Beside the hole, a wet
partial footprint, the ball of a huge foot and toes with long,
clawlike nails, was clearly visible.

"I always thought the devil had cloven hoofs," Allen muttered. "Over there! Looks like there's another—"

Montoya and Gordon spotted it at the same time—the partial print of a boot with heavy tread.

Gordon glanced at his detectives. "You two mind giving me a moment alone?"

Montoya gaped at Gordon.

"Sure, sir," Allen said.

When Montoya didn't move, he grabbed her by the arm and dragged her toward the stairs. Their retreating flashlight left Gordon in partial gloom.

"It's Batman, isn't it?" Montoya hissed, craning her neck to look backward. But Gordon had disappeared behind one of the thick arches. "Darn! Cris, cut it out! I want to get a look him."

"Well?" Gordon murmured. "You thinking what I'm thinking?"

"Careless of me," Batman said, his voice rueful. "If that's what you're thinking."

Gordon shrugged. "It is raining out there. Your feet were wet. Or did you come in through the sewer . . . ?"

He waited a moment, but Batman didn't answer.

"The use of a hallucinogen suggests Jonathan Crane must be involved," Gordon continued. "But Crane is slight. Certainly not strong enough to shift that stone. Or carry off O'Fallon. And that's definitely not his footprint. Which means Crane's working with someone else."

Batman stepped forward. Lit up by the beam of the flashlight, he looked almost demonic. Gordon could see how his very appearance might strike fear into the hearts of criminals.

"The lizard man," Gordon said. "He's the monster who has O'Fallon. And is in league with the Scarecrow."

"You read the files, then."

Gordon nodded. "Yep. Waylon Jones. Serial killer and

cannibal. Mad enough before he was incarcerated for life in Arkham Asylum. An inmate during Jonathan Crane's stint as the asylum's head. And a . . . special participant in Dr. Crane's advanced fear-aversion therapy program."

"Which means he's twice as twisted as he was before," Batman said.

Gordon thought of the bodies that had washed up, half-eaten, onto Gotham's shores. "Given Jones's proclivities, O'Fallon probably doesn't have much time."

Batman crouched, peering into the hole at the water rushing past fifteen feet below. The shower had been heavy but brief. The sewers would be passable.

"The cathedral has a long and proud history of aiding the disenfranchised. This false gravestone must be left from the days when the church was a stop on the Underground Railroad, providing sanctuary for escaping slaves. In case of trouble, the fugitives could slip away through the sewers and out onto the shore," he said. "I'll follow the trail. See if I can catch up with O'Fallon's abductor." He took hold of the rim of the opening.

Gordon put a hand on his shoulder. "You remember Crane's code name for Jones?"

"Killer Croc."

"I don't like the idea of you tangling with that monster alone. Or with the Scarecrow, for that matter," Gordon muttered. "Let me send—" He stopped. He couldn't very well send the police to follow Batman, a known vigilante. "Never mind. I'll come—"

"You're not dressed for a trek through the sewers, and we don't have time for you to get suited up." Batman could see that Gordon was readying another protest and shook his head grimly. "Don't worry. I'm probably better prepared than you think. I've carried the antidote to Crane's hallucinogenic gas with me ever since he escaped from Arkham. And I doubt even 'Killer Croc' would be able to bite through my thick armor. But I appreciate the thought."

He rose to his feet, unclipped something from his utility belt, and handed it to Gordon.

Gordon studied the object. It appeared to be a tiny earbud.

"I'll keep in contact through this," Batman said. "It's a wireless relay system, slaved to the communicator in my mask." He smiled wryly. "It's not a GPS system. Don't bother to try and track me with it. Signals are locked with quantum cryptology, bounced through a dozen different satellites. You'll never be able to follow it."

As Gordon watched, Batman climbed down the ladder and dropped into the water. Then he looked up into Gordon's anxious face. "I'll be fine. You have enough to deal with here." He paused. "You read Crane's report on Waylon Jones. You remember what he was most afraid of? What his nightmares showed him?"

"I remember." Gordon grinned down into the manhole. "He was afraid of bats."

22

Batman landed in brackish water up to his knees. Its surface was slicked with oil and other runoff from the streets above. He engaged the infrared lenses built into his cowl and looked around. The combined body heat of Waylon Jones, aka Killer Croc, and Cardinal O'Fallon left a visible trail for him to follow.

"I'll keep in touch," Batman shouted up to Gordon.

He switched on the xenon-powered beams in his cowl and began to follow in Croc's footsteps.

Slick slime covered the brick beneath the calf-deep water—a noxious mixture of sediment, mold, and decaying matter. He'd definitely have to watch his step. He smiled grimly, thinking he'd have to thank Lucius, once again, for the imperviousness of his thick-soled, waterproof boots and Kevlar armor.

The vintage sewer pipes in this part of Downtown were brick and mortar, installed during the early 1850s, during a building boom when the cathedral was also under construction. Here and there, patches of cement showed against the curved brick wall, places where sewer-maintenance workers had mended leaks and cracks, but, for the most part, the old storm drains appeared to have held up well through the ensuing century and a half.

Gotham's sewer system was both an engineering marvel and a work in progress. It consisted of nearly six thousand miles of mains and pipes, the shapes, materials, and sizes of which varied wildly.

Nearly 60 percent of that vast, mostly invisible underground network was made up of combined sewers that carried runoff from storms as well as waste from sinks, tubs, and toilets. Most of the time, its contents flowed toward treatment plants. But when huge storms hit Gotham, as they had for the past week, the water rose too rapidly for the plants to handle the influx, and thousands of gallons of untreated trash, chemicals, and raw sewage spilled into Gotham's rivers and bays. For years, Gotham had debated the construction of underground reservoirs where the overflow could be held for treatment, but political wrangling had stalled the project. Now at last, the work had begun. Personally, Batman thought that the Gotham Waste Water Reclamation Project was going to make Boston's Big Dig look like a walk in the park.

The good news, from Batman's perspective, was that the swiftly flowing current from the recent storms had left the mains he traversed in relatively clean condition.

They stank. But, for now, the stench was bearable.

He heard the *thump thump* of cars and louder *whamp rattle thwump* of trucks as they bounced over a manhole cover. He looked up. A concrete shaft rose over his head with hand-over-hand rungs embedded in its side. He estimated that he was about two stories underground.

He switched off the xenon lights and, for the moment, was enveloped in darkness. In the pitch black, his other senses sharpened. The susurration of moving water echoed softly around him in the endless tunnels. The smells—damp brick, salt water, decay—seemed more intense. It was another world down here.

He engaged his infrared lenses and checked for a heat signature. In theory, Killer Croc could have carried the

cardinal to the surface through any of the auxiliary connecting tunnels. But the heat trail continued down the sewer
main.

As he reached each connecting shaft or pipe he stopped
to double-check Croc's trail.

Eventually, he reached a point where the wide brick
main split into two narrower tunnels, one an arched brick
construct and the other a round cement pipe. The heat trail
turned left into the lower, narrower brick sewer that seemed
to lead slightly downhill. He had to walk with his head bent
because, when he stood upright, the ears of his cowl scraped
against the ceiling.

A child's plastic doll bobbed past him, carried along on
the diminishing current. The water was only calf high, now,
and was receding fast.

The light from his xenon-powered spotlights caught
something white—albino crayfish, he realized, trapped in a
shallow pool, moving sluggishly.

As he walked on, small eyes glowed green, reflecting
back the spotlights from his cowl. The splash of his boots
ricocheted around the tunnel.

He stopped, switched off his xenon beams, and waited
in darkness. Was that the sound of someone coming toward
him? Had Croc realized he was being followed? Had he
doubled back?

Then the sound died, and he realized he was hearing an
echo of his own footsteps, not those of an approaching
stranger. He switched the beams back on and sloshed forward.

A dull roar was coming from somewhere up ahead.

As Batman got closer, he saw that the noise was made
by the runoff from the earlier shower, pouring from a dozen
circular openings into the larger pipe he was following.
Noisy, but not dangerous. During a heavy and prolonged
storm, runoff would pour through the grates in the street
above and flood into the storm drains. The water could rise
faster than a foot per minute. He hoped that the evening

weather forecast—a 30 percent chance of light, sporadic showers—would prove accurate.

He trudged on. The enveloping darkness became his world.

The movement of the narrow beams threw nearby objects into bright relief and cast dancing shadows across the brickwork. He barely noticed the smells now, of damp, mold, and decay. The drips, slaps, and trickles of sluggishly moving water became his new reality. It sounded rhythmic, lulling—almost as if the pipes were whispering words that were just beyond his understanding. The overall effect was near hypnotic.

He snapped himself to attention, refusing to let his mind drift into limbo while he was on the hunt. In his line of work, it took little to turn predator into prey. He noticed that the murmuring sounds around him had been joined by a gushing deep bellow.

Minutes later, he discovered the source of the sound. The tunnel he was following ended abruptly, opening some feet above the floor of a large concrete chamber that seemed to be a combination junction room and catch basin. The runoff ran over his feet and fell to a pool below. Miniature waterfalls from a dozen other openings around the chamber cascaded down the walls, adding to the clamor. More of the climbing rungs rose along the walls. At the far end of the chamber, the pool was emptying through a corroded metal grill into a large opening that led away and downward—probably carrying the overflow toward the river.

A stench, worse than any he had smelled before, assailed his nostrils. When he got home, he was going to need more than one hot bath to wash away the stink of the sewers.

He took a small, battery-powered combustible-gas detector from his utility belt and switched it on. A red light flashed, indicating the presence of methane.

He touched a small button near the chin of his mask, keying his communicator.

"Can you hear me, Gordon?"

Gordon's voice sounded in his ear. "Loud and clear."

"I'm still on Croc's trail. There's methane in here. I'm switching to air assist, so I may be out of touch for a while," he said.

"Roger that," Gordon answered. "Be careful down there."

He unclipped a miniature breather mask from his utility belt, unfolded it, and secured it over his nose and mouth.

He followed Croc's heat trail up the climbing rungs and into another of the pipes that spilled its torrent from the center of the wall. It amazed Batman that Jones could have carried the cardinal up the ladder and into the pipe, but it was a feat he appeared to have managed.

Batman knew Jones was large—near eight feet tall, the report had said. He must also be immensely strong.

He thought about the information that he had found in Crane's—the Scarecrow's—secret file.

"Waylon Jones . . . a former circus sideshow freak . . . Suffers from a rare skin disorder known as epidermolytic hyperkeratosis . . ."

Epidermolytic hyperkeratosis was a rare, hereditary, congenital skin disease characterized by thick, warty, blistering skin with large red patches and an overgrowth of the horny layer of epidermis. In the condition, thick, generally dark scales formed parallel rows of spines or ridges, especially near large joints. There was often thickening of one or more of the nails, and hair was usually sparse.

But as the disease typically presented, the skin was fragile and blistered easily following trauma. The way Jones was moving through the tunnels, carrying the heavy O'Fallon as if his weight meant nothing, made Batman wonder if there had been a misdiagnosis. Because, for Jones to walk and climb barefooted through these tunnels, his skin would have to be as tough as alligator hide.

Besides, Batman had seen a picture of the man. The picture was small, and in black-and-white, but Jones's skull had appeared misshapen, with a receding forehead and a nose and a jaw that jutted forward, like an animal's muzzle.

His pupils were slitted instead of round. And his teeth looked abnormally pointed and sharp. Except for his ears, his face looked as much reptilian as human.

Congenital, yes. But not epidermolytic hyperkeratosis. Probably some bizarre mutation, possibly with mental as well as physical manifestations.

Killer Croc, indeed.

Water flowed down past him as the round concrete pipe rose at a shallow angle toward the surface. His steps echoed faintly as he walked uphill beside a rushing rivulet of water.

A glance up a manhole shaft told Batman he was only about a story below street level now. He tested the air again, found it fit to breathe, removed his breathing mask, and walked on.

More often now, he began to hear the sporadic *thwumps* and *bumps* as cars crossed manhole covers. Slivers of light from a streetlamp drifted in through a barred grate overhead. Once he smelled the scent of cooking meat. A little farther on, he heard the voices of two men on the street above discussing politics.

He thought he must be in western Downtown beneath the restaurant district near City Hall. The possible points of egress were increasing. He decided to shift to infrared.

About five blocks farther, the heat signature began to climb upward toward a manhole. Batman mounted the rungs to follow. He stopped near the top of the shaft and listened. No traffic rumbled. No lights flashed.

He shoved at the manhole cover and it lifted easily.

He climbed out onto a derelict, cement-paved courtyard, still damp from the earlier rain shower. He stared up at a looming two-story brick building, feeling slightly disoriented while his eyes adjusted to the ambient city light. It felt odd, to stand on ground that didn't rise or curve. Strange to hear the crisp slap of footsteps on dry pavement. Blessed relief to smell the fresh, clean river air.

Even if he hadn't seen the huge smokestacks towering

above the gabled roof, he would have recognized the location—the Miller Power Station, on the shore of the Gotham River. He had come here on a school trip as a young child, before the plant had been placed on standby. The obsolete power station had been decommissioned soon after his visit, when the newer Gotham Light and Power Station came on line across the river. The older structure had been scheduled for demolition. A sign posted over the main door told him that this was yet another Ronald Marshall project. He was unsurprised.

After his dark, claustrophobic travel through the sewers, the details of the building stood out in sharp relief. The red-brick edifice was wrapped all around with two rows of windows. The upper windows were huge—twenty feet tall and arched, with red terra-cotta trim and corbelled cornices. The smaller windows below were square and built to a more human scale.

The windows that weren't broken, like the exterior walls that surrounded them, were covered with graffiti to a height of twelve feet: gang symbols, personal handles, art that overlaid other graffiti going back over the past twenty years. This alone made it apparent that the buildings had been abandoned for a long time.

Killer Croc's heat trail led through the front entrance. Its double doors, capped by a decorative gable and more of the red terra-cotta trim, were flung wide, their wooden surfaces covered with the same painted scrawls that coated the rest of the first floor's exterior.

The interior was a vast, dramatic, open space, rising like the nave of a church, past the arched windows to a row of massive skylights that lined the roof gable. This had been a cathedral to progress, Batman thought. And though its boilers and turbines had been taken for scrap long ago, it still held a strange and terrible beauty.

A rusted metal catwalk stretched the length of the space, maybe five stories above. Rain had come in through broken windows and skylights, and puddles and pools reflected the ambient light that shone through the windows.

The building reverberated with small noises made larger by the vastness of the space. *Clicks, clangs, drips, creaks.* The cooing of roosting pigeons. The flutter of bats' wings.

Bats, Batman thought. *What Killer Croc fears most. The stuff of his nightmares. Let's hope Crane hasn't managed to cure him of that particular obsession.* Needing to be sure of his footing in the derelict building—he definitely didn't want to fall through a hole into the level below—Batman switched on his small headlights once more. There, on the slate floor, were several wet footprints—huge, clawed, the distance widely spaced, even for an individual who was eight feet tall. For some reason—maybe because bats were roosting in the building or because Cardinal O'Fallon was beginning to awaken—Killer Croc was moving fast.

Batman picked up his speed as well, followed Croc's trail across the debris-covered floor. He switched to infrared intermittently, following the heat trail past the pits where the huge boilers had once heated and the great turbines had once spun, manufacturing the electricity that had run this part of Gotham.

Pipes jutted from the floor at odd angles. In several places, he narrowly avoided large holes in the floor.

The trail led down more rusted steps, then out a smaller door in the back.

This was the blackened area where coal, the energy source for the plant, had been stored in huge bunkers. Ships had once delivered a seemingly endless stream of coal via the river to Gotham's "Little Coaltown." Coal heated the boilers that turned the turbines that produced electricity. And river water cooled its machinery and was the source of the steam that was the plant's by-product.

In the middle of a cement lot, pitted with broken slabs and stagnant puddles, the trail disappeared into another manhole.

Batman pulled it open—it was the entrance to another steam tunnel. Given the location, he guessed that wasn't surprising. Nor was it surprising, he thought, that the tunnel was still active though the plant was closed. Vast sections of the old network were still in use, carrying steam from the new plant as easily as they had carried it from the old.

With a quick look at the manhole cover, Batman dropped into the steam tunnel—more brick—and pulled the hatch shut behind him with a *clang!* Again he activated his infrared vision. But the heat from the pipes obscured Croc's heat signature. Batman couldn't tell which way he had gone.

He switched on the xenon beams and scanned the tunnel floor carefully. Toward the north, he spotted a series of scuffs in the dust.

Batman crouched and studied the prints. Big. Damp. Barefoot. Marks made by clawed nails.

He touched a small button near the chin of his mask again, keying his communicator. "Can you hear me, Gordon?"

Gordon's voice sounded in his ear. "Loud and clear."

"I've found more footprints. Based on the size and depth of the depressions, I'd estimate our Killer Croc weighs more than three hundred pounds.

"He came out in the grounds of the Miller Power Station, but he's gone to earth again, through one of the active steam tunnels. Stay tuned."

Batman followed the steam tunnel, relying on observation since infrared was virtually useless. Occasionally, he spotted the scuffs in the dust that told him he was still on Croc's trail.

At one point, the walls of the tunnel became concrete and dipped, dropping beneath the Narrows Channel, he thought, then up under Midtown.

Finally, at a large junction where two tunnels met, he lost the trail completely. The dust on the floors of the tunnel ahead and the one to the right were crisscrossed with clawed tracks—a major thoroughfare for Killer Croc. But which way had he gone this time?

23

Batman lost time while he scouted the tunnels, first forward through the passage that continued north, then down the section that turned off to the east.

Finally, when he had almost given up, he found a scarlet thread snagged on the fastening of a pipe up near the ceiling.

He keyed the communicator. "Gordon, are you there?"

"I'm here," Gordon said.

"What was Cardinal O'Fallon wearing when he was taken?"

"Let me check." In a moment Gordon was back on line. "Black cassock trimmed in scarlet, a fringed silk scarlet sash, and skullcap. Oh, and a pectoral cross and his ring of office."

"Thanks," said Batman. "I'll be in touch."

Scarlet, he thought, fingering the silky filament. Probably fringe from the cardinal's sash.

An image resolved in his mind—the old cardinal, dressed in black and scarlet, flung over the shoulder of the monster who was carrying him. Only . . . if Batman remembered right, a cardinal's sashes hung down the front of his cassock. How did a thread get hung up near the ceiling unless . . .

Had O'Fallon awakened? Had he managed to lift or tear the sash, to deliberately snag a thread on a rough nail near eye level where anyone looking for him might spot it? Was he aware enough to leave clues for rescuers to follow?

Several minutes later, Batman had his answer. Another clue—the cardinal's skullcap—dropped before a ladder that ran up a shaft beside a series of pipes. He climbed the shaft and pushed open a square metal hatch.

Batman found himself in a small dusty storeroom. Rusty equipment was piled against one wall. The steam pipes continued upward, past metal girders and horizontal pipes, and through the ceiling. Before him was a metal door. He shoved it and it creaked open.

The beams from his light caught a graffiti-covered sign and, suddenly, he knew where he was—in western Midtown, on the lowest level subway platform of the Terminal Street Station.

The three-level Terminal Street Station, which lay beneath the Gotham City Central Terminal, had been built originally during the early 1930s as part of an effort to link the subways with commuter rail and bus lines. Levels one and two had carried passengers up- and downtown for more than seventy-five years. No one knew why the third level—a single platform with uptown trains on one side and downtown trains on the other—had been built, though it may have been part of a make-work program during the Great Depression. At any rate, it was never completely finished, and was eventually used for only a few years during the late 1930s, then, again for reasons unknown, abandoned.

But not by everyone. The graffiti that covered the station's tiled walls and girders made that clear.

He checked the area with infrared. Killer Croc's heat trail led down the platform, then merged with the heat signatures of a group of figures. People . . . but what were they doing down here in darkness? Where there were people, he

would have expected some kind of light source, if only
from candles or battery-powered lanterns.

He activated his flash beams and stepped forward. The
light hit a jumble of cardboard shanties and blankets . . . a
small tent city erected on the center platform.

Huddled behind them, a dozen people—mostly men but
a few women—blinked fearfully up at him, shielding their
eyes from the burning glow of his lamps. Some were
dressed in thin rags, others were swaddled in thick layers,
obviously wearing every piece of clothing that they owned.
Caught by the harsh glare of the xenon beams, they hardly
looked human.

He could only imagine how, in his cowl and cape, he
looked to them.

He keyed in his communicator and murmured, "Gordon.
I'm on the third level of the Terminal Street Station."

"The abandoned level?" Gordon's voice said in his ear.

Batman smiled. Trust Gordon to catch on quickly. "You
got it. I just found at least some of our missing homeless."

He stepped forward, and the smell hit him. The stench
of human waste. Of decaying garbage. Of unwashed bodies. Of sweat and fear.

A skinny wraith in rags sidled toward him—an old man,
chin covered with a scraggly beard, wearing a stocking cap
pulled down low on his forehead. He squinted up into Batman's face, then looked him down and up again.

"You Batman," he said. "You supposed to be up in the
sky. Why you underground? You break your wings?"

"I'm looking for a monster," Batman said.

"We all monsters here." The mole man cackled. "Monsters . . . an' maybe a few ghosts, too."

"This one's different," Batman said. "He's a predator.
He just came this way."

The mole man nodded. "Killer Croc. They say his
momma didn't want him. Flushed him into the sewers. All
that toxic waste done turned him. Made him ugly. Made him
strong. We see him, we kill the fire. Croc don't like it when
folks look at him."

"We don't like it when Croc looks at us!" A gray-haired woman stomped forward into the light. She was larger than the man and stood with arms crossed belligerently over her large bosom. Her thick legs were below several dresses worn one on top of the other. "That monster had somebody. Saw him 'fore we killed the light. Old guy. That Croc—he's bad news."

"Then why do you stay here?" Batman asked. "With Croc nearby?"

"This is our spot," the woman said. "We were here first. Before the others came." She spat on the platform.

"Got no choice, anyway," the man mumbled. "Demons're up there."

"Demons down here, too," the old woman snapped. "Scarecrow tells us stay, so we stay. Most of us. Ones that run, he sends Croc after 'em. Rest of us too scared to run. Besides," she said again, "this is our spot."

"I'm gettin' hungry," a tattooed teenager in a leather vest chimed in. "I'm tired of eatin' rats. Somebody's gonna need to go into the upper levels. Need to get us some real food. If Scarecrow finds out, though, he won't like it." He frowned. "Maybe *you* can get us food."

Batman frowned. "Maybe I can get rid of Croc for you. Where did he go?"

The old man pointed a rag-wrapped hand toward the mouth of the downtown tunnel. "He gone down the coffin road."

Batman shined his beams toward the opening.

"Thanks." He turned, leapt down onto the tracks, and began to walk toward the tunnel.

"Hey, Bat," the man called out. "When you flyin', what the city look like from up on high?"

"Light and dark," Batman said. "A few bright spots. And lots of shadows."

As Batman followed the track, he switched to infrared. Yes, there was the heat signature, faint and fading fast. He had lost time as he checked the steam tunnel, trying to determine Croc's direction, then talked to the mole people. Now the monster had gotten even farther ahead of him.

It could be worse, he thought. Without the clues O'Fallon's had left, he could have veered off down the wrong tunnel. It might have been hours before he came this way. Or days.

He flipped on the xenon flash beams. A little farther on, the tunnel split—the main track rose toward the upper level. Somehow he didn't think that was the path Croc had taken.

He checked via infrared, then turned left into the narrower offshoot tunnel.

The subway tracks sloped downward and, as the tunnel dropped, he noticed that the steel tracks were rusty with disuse. In spots, the wooden ties that supported the tracks had rotted away to dust.

He began to walk through water, overflow from the storm, he surmised, that had run into the tunnel and hadn't had a chance to drain out. If it ever drained down here. It smelled moldy and dank.

Water rose to his ankles. To his calves. Nearly to his knees. What was this track? he wondered. Where did it lead?

Abruptly he came upon a wall of dirt, fallen brick, and boulders that blocked the passage. Had the builders gone this far and just . . . stopped digging? No. The track ran under the dirt. Clearly, there'd been a cave-in. So where was Killer Croc?

Batman checked with infrared. The heat trail ran up the pile of debris—and, yes, he could see the clawed prints where the ground was soft.

And there, half-buried in the dirt, a gold ring gleamed.

He scooped it up. It was the cardinal's ring of office. The old man was still alive . . . still doing his best to assist in his own rescue. Batman stowed the ring in his utility belt and ran his light beam up the barrier, following the footprints.

There, at the top of the tunnel, was a hole that looked as if someone—Croc, probably—had dug it out from the other side.

Batman climbed the rocky slope, following in Croc's footsteps—if this rubble was stable enough to hold Croc and his burden, it would surely hold him. At the top of the barrier, he shined his xenon beams through the hole into the darkness beyond.

He could hear the trickle and slap of moving water. There was a jumble of something indistinguishable—boxes, maybe, and a scattering of white shards that reflected back the light. He couldn't make sense of what he was seeing. There was the faint rotten-egg smell of hydrogen sulfide. It was almost certainly accompanied by the odorless but equally flammable methane, produced by bacteria from decomposing organic matter.

He checked with infrared. Croc's heat signature seemed brighter there. Maybe he had lingered on the far side of the cave-in for a while.

Maybe he was entering Croc's lair.

Batman climbed through the hole and slid down the rocky slope. He landed in water up to his waist and stood there, looking around.

The side tunnel was roughly fashioned—blasted out of rock, then reinforced with the wooden beams. He could see places where large chunks of rock had crashed from the rocky ceiling onto the floor below. Here and there, jagged chunks of stone stuck up through the surface of the water.

The boxes he had seen were rough wooden coffins . . . some intact, some broken by slabs of rocks that had crashed down from the ceiling. The light-colored shards were bones—parts of moldering skeletons that had spilled from the shattered caskets.

"Gordon? Can you hear me?" he said into his communicator.

"There's static." Gordon's voice crackled in his ear. "But I can make out what you're saying."

"Good. I'm pretty far down. I entered an old subway siding and followed it past a cave-in into a flooded area."

"A cave-in?"

"There are flatbed cars, some of them half-buried in rubble. Jim . . . remember the story of the missing bodies from the Great Flood of 1939?"

"The urban legend about the poor squatters who died when flood waters buried the bog that used to be Robinson Park? The ones who were being transported out of city for burial when a tunnel gave way?"

"And whose spirits haunt the rail lines," Batman said. "There are coffins down here. And skeletons. Dozens of them, spilling off the flatbeds and into the water. They've been here quite a while."

"Maybe that explains why they quit using that level," Gordon said.

"City government must have covered it up pretty thoroughly. Probably didn't want to risk more lives in an unstable tunnel to disinter the already dead but didn't want to anger the populace by their callous abandonment of the corpses."

"But the story survived as urban legend, like the tales of the crocodile in the sewers."

"Just when you think you know all of Gotham's secrets." Batman sloshed down the tunnel beside the flooded track. Up ahead there was movement—a skeleton, floating on the surface of that black water, its arm waving in the current.

A current meant the water was moving. That meant—
Whoosh!

A large shape erupted from the water.

For barely a second, harsh light from the headlamp struck the glistening hide, sending the scales that covered Killer Croc's nearly naked body into sharp relief. His pupils were vertical slits. His nostrils were flaring holes. His mouth gaped wide like a striking snake's.

Then Croc grabbed Batman around his torso, forcing him backward. Croc's teeth raked the side of Batman's protective cowl, slid off the slick surface, and ripped a row of searing furrows across his unprotected cheek. Croc's teeth settled on Batman's throat.

The cowl was tough, Batman told himself. Croc would never break through. He just had to—

The monster threw his massive body against Batman, toppling him backward into the dark pool. As the water closed over Batman's head, he heard Gordon's voice yelling in his ear. "What's happening? What's going on?"

Batman, submerged in that cesspool, was in no position to tell him. For a moment he struggled against the living weight pressing down on his chest. And then he understood.

A crocodile gobbled up its small quarry. But it grabbed its large prey, jerked it underwater, and rolled over on it, holding its struggling victim beneath the surface until it drowned. Only then did the croc begin to tear off chunks of flesh.

Killer Croc patterned his attacks on those of his name-sake.

Batman's utility belt was loaded with weapons he might have used against his attacker, but Croc body blocked his access.

He held his breath, pulled up his legs, and kicked up at Croc with all his might. The blow landed on skin as slip-pery as moss-covered rock and skidded off. Strong as he was, Batman couldn't get any leverage against that slick, hard hide.

He was forced even deeper. Croc was a weight on his chest. He had to find a weapon—any weapon—that would force Croc away from him.

He felt around on the bottom of the pool. His gloved fin-gers burrowed through mud, silt, and slime, then closed on something hard and rounded. The head of a railroad spike. Thick. Pointed. Sharp. Hammered through the track.

Outside in the tunnel, the track had been rusted and crumbling. Here, maybe . . . just maybe . . . He tugged at the spike. It slid from the friable track into his hand. He prayed the spike itself wouldn't crumble into rust when he tried to use it.

He swung the pointed spike as hard as he could and buried it, like a dagger, in Killer Croc's side.

Croc's mouth opened—a shocked, silent scream—and suddenly Batman was free of that smothering bulk. He lunged upright, gasping for air, swinging his head left and right, searching for the monster. But the water around him slowly stilled. Nothing moved.

Had he killed the monster, or was Croc just lying in wait for him?

"Batman! What's going on?" Gordon's voice had been there all that interminable time he was underwater, Batman realized, just another meaningless roaring in his ears. Now it became distinctive once again. A human voice. Gordon's voice.

"I found Croc," Batman gasped. "Or rather, he—"

He blinked, suddenly unsteady on his feet. His vision blurred. The tunnel, the flatbed cars piled with broken coffins, the skeletons in the water all pulsed and shimmered. And moved.

The skeletons stretched out their arms . . . called to him.

"Something's wrong," he croaked. "Vision's all twisted inside out . . ." Batman felt his cheek. "Croc bit me. Not bad, I think. Scratches but . . . may be contaminated with some kind of venom." Before his eyes, the skeletons seemed to sway. Back and forth. Grinning. Beckoning. "Seeing . . . monsters."

24

Monsters.

He's small—a boy—young and scared and falling down a dry well. He lands hard, knocking the air from his lungs. He can't breathe. He hears a rustle. A high-pitched shriek. There are monsters in the darkness. Bats! Thousands of them! They roar past him. Their flapping claw wings brush his cheeks and tear at his hair. He slaps at his own head and shrieks along with them. But they envelop him.

In his terror and his pain he becomes one with them. His hands extend. Webbing stretches between elongated twiglike fingers. Bat hands. Monster hands. He becomes one of the monsters.

But he can fly . . .

"Venom?" Gordon's voice brought him down to earth. "Maybe. But maybe Killer Croc's got the Scarecrow's fear toxin running through his veins—maybe he's somehow infused with it."

"Fear toxin," Batman muttered vaguely. "Monsters . . ."

"You said you carried an antidote with you, man! Use it!" Gordon shouted.

Antidote.

The world stabilized around him. His hands and arms became normal human appendages again . . . almost. He was no longer flying.

"Antidote's for gas," he tried to explain, as if to someone very dim. "Told you. He bit me . . . venom . . ." His voice trailed off. He was watching the skeletons rising from the water once again. The teeth in their skulls were elongating . . .

"Try it anyway, dammit," Gordon's voice said in his ear. "Hurry. Before Croc comes back."

"Stabbed him with a railroad spike," Batman muttered. "Not coming back."

"You can't take that chance," Gordon answered. "Batman. Use the antidote. Now."

"Okay." Sure. Anything to stop Gordon's voice from yammering.

Batman reached into his utility belt, pulled out a hypodermic syringe, and held it in his teeth as he fumbled with his glove.

"What are you doing?" Gordon asked.

Batman spoke around the syringe. "Got to get my glove off. Need to inject the antidote into muscle."

He yanked at his glove again and the seal that attached it to his armor finally gave. He slid it from his hand and stuffed it beneath his arm. "Glove's off. Don't want to drop it."

"Screw the glove," Gordon yelled. "Take the shot. And keep talking to me!"

Batman pulled the cap off the needle, punched the needle into his forearm, and pushed the plunger. The antihallucinogen burned into his veins. He pulled the needle up and away . . . and saw a spot of blood on his arm where the needle had pierced his skin.

* * *

Blood . . .
The spot grows until his entire hand is crimson.

"Not working . . ." he said to Gordon. **"Antidote's not . . ."**
"Wait," said Gordon's voice. "Give it time."

He bends over the bodies of his parents. He puts his child's hands on their chests and presses on their deep wounds, but their blood pumps beneath his fingers. His hands are too small to staunch the hemorrhage.

So much blood . . . turning the ground around him wet and red. Filling the air a metallic smell.

He looks up into the face of their killer.

The warm liquid laps around his legs. His waist. His neck. He's drowning . . .

"Drowning in their blood . . ." he said. **"Not working."**

"Listen to me, Batman. There is no blood. You're not drowning. But maybe you're right. Maybe it isn't the Scarecrow's poison. Probably why the antidote doesn't work." Once more, Gordon's calm, matter-of-fact voice pulled him back from the edge of madness. "What do you think? Could Croc have developed venom naturally?"

Gordon had done the right thing—had invoked his ability to reason. As his mind grappled with the puzzle, he took another mental step toward clarity. The blood around him receded.

"Possible," he said in a voice that was more like his own. "Or maybe the poisons Crane fed Croc for years have infused his cells, altered his body chemistry."

"But long story short, the antidote doesn't work on it."

"I'm not sure. I'm . . . better," Batman said. "Still seeing things, but I'm on top of it now. Know some of what I'm seeing isn't real. I know where I am."

"In a tunnel," Gordon agreed. "Following Croc's trail."

"I need to find Cardinal O'Fallon. Need to save him."

As he watched carefully, the blood was disappearing back into the needle puncture in his arm. He looked around the tunnel. It seemed ordinary again. The water in the tunnel was just that, dirty water.

The cardinal's danger. That had to be his focus—his anchor to reality. Batman took a deep breath and concentrated. Not just on what his eyes were seeing but on what his mind told him was possible. The blood was gone. The wound in his arm merely a slightly angry-looking dot.

Slowly, carefully, he pulled his glove back on his hand and depressed the seal that locked it to his armor. Instinctive movement and reaction were unreliable while he couldn't trust his senses. Every action would have to be filtered through his consciousness until the hallucinogen wore off.

Rā's al Ghūl, his great enemy, had trained him to keep his focus. To fight—through fire and ice and through a haze of drugs nearly as potent as whatever it was Croc had infected him with. And he had had other teachers . . . before Rā's. Many of them. Good and bad.

Remember them, he told himself. *They're what's real.*

They slogged beside him now through the waist-deep water. He held tight to them . . . another kind of antidote.

Rachel Dawes, his childhood friend, now an ADA, who had made him understand that an avenger was just another coward with a gun. But that a bringer of justice could change a city.

The mob boss Carmine Falcone, who had slain his parents' murderer before Bruce himself could carry out the deed. Who had led young Bruce Wayne to take that first step into vigilantism. Who was the first to show him his weapon of choice—the power of fear.

Other teachers he had met on his journey of discovery.

Other lessons . . .

His cheek stung where Croc's teeth had raked it.

"Once I get out of here . . . going to need antibiotics," he said to Gordon.

"I hear you," Gordon said, staying with him. "I don't even want to think about where Croc's teeth have been."

"We're going to need more antibiotics," Dr. Frederick Avery *yells above the constant* crack-pop *of gunfire.*

Bruce is in a makeshift medical facility in Sudan staffed by international volunteers—doctors and nurses, trying to save the catastrophically wounded victims of a terrible tribal war. He is one of those volunteers. Barely out of his teens, still unsure of where his life is headed but convinced that being schooled in triage will be a necessary element in his future.

Around Bruce, people scream. People die.

Dr. Avery, an African-American in his late forties—thin, short, round glasses, serious—heads their overworked field-hospital unit. One of the toughest men that Bruce has ever met. A hero in the realest sense of the word.

He, Avery, and a Sudanese nurse named Anna Deng— another hero—work over a moaning man. Gut-shot. Thrashing about as Avery tries to sterilize the wound. Without anesthetic. They ran out of that two days ago, soon after the relief agencies were forced to pull out because of the escalating violence.

They have begun to run low on antibiotics, as well.

"Bruce! Strap his legs down!" Avery snaps.

"I'm trying!" He throws his body across the wounded man's legs and fumbles for the fastening.

"So—was this what you expected when you volunteered for the relief effort?" Avery asks.

Bruce grits his teeth as he tries to secure the buckle. "I knew . . . it'd be bad."

"This bad?"

"This defies imagination." Bruce finishes strapping the wounded man's legs down. "But I'm here, for what that's worth . . . and I'll do whatever I can."

"All right. Got the artery. No perforation of the bowel. Gimme a clamp."

The nurse hands Avery a clamp. Avery closes off the vein.

He cuts away a jagged shred of flesh, and the wounded man screams again.

"Okay. Bruce, sew him up!"

"Keep the sutures loose so the wound can drain," the nurse reminds him. "Then inject the antibiotic . . . he's lucky we have some left."

Bruce looks from Avery to Anna Deng, shocked. "Me? I've never—"

But Avery and his nurse are on to the next emergency— a guy about Bruce's age. Head wound. Ear and part of his cheek shot off, pumping blood onto the examination table.

Bruce grabs a kit and threads a needle with shaking hands. He's watched Avery and the nurse suture wounds for days. Avery has explained how it's done. Has shown him on patients who were properly anesthetized. He isn't ready for this . . . but if he doesn't do his part, the man will die.

As Bruce thrusts the needle through the raw flesh, the wounded man screams again. Bruce glances at his face. It is a mask of pain. A rictus of suffering.

Sweat runs down Bruce's forehead and into his eyes.

The exhaustion. The constant danger. The cramped muscles. The sleepless days and nights. The heat. The flies that buzz and sting. The fear of injury and disease. His own ignorance. His helplessness as men die beneath his hands.

Ignore it.

Focus.

Learn.

He can't save everyone. But he can save this one man lying on the table before him. He hopes. He reaches over, grabs a dirty towel, stuffs it in the man's mouth. "Bite on this," he says in perfect Arabic.

Bruce swipes the sweat away with his forearm and punches the needle, once again, through the man's ragged flesh.

He almost felt the tug of the thread in his own cheek as he moved through the waist-deep water. Like the needle.

One stitch. Then another. One step. Then another. Avery and Anna Deng by his side.

"Save the life . . . of that one man," he muttered.

"That's right. We need to find O'Fallon," Gordon said. "Where's Croc? Have you seen him?"

Batman swept the xenon beams across the surface of the dark water. He half staggered past the final flatbed car with its burden of the dead, his movement causing ripples in the water as he felt the ground move under his feet.

The water danced and shifted . . . the skeletons sat in their coffins, watching him and waving like the Queen of England . . . slowly but relentlessly.

They're persistent, he thought. *Ignore the dancing water. Ignore the beckoning skeletons. Skeletons don't wave.*

"No Croc," he said to Gordon. He swept the area with infrared.

"You think Croc's still in there with you?"

"Probably," Batman said. "Hurt, though. Maybe dead. Maybe—"

Roaring like a wounded lion, Croc broke through the surface of the pool and slammed like a battering ram into Batman's chest.

Once again, Batman toppled backward. Dark water closed over his head, but this time he knew what to expect. Even as he fell, he threw up one arm to protect his face, while he reached with his other hand for his utility belt. Before he hit bottom he had a small concussion bomb in his hand.

Croc's teeth closed on his forearm. Even through his armor, he felt it—a crushing weight as if his arm was caught in a vise. Despite Croc's inhuman strength and the sharpness of his teeth, the armor didn't break, but Batman didn't think this was the time or place to test it to destruction. Croc pulled backward and down, trying to drag Batman underwater.

He slammed his free fist into Croc's side, hard, trying for the area where he'd stabbed the spike.

Croc roared, freeing Batman's arm. Howling in pain and

fury, Croc grabbed Batman around the chest in a crushing grip and twisted in Killer Croc's own version of a death roll, designed to disorient his prey and begin the process of ripping him into pieces.

As he whirled, submerged in roiling blackness, Batman reached up with one hand, feeling for Croc's throat, his jaw, his mouth.

Open! Waiting!

He shoved the small spherical concussion bomb between Croc's teeth and deep into his gullet.

Croc choked and released his victim.

Batman surfaced, gasping, and took off through the water, partly running, partly swimming, moving as quickly as he could. His infrared lenses were still engaged, and he followed the heat trail that led deeper into the tunnel away from the caved-in entrance. He needed to get clear before—

Behind him, Croc broke the surface, tearing at his throat, trying to cough up the sphere.

"What's going on down there? Dammit, Batman." He heard Gordon's shout. "Are you all right?"

"Later," Batman panted. He pushed off hard to his left, climbing the side of the tunnel. Above him, the rocky irregular surface of the tunnel offered several handholds. Batman reached out, grasped a projecting rock and hoisted himself as high as he could out of the water. He had to get clear before—

Boom!

The sphere exploded.

Croc screamed.

With a crack, Batman's handhold let go of the wall and fell, taking Batman with it. He hit the water and dove for the far end of the tunnel as several large chunks of rock came loose from the ceiling and splashed down into the water behind him. He waited, afraid the whole tunnel might collapse, but nothing else happened. For now, at least, the tunnel held.

Croc thrashed about, roaring—in pain or anger, he couldn't tell—then bounded away from Batman, through the water, past the flatbed cars and their grisly burdens, and up the pile of rubble toward his bolt-hole and the abandoned subway platform beyond.

Halfway up the pile of rubble, he collapsed.

The monster was still breathing in rapid and shallow pants. Croc must have regurgitated the bomb before it had detonated. Maybe the concussive blast had knocked the air from his lungs. Or maybe it had actually damaged him. Batman couldn't tell. Croc was an enigma. For all Batman knew, his interior organs were as nearly impervious as his skin had been.

Batman felt torn. He needed to go on . . . to find Cardinal O'Fallon. He also needed to go back and secure Killer Croc. He didn't want him roaming free to kill again.

"I'm okay," Batman answered Gordon's shouted question. "I used a concussion grenade on Croc. A few rocks shifted, but the tunnel held. Croc's down. I need to—"

Batman looked back over the threatening water, past the coffins where the dead were still beckoning to him. During Croc's attack, his mind had cleared—maybe the effect of that extra kick of adrenaline that had shot through his veins—but the effect was temporary. He could tell he was losing it once again. He'd have to work fast.

He pulled handcuffs from his utility belt. But as he took a step toward the fallen monster, Croc pushed himself upright and began to stagger up the pile of rubble. He wiggled through his bolt-hole into the siding tunnel and disappeared.

"Never mind," Batman said. "He's gone. Got away. One tough monster."

"I hear you," Gordon said.

He turned and, once again, began to follow the heat trail that he hoped would lead him to O'Fallon. Now that he had actually tangled with Croc, he was more worried than ever that the old man might not be alive.

"I'll send down a troop of officers for him," Gordon said. "At least we know where Croc's lair is and—"

Another chunk of tunnel ceiling cracked free overhead, smashed into the coffins, and toppled into the water.

"Check the abandoned station, if you want," Batman told him. "But don't risk your men going on past the caved-in section. Tunnel wasn't all that stable to begin with. Concussion bomb shook it up some more. Probably another entrance farther on . . ."

He sloshed through the water, consciously putting one foot before the other. The slope rose slightly, and the water level dropped. Eventually he was walking through water that was only ankle deep.

As the adrenaline faded from his system, the hallucinogenic effect of the venom returned in force. The walls, ceiling, and floor of the tunnel seemed to move—in and out, as if he were traveling through the innards of some living, breathing monster. As the floor shifted, he put out a hand, touching the tunnel wall to steady himself.

Something crunched beneath his palm. Quickly, he shifted from infrared to xenon spots. When he turned to look at the wall, bugs, hundreds of giant sewer roaches, skittered in a wave of movement across the rocky surface and away from the light.

Real or imagined? It was hard to tell.

"Just bugs," he muttered. "Doesn't matter." But his stomach clenched and roiled. He was beginning to feel sick. Probably a reaction to the combination of venom and adrenaline. Shifting walls and floors weren't helping. Hard to stay upright.

"Eyes open," he told himself. "Just follow the trail." He went back to infrared.

The heat trail led to a grimy wooden ladder propped against a hole at the end of the shaft—probably left over from when the shaft was blasted three-quarters of a century ago. A rough hole had been excavated, up through the ceiling and into another tunnel above.

"Found another bolt-hole," he muttered.

He climbed the filth-encrusted ladder, feeling light-headed, pulling himself up one step at a time. He was halfway to the top when a rung cracked beneath his weight. He slipped and lurched off balance. The rickety ladder toppled, and he fell, landing on his side in six inches of water, hitting the ground hard.

For a second or two, he lay motionless.

He heard a skittering slither to his left. Immediately, adrenaline shot through his system. Alert again, he rolled over, reaching for his utility belt, expecting Croc. Instead, he found himself nose to nose with a large rat.

Just a rat.

He'd seen that expression on a furred and pointed face once before.

In India . . .

The prospective combatant is a mongoose—a small ferretlike animal with rounded ears, thick fur, and a broad, fat tail. It waits with apparent indifference by its master's sandaled feet, seemingly unfazed by the people thronged around it. A string knotted around its neck is tied to the wrist of its master, a bearded old snake charmer dressed traditionally in bright yellow-orange: a rumal—*a cloth wrapped like a turban around his head; a long, ragged shirt; and a trailing loincloth. He exhorts the crowd in a shrill voice to pay to witness a* tamasha—*a show, a fight to the death between the mongoose and a cobra. He pulls the cobra from a flat, cylindrical straw basket and waves it before his audience.*

When the men in the crowd proffer sufficient money, he places the snake on the ground and looses the mongoose.

The spectacle is against the law, Bruce knows, condemned by a wildlife protection law enacted back during the 1970s and strictly enforced at present. He knows that this disgusts the snake charmers, who form a Hindu caste of Untouchables all their own, and who support their families by this traditional method. Bruce notes that this particular man is keeping an eye out for the police even as the battle between snake and mongoose commences.

The mongoose chatters as it faces the rearing hooded

cobra. The cobra hisses and spits. The crowd roars encouragement.

Around Bruce, the Old Delhi bazaar is a moving kaleidoscope of humanity: men wearing clothing that ranges from Western to traditional to the rags of beggars; women garbed in brilliantly colored saris and festive shawls; holy men draped in golden robes. Some people wear Western shoes. Some wear slippers or sandals. But some feet are bare, despite the garbage and offal littering the streets.

The noise is constant and nearly overpowering: hawkers shout the virtues of their wares; customers bargain, yelling to be heard above the din of blaring horns, bleating goats, and screeching birds.

The air is thick with odors. Human bodies. Animal smells. Cooking spices. Cheap Indian cigarettes. Exhaust from a million engines.

Car and trucks, motorcycles, scooters, and bikes, auto and bicycle rickshaws, veer through narrow lanes.

Sacred cows wander the marketplace at will.

Bruce is one of the few Westerners in the crowd.

He glances to the left. Ten yards away, his rotund and mustached Indian guide Arman is in deep discussion with three orange-garbed fakirs, crouching before a small stall tent. Bruce wants these mendicant Sufic ascetics, renowned for the mystical control they exert over their bodies, to teach him what they know.

He ignores a group of young men wearing shorts and short-sleeved Western shirts—members of a local gang, Arman had told him—who have been eying him suspiciously since he arrived at the bazaar.

Bruce glances back at the cobra and mongoose, locked in the dance of death immortalized over a century ago in a story by Rudyard Kipling. The mongoose zigs and zags. The cobra strikes. And misses. The mongoose darts, quick and alluring, offering his body as a target, daring the cobra to try to strike again. After the snake tires, the mongoose will

*leap on its back, bite down into the flesh beneath its head,
and break its neck.*

If it survives the cobra's attacks.

*For several moments, the fakirs, with Arman beside them,
watch Bruce watching the combat. Then the old men rise
and go inside their tent.*

*Arman joins Bruce as the mongoose nimbly leaps aside,
once again avoiding the cobra's strike. The snake is tiring,
slowing down.*

*"Despite Kipling's tale, the ending is not certain," Ar-
man says somberly. "Sometimes, despite the quickness of
the mongoose and the thickness of its fur, the cobra still
wins. Cobra venom is very poisonous . . ."*

"Batman! Talk to me!" Gordon's voice in his ear
sounded tense. "What's happening?"

Batman blinked and sat up in the water. At some point,
the rat had disappeared.

"Slipped," Batman said. "Just . . . need to catch my
breath."

He climbed to his feet, reset the ladder at the hole, and
began to climb consciously, one foot in front of the other,
avoiding the broken rung, until he was in a much larger
passageway up above.

The last—what was it? Flashback? Premonition?—had
been apt enough. Like Kipling's mongoose, Rikki-Tikki-
Tavi, he had gone into a tunnel after a venomous reptile.

The first round had been a draw. But later . . .

He shook his head. "O'Fallon first," he muttered. "Then
Croc."

25

Batman climbed up into a vaulting, elliptical, brick-lined tunnel that was over eight feet tall and close to nine feet wide. He flashed his bright beams around, studying his surroundings. A course of somewhat lighter-colored bricks, darkened with age and wear but still visible against the other masonry, ran down the centerline of the ceiling like a spine. He had never been in this particular tunnel before, but he knew instantly where he was.

"I'm in part of the old abandoned Mooney Aqueduct," he told Gordon. "Someday, when I'm not hallucinating, I'll have to come back and get a look at this place. It's falling down now, but in its heyday, it must have been amazing."

There was very little about the intimate structure of Gotham that Batman didn't know. The aqueduct had been built during the 1830s, when Gotham City's rapidly growing population was in dire need of drinkable water—not to mention water for industry and fighting fires. The aqueduct carried thirty-eight million gallons of potable water a day, fifty-three miles from the Concord Dam upstate, to a massive reservoir built in what was now Midtown Gotham. In addition, the engineers had built a huge underground storage tank below the Reservoir to hold additional water.

The city grew by leaps and bounds. Within fifty years it became clear that the Mooney Aqueduct was inadequate to supply the needs of Gotham's burgeoning population. Two other, larger tunnels were built in the late 1800s.

By the mid 1950s, the decrepit Mooney system, with its miles of brick tunnels, had begun to crack and leak. These were drained. A portion was repurposed. But a five-mile-long section that ran below the Narrows Channel and beneath lower Midtown was abandoned and eventually forgotten.

The holding tank itself had been sealed off when the old Reservoir above had been converted into a shallow man-made lake. Robinson Park, created in the area surrounding the old Reservoir, had become an important destination spot for tourists as well as a place for city dwellers to commune with nature—at least during the daylight hours.

Few people realized that the old aqueduct and storage tank below had ever existed.

Batman ignored the subtle pulsating of the tunnel's ceiling and walls. He was working hard to keep the shifting surfaces, capering monsters, and ghostly shadows firmly locked away on the far edges of his consciousness.

More rats skittered. More roaches clustered. Stalactites clung to the ceiling. Roots and slime molds covered the begrimed walls. He welcomed them. These were real obstacles he couldn't will away. And, while they could make traversing the tunnel treacherous, concentrating on evading them was helping him keep his focus on the here and now.

"I'm moving north toward Robinson Park and the Reservoir," Batman said to Gordon.

He followed the heat signature toward Midtown. Two separate signatures, actually—he could distinguish that now. One faint, the other sharp and clear. Croc had carried O'Fallon along this path to some destination, then retraced his steps to return to his lair past the coffin train where Batman had found him. The Dark Knight hoped that wherever he had abandoned the kindly old cardinal, he had left him alive.

Twenty minutes later, he came to a section that leaked badly. Water trickled down the bricks and dripped like rain onto the floor of the tunnel. The sound was hypnotic, like whispers on the edge of his consciousness.

Like the voice of India, speaking longingly of rain . . .

"The monsoon season will begin in a few months," Arman said, as they turned from the battle between mongoose and cobra. The winner was still uncertain.

Bruce swiped his arm across his forehead, wiping away the sweat. He had arrived in India in March, when the temperature was more moderate. But this year summer had come to New Delhi earlier than usual. As he baked beneath the scorching sun, it was hard to imagine the city deluged with driving rain. Or freezing beneath blankets of fog, as it would be in December.

Bruce shrugged. "The monsoons shouldn't stop the fakirs from teaching me. When do I get started?"

"Um . . . you don't," Arman said. "Ever."

"They've made me wait months for this opportunity!"

Arman shrugged. "They said . . . they will not train you."

Bruce frowned. "Why? Is it a question of money?"

Arman shook his head emphatically. "No, Mr. Wayne. They're not concerned with your money—or anyone's, for that matter."

"Then what is it?"

"Temperament, Mr. Wayne. The fakirs said you haven't the temperament to learn what they have to teach."

"But I've never spoken to them! They insisted our business be arranged through liaisons!"

"It's impossible to say, Mr. Wayne. But I have always suspected that their sympathies, if they have any, lie with the cobra. I watched with them as you watched the match. If I may be permitted as to say so, I believe your sympathies lie with the mongoose.

"Perhaps . . . that was reason enough." Again Arman shrugged. *"But perhaps . . ."* he hesitated. *"There is another who possesses the knowledge you seek. Not a fakir, but . . . she may be willing to help you."*

"This should help! I've located a map that marks the line of the old aqueduct," Gordon's voice said in his ear. "Up ahead on the right, you'll find the opening into the Reservoir holding tank. Be careful. Looks like a big drop."

"Great," Batman said. "Thanks."

He was walking through the tunnel, avoiding the obstacles, but his mind had slid into another time. Another world.

Was halfway there still.

Killer Croc's venom was more LSD than fear poison, he thought. It seemed to be distorting his senses even as it evoked waves of memory so vivid he felt as though he were reliving the experience. Classic drug-induced flashbacks.

He supposed it could be worse.

Now another teacher walked beside him.

Cassandra.

He smiled at her; welcomed her presence. He remembered the day they met . . .

He steps from the bright sunshine into in the dark interior of a wide hut, waiting for his eyes to adjust. The little house has no windows. Its walls are constructed of bundled reeds plastered with cow dung. When the monsoons come, the woven grasses that make up the roof will leak, the hard-packed clay floor will turn to mud, and the damaged hut will have to be repaired. Luckily, in the area outside of Delhi, cow dung—the cement of choice—is free and plentiful.

A woman crouches near the back wall, before a small fire pit set into a mud hearth. She is making chapatti—flat bread—on a metal griddle. Nearby, a few cooking pots and several vessels filled with water are stacked neatly.

As Arman makes the introductions, she stands and looks Bruce in the eye.

"And this is Cassandra," Arman says. "She may be willing to help you."

"Why would I want to do that?" she asks in accented English.

She is a striking woman with pale, luminous skin, dark hair, and green eyes. Probably half-Indian, Bruce thinks— Cassandra is hardly a common Indian name—and a few years older than he is. She is wearing the traditional female clothing of India—a long skirt called a ghagra *and a short-sleeved, fitted shirt, or* choli, *that leaves her midriff bare. Over this she has wrapped a graceful sari. Unlike the women in the marketplace, with their colorful saris and shawls, she is dressed entirely in black.*

Arman smiles slyly. "You may want to help him because, after agreeing that they would teach him, the fakirs have refused."

Cassandra darts a glance at Arman. "What made them change their minds?"

Arman raises an eyebrow in Bruce's direction and shrugged. "Perhaps there's more to him than meets the eye."

"Perhaps." Cassandra smiles fleetingly, and for a moment she looks mischievous and much younger. Then she frowns at Bruce. "What is it you seek?"

The tunnel grew drier. The sharp imprint of several massive clawed footprints in the sticky slime drew him from his waking dream. Beneath Croc's tracks were prints from shoes in different styles and sizes. Sneakers. Leather-soled. Flip-flops. Even bare human toe prints.

People had come this way. Ordinary people. Lots of them.

Bruce relayed the information to Gordon. "There must be an exit from the aqueduct somewhere beyond the hole to Croc's lair."

"I'll check," Gordon said. Batman could hear the rustle

as Gordon consulted a map. "Nobody in their right mind would enter that monster's lair on purpose."

"I hear something, Gordon," Batman said quietly. "Sounds like voices up ahead."

A dim light—green and eerie—shone farther down the tunnel. Batman killed the xenon beams and moved forward cautiously.

Thirty yards later, he stood at the junction Gordon had mentioned, where the aqueduct had once spilled its water into the massive Reservoir holding tank.

By the pale neon glow of luminescent lichens growing on the leprous chamber walls, he saw that he was standing at the top of a brick spillway a full story above an assembled throng.

"What about the toxin? You still seeing things?" Gordon asked in his ear.

"Probably. But the hallucinations are definitely taking a backseat to reality at this point."

In his comprehensive studies of Gotham City, he had read about the Reservoir and its history, but no description had ever done the magnificence of the old structure justice.

The chamber had once been inspired, not by the Roman aqueducts, but by ancient Egyptian temples. Carved palmiform pillars—he had seen similar columns in the fifth-century pyramid-mortuary complex of the pharaoh Unas at Saqqara in Egypt—rose from floor to ceiling. The walls even had a shallow bas-relief design, though nothing as elaborate as the decorations in that distant tomb.

The undertaking was architectural madness, of course, since the interior of the tank was meant to be completely underwater. Under normal circumstances, no one but the people who built it would ever have known it was down here.

Now, seepage from the Reservoir above, the stalactites clinging to the ceiling, and the slime and glowing mold that covered the brick and bas-relief on the walls made it look like something out of Dante's *Inferno*. The people crowding the floor of the chamber—Gotham's homeless in all their various manifestations—added to the illusion.

And as his eyes reached the center of it all, at the focus of the attention of the multitudes, Batman saw that once again, he was in the presence of genuine evil. The Scarecrow, bizarrely garbed in a rumpled suit with a roughly stitched burlap mask covering his face, slouched negligently on a raised dais composed of a mad jumble of architectural castoffs and Gotham's garbage, topped by a makeshift throne.

As Batman watched, the Scarecrow's burlap mask became a torn sack of writhing maggots. His body was a jumble of ancient bones. Then his writhing mask morphed into a skull with worms crawling from empty eye sockets. Batman squeezed his eyes shut for a moment and clenched his jaw, willing the nightmare back into the dark. He forbore sharing these particular illusions with Gordon. The reality before him was bizarre enough.

Three Arkham escapees in orange jumpsuits stood between the Scarecrow and the crowd. Batman couldn't tell if they were a guard of honor or bodyguards to keep the masses at bay.

"Do you see O'Fallon?" Gordon murmured in his ear.

Batman scanned the crowd, trying to separate reality from the haze of venom-induced phantasms. "Not yet."

He sniffed. "I smell gas—hydrogen sulfide and"—he hesitated while he checked his meter—"there's methane. A lot of it. Probably worse up here near the ceiling. I'm going to put my breathing mask back on—Hold on. Something's happening."

Below, the Scarecrow's orange-clad minions raised cylindrical vessels that looked like censers and began to swing them in a twisted parody of the dispersal of burning incense that was part of many religious ceremonies. Mist wafted from the censers. But instead of incense, Batman was pretty sure the Scarecrow was infusing the crowd with hallucinogenic vapor.

He was suddenly glad that he had injected himself with the antidote to the Scarecrow's fear poison earlier. If he had to breathe in that toxin on top of what Croc's venom was doing to him, he'd be in serious trouble.

Under the hallucinogenic influence of the gas, the crowd gazed raptly at the Scarecrow as he stood on his throne, a scythe raised above his head like a military standard.

"You are my army!" the Scarecrow shouted. "Soon I will lead you through the streets of Gotham. We will take the city from our oppressors and we will become Gotham's worst nightmare."

The crowd began to sway, parroting, "Gotham's worst nightmare!"

"We will take whatever we want. Food. Money. Clothing. Jewels. Cars. Women. Men. All Gotham's riches will be ours. Like these most loyal—most honored—of my followers, you will wear orange. And, beneath your feet, Gotham will sink into ashes and dust. We will transform the city into New Arkham! The surface dwellers will become our slaves or they will die—huddling in fear, waiting for my scythe to fall! And I will send my loyal Killer Croc to devour them, as he devours all who oppose me."

The crowd roared its approval.

Again the Scarecrow raised his scythe. "Bring in the prisoner!"

A fourth orange-suited Arkham escapee dragged O'Fallon onto the dais. The old cardinal stood before the swaying crowd, pale and trembling. Their roar hushed to a confused babble of voices—excited, angry . . . perplexed.

"I've spotted O'Fallon," Batman murmured as the Scarecrow's minion flung the old man at the Scarecrow's feet.

"Here is one of them!" the Scarecrow shouted. "One of those who has dared to defy me! You will watch as he pays the price!"

Obediently, the crowd shouted its support.

The cardinal blinked up at the Scarecrow. Then he turned his head to stare out over the angry crowd. He stood shakily.

"O'Fallon's trembling," Batman said.

"I don't blame him," Gordon said. "He's breathing in the Scarecrow's toxin . . . maybe has been for a while. God knows what he's seeing. Even without the toxin, with what he's been through, I'd expect him to be a blithering wreck. It's a miracle he's still upright."

Below, the Scarecrow was strutting back and forth before the cardinal, pointing dramatically and gesturing wildly with his scythe. "This . . . bombastic cleric claimed he was trying to help you—the city's homeless. He gave you a place to sleep. He fed you from his own kitchen. He tried to make you believe that none of you wretched was truly abandoned or forgotten.

"He lied! He wanted only to encourage your desertion. To steal you from the Scarecrow's army. To make you look to Heaven for your salvation when you know that—for your kind—there can be only Hell!"

"Hell!" His voice echoed around the chamber.

"Hell!"

"Hell!"

"NO!" The cardinal shouted in a voice honed to fill a cathedral. His shout boomed and echoed over the heads of the audience.

"No!"

"No!"

"No!"

O'Fallon coughed.

There was a dead silence throughout the length and breadth of the great Reservoir. Even the Scarecrow seemed taken aback by the sudden outburst from the old man.

"He's having trouble breathing," Batman whispered. He could practically see the thick tendrils of hydrogen sulfide and methane gases pooling near the ceiling, gases that were highly flammable.

"He's got guts," Gordon muttered. "But it's going to take more than sheer backbone to keep him alive. I've dispatched reinforcements. They should be there in fifteen minutes."

"I don't think we've got the time," Batman said.

O'Fallon coughed once more, then turned his back on the Scarecrow and, facing the crowd, held out his arms. When he spoke again, it was in a softer tone but because of the silence, it carried out across the heads of the crowd clearly.

"God will forgive his children," he said. "You have but to ask." And the old man crossed himself.

"Yea, though I walk through the valley of the shadow of death, I will fear no evil: For thou art with me . . ."

The Scarecrow recovered himself. "Shut up," he cried.

The cardinal continued as though the Scarecrow hadn't spoken. "Thy rod and thy staff, they comfort me. Thou pre- parest a table before me"—*cough*—"in the presence of mine enemies—"

The Scarecrow was practically dancing with fury. "Shut him up!" he screamed.

The orange-garbed guard nearest the cardinal cuffed him hard across the face. O'Fallon fell sideways, landing heavily on the stone floor. His face was bleeding. His voice was fainter, but quite clear.

"Thou anointest my head with oil"—*cough cough*—"My cup—"

"Your cup is empty!" the Scarecrow shouted. He raised his scythe. "Cardinal O'Fallon—your own words condemn you! I sentence you to death for your crimes against me! You will be torn apart before this multitude by"—he held out his arm, the ringmaster announcing his starring act— "Killer Croc!"

There was absolute silence. Everyone waited.

Nothing happened.

The audience looked around. Batman could hear their sibilant whispers.

"Croc's not here."

"Where is he?"

". . . 's gone?"

For a moment, Batman hoped Croc's absence would stay the executioner's hand.

No such luck.

The Scarecrow, balancing atop his throne, stared around the room wildly. "Croc isn't here? He'll pay for this dereliction! But you shall take his place! All of you! You will become the Scarecrow's monsters!"

With a low growl, the Scarecrow's mesmerized army lurched forward.

O'Fallon's lips were moving. As Batman lip-read, the old Cardinal completed the Twenty-third Psalm. ". . . runneth over."

"Hold a moment!" the Scarecrow called out. "We must observe the form!" He lifted the scythe high above his head, signaling for silence. "O'Fallon—the good shepherd—has fed and sheltered many of you," he said in a kindly voice. "Is there no one here willing to speak for the holy man?"

Silence.

Then someone shouted, "Death!"

Others took up the chant.

"Death!"

"Death!"

"Death!"

"The jury has spoken!" The Scarecrow swung the scythe high into the air behind his head. "I myself will strike the first blow!"

"I'll speak for him!" Batman shouted.

As all heads turned, looking for the source of the cry, Batman hurled a Batarang. It spun over the heads of the mob with a faint keening sound and lodged in the Scarecrow's upraised wrist. The Scarecrow screamed and dropped his scythe.

Batman snapped out his cape and launched himself toward the Scarecrow. As he neared the throne, he switched off the glider and dropped like a stone, feetfirst, and slammed into the Scarecrow's chest. The Scarecrow toppled backward off his throne and onto the rubble piled high behind it.

The Scarecrow jerked the Batarang from his wrist as he scrambled to his feet. "Kill him!"

His jumpsuited bodyguards trampled O'Fallon in their

haste to obey, leaping forward, snatching at Batman, swinging their censers like medieval flails. The old man lay, un-
moving, before the Scarecrow's throne.

Batman ducked a blow from a censer, then high-kicked
with his right leg fully extended, sending the hulking madman who wielded it sailing off the dais. Batman snatched up
a length of one-inch pipe from the rubble and swung it
around like a quarterstaff, knocking two more would-be as-
sailants backward into the surging crowd. He snap-kicked a
fourth, sending him sprawling into a pile of rubble.

Standing over the fallen cardinal, he turned toward the
Scarecrow. But the madman had scrambled higher on his
pile of garbage, capering to the very top of the trash heap
mounded behind his throne.

"You will die—you son of darkness!" the Scarecrow
shouted. "You will die by fire!"

He pulled a cigarette lighter from his pocket, flicked it
on, and tossed it on top of the debris.

Batman knew what was coming. He threw himself face-
down on top of the fallen cardinal, covering them both with
his cape.

There was a loud *whumph!* as the flammable gases
trapped in the roof of the cavern ignited, and the world
around him exploded in searing brightness.

With a twitch of a finger, he activated the smoke shields
that would protect his eyes and glanced upward. Cracks
were forming in the ceiling. The Reservoir was directly
above them. Annihilation was seconds away.

Below the dais, people were screaming and running.
Some were on fire. A large chunk of ceiling fell, crushing
others. Water began to drip from the ceiling into the cavern. Soon it would be a deluge.

Batman grabbed O'Fallon and threw the old man's limp
body over his shoulder.

He pulled his grapple gun from his utility belt and fired a
grapnel at the carved palmate capital of a column that stood
near the spillway where he had been standing, praying that
the roof would hold a few seconds longer. The grapnel

caught on a decorative carving. He punched the retractor and, with a hissing *whirr*, he and O'Fallon soared upward, then swung like a pendulum to land in the tunnel entrance. Water was coming from the ceiling in streams now.

Below him, homeless men and women and Arkham escapees ran toward a narrow stairway that climbed the side of the cavern toward the aqueduct. Some made it and began to race upward. Others fought for position, toppling their neighbors off the steps in their own desperation to escape.

Another large chunk of roof broke loose and crashed onto the cavern floor. Water poured through the opening. The screams of the drowning mixed with a shuddering roar as the entire chamber roof gave way. Huge chunks of masonry and tons of water from the Reservoir thundered down into the holding tank.

There was nothing Batman could do for any of them— Arkham escapees or homeless victims.

He released the grapnel and raced into the aqueduct tunnel, shouting to Gordon, giving him his location, telling him what had happened. The lake the city called the Reservoir was flooding into the old tank and—when that was filled—would pour into the tunnel behind him.

O'Fallon hadn't been burned—Batman had made sure of that—but he was in bad shape, moaning about demons and the fires of Hell but too weak to do more than struggle feebly. Batman held on to him tightly as he tried to outrun the waters that would soon surge into the tunnel behind him. He didn't have any breath left to reassure the cardinal, even if the old man was in any state to understand what he was saying.

"Follow the aqueduct," Gordon shouted in his ear. "There's a manhole that leads up into the east side of the park. We'll have it open and ready to get you out of there."

"Good. O'Fallon . . . needs an ambulance," Batman panted as he ran. He could hear the shouts of people pouring into the tunnel after him. "Others escaped . . . coming behind me. Homeless. Some burned in the explosion. Some

hurt. A few Arkham escapees. Got O'Fallon. Couldn't save
the others."

"You did what you could. Just get O'Fallon here," Gordon said. "We'll take care of the rest."

Batman reached the manhole entrance. The cover was
open and, as he looked up, he saw Gordon waiting. With
O'Fallon over his shoulder, he clambered up the long lad-
der. He stopped at the top and waited while Gordon lifted
O'Fallon from his shoulders and handed him to waiting
EMTs.

"Get him into the medevac chopper on the double,"
Gordon shouted. "He's had a pretty heavy dose of the
Scarecrow's toxins."

He turned back to look down at Batman. "Amalgamated
Water was able to open one of the old floodgates on the
other side of the underground Reservoir. Pure luck. One of
the old hands was pulling the graveyard shift and knew
what to do. This tunnel at least should offer relatively safe
passage to anybody else who got to it." He held out a hand
to haul Batman out and saw the vigilante hesitate.

Beyond Gordon, the park was a madhouse. Cop cars
and ambulances flashed lights and blared sirens. Another
medevac chopper was just landing. Police and EMTs hauling gurneys rushed forward to help the survivors. News
vans screeched up, ignoring the parking rules, letting off
reporters and cameramen, who immediately began to vie
for the best shots of O'Fallon and the rest of the emerging
victims.

"I'll skip the media circus, if it's all the same to you.
Keep your earbuds fired up. I'll help whoever's left alive
down here get out. And then—"

"What about the Scarecrow?"

"No idea. MIA. But Killer Croc is definitely still down
here somewhere."

Batman dropped down the ladder and stepped back into

the darkness. He watched a flood of humanity rush toward the long ladder. He helped the weaker ones among them climb toward the flashing light, blaring sound, and fresh night air.

Then he faded back into the darkness.

O'Fallon looked up blearily as EMTs strapped him to a gurney and rolled him toward a waiting helicopter. A monster had kidnapped him. And a demon had rescued him.

He had seen his savior, lit by the terrible green glow in that monstrous cavern. The demon had flown at him, dark wings spread. Horned. Frightening.

There had been a terrible conflagration . . . but the demon had carried the cardinal from the fire and darkness and had delivered him into the light.

Not a demon, then. An angel, not quite fallen . . .

As the effect of the Scarecrow's fear toxin began to fade, O'Fallon closed his eyes, not sure exactly what had happened. What had been real and what was drug-induced nightmare.

As EMTs loaded his gurney into the waiting chopper, he glanced back at the chaos that was behind him. The city loomed beyond the park—shadowy buildings against a threatening sky, their shapes defined by the light from a million windows.

"Appearances can be deceiving," he murmured.

He thought of all those poor, hopeless, deluded souls that that monster—the Scarecrow—had lured underground, then destroyed. He would pray for the souls of the dead. And for the Scarecrow. And he would do whatever he could to aid the survivors.

"Did you see him?" Detective Allen asked Montoya as they helped another of the Scarecrow's victims climb from the hole.

They passed the man—filthy, wild-eyed, and wet up to his waist—on to a couple of waiting EMTs, then reached for the next escapee. The water was still rising in the tunnel below.

"No!" Montoya sounded so disgusted that, despite the insanity surrounding them and the tragedy that had just taken place, Allen almost smiled. "He was right there. At the mouth of the manhole. I heard him. I turned to signal the EMTs forward, and when I looked back, he was gone."

"He tracked the cardinal all that way underground and saved him," Allen said.

"And he's going back for Killer Croc," Montoya said. "After all he's been through, to do that—he must be some kind of superman!"

Allen grinned. "Next time I bump into him, I'll get you his autograph."

26

His cape and cowl tossed carelessly over the back of a
chair, he had been studying his extensive collection of
Gotham City street diagrams, blueprints, and maps. He had
concentrated on the cutaways and section views that showed
the hidden arteries of the living city, the storm drains, gas
lines, electrical conduits, and steam pipes that laced their
way beneath Gotham's streets.

His eyes were beginning to ache but he was confident
that he now knew the underground layout of the city almost
as well as he knew her ways and byways.

The walls and floors had stopped shifting. Well . . .
almost.

And the monsters were keeping just on the edge of his
vision now.

But flashes of imagery kept tugging at him . . . pulling
him backward, toward the past. Whatever toxin was in
Croc's venom, its effects were persistent.

Bruce shoved the maps across the table and sat back,
stretching his neck from side to side.

Lucius Fox came in from the shop, carrying a sizable

black shoulder pack. He set it down on the table in front of Bruce with an audible *thunk*. Then he laid a small black box on the table next to the shoulder pack.

"Everything you wanted," he said. "Pitons. Sharpened and reengineered so that you can attach the clip to your grappling gun here and fire them, one after the other, until you're empty."

Bruce studied the arrangement with interest. Slender strands of wire were attached to the metal head of each piton. The wires came together, forming a little river of shiny blue skeins that flowed up and into the top of the shoulder pack.

"Lock and load, Bruce," Fox said. "And for God's sake, don't miss."

Bruce smiled slightly. "Be a pity to waste all this effort if I don't hit the target. No worries. I'm not apt to miss at that range."

Lucius did not return the smile. "It's not the range I'm worried about. After your last encounter with Killer Croc, you're putting yourself in real danger trying to take him alive."

Bruce stood and took a last sip of his cold coffee, then set the cup back on the table.

"I expect you're right, Lucius. But I can't just put him down. Whatever he is now, he used to be human. And the Scarecrow had a lot to do with turning him into a monster. He's done terrible things, but maybe there's still a path of redemption for him somewhere, even if I can't see it. If I have to kill him, it's like the cliché about terrorists. The Scarecrow wins."

He scooped up several extra pitons and shoved them into his utility belt.

"Are you planning on reloading?" Lucius asked dubiously.

"You never know," said Bruce. "I'm a big fan of the Boy Scout motto: 'Be prepared.'"

He pulled on his gauntlets and snapped them into place over his forearms. Tonight, he would be fully armored with the finest protection he had available.

Picking up the shoulder pack, he walked over to the Batmobile and laid the pack in the passenger-side front seat.
Then, with a nod to Lucius, he fastened his cape and cowl
into place.

A moment later, Batman slid behind the wheel, and,
with a rumble like thunder, the low-slung vehicle moved
off into the darkness of the exit tunnel and out into the
world beyond.

A few minutes later, Batman eased himself through one
of the manholes that led into the storm drains. He was carrying the shoulder pack. The air was still and oppressive,
even at three thirty in the morning. The storm drains, he
thought, were going to be a real treat.

As hot and humid as the city streets had been, the tunnels felt like a convection oven. Batman dropped the last
few feet into the ankle-deep water flowing sluggishly along
the bottom of the great drains to the river.

Batman activated his night-vision lenses. The absolute
darkness turned to green images, and he began moving
cautiously down the tunnel toward the Reservoir. Once the
water from the Reservoir had receded, Killer Croc would
probably have returned to his lair in the subway siding. Unless it had been destroyed in the flood.

Batman was moving without visible light. He didn't
want to let Croc know he was coming for him.

The hunter was about to become the prey.

Moving as quietly as he could, Batman finally reached
the intersection of several sewer mains near the Terminal
Street Station. They all debouched into a large cylindrical
vault constructed of granite blocks taken from the old Car-
lini quarry some thirty miles west.

The storm drains here mainly carried overflow volume
from the Reservoir in times of flooding. A number of
smaller tunnels entered the vault at different levels. During

storms, water poured out of them into the chamber, then emptied through an enormous grate at the lowest point of the vault. Then it flowed through the massive tunnel that carried the onrushing water to the river.

He stood in four feet of water and checked the grate. Its metal bars were badly rent near the top as if they had been torn apart. Batman double-checked via infrared and saw Killer Croc's familiar heat trail. Croc had passed through here within the last twelve hours. Batman guessed that his quarry would be coming back this way sooner or later.

The spot was perfect for his purpose.

Debris piled up against the bottom of the grating was acting as a dam, and the incoming water had formed a pond about four feet deep at the bottom of the vault.

Batman listened carefully but heard only the soft trickling of the slowly moving water. He unhitched the heavy shoulder pack and set it down on a small raised concrete platform at one end of the vault. He pulled out a carefully stored roll of black velvet from the top of the pack, unwound it, and spread out its contents—a dozen small black disks.

He scooped up the disks and levered himself into one of the smaller storm drains.

He paced off a hundred feet. Then he took one of the disks, peeled a circle of paper off the bottom, and pressed it against the side wall of the tunnel. The glue bonded instantly, and the disk remained in place when he let go. He tapped the center of the disk, activating the circuitry inside.

Then he entered each of the remaining auxiliary tunnels and left one of the disks in each of them. After he had fastened the last one into place, he slid back into the vault, produced a small black box from his utility belt, set it on the platform, and flipped a little switch on one side. A dozen green LEDs lit up in a grid. His motion sensors were active. He'd know in advance which way Croc was coming.

Moving rapidly and with an economy of motion, Batman carefully unpacked the rest of the bag's contents. He laid out the magazine with its reengineered pitons, several coils of monofilament, and other assorted odds and ends. Finally, he pulled the last of the contents from the shoulder pack, a tightly wound plastic web.

Hoisting the web over his shoulder, he climbed to the top of the vault, using the smaller storm drain openings as hand- and footholds.

In another twenty minutes, he had the net strung across the top of the vault. Wires from the various ceiling mounts ran down the edge of the vault to the magazine, where they were attached to the pitons.

Batman pulled out his grappling gun and snapped the magazine into place.

The trap was set.

The net would fall when Croc entered the vault. Batman would fire the wired pitons all around the floor of the chamber, pinning the net to the stone walls. Then he would toss in grenades filled with knockout gas, which were hooked to the back of his utility belt.

All the net had to do was hold Croc in the chamber long enough for the anesthetic to take effect. In the relatively small, poorly vented chamber, that wouldn't be long.

He put the gun down on the concrete apron and waded over to the torn grating. He fished a small BlackBerry-like device out of his utility belt, peeled off the paper backing, then reached through the opening in the torn grating and fastened it to the roof of the large drainage tunnel. A quick glance over his shoulder assured him that he was as prepared as he was going to be. With that, he pushed the small button on the bottom of the device.

A moment later, a soft sound like distant footfalls began to echo gently down the tunnel. Though Batman couldn't feel it himself, he knew that minute vibrations synched with the sounds were now traveling through the tunnel walls. If Killer Croc was somewhere in the storm drains, his heightened senses would tell him that there was prey loose in his domain. And he would come hunting.

There was no telling how long it would take Croc to arrive. Batman sat down on the small concrete apron and folded his legs, assuming the lotus position. He regularized his breathing and emptied his mind of extraneous thought. He had learned much during his travels before he first donned the cape and cowl and identity that now gave a city new hope. And that knowledge served him well.

He heard the water around him on its journey to the distant river. He felt the weight of the bedrock, asphalt, and soaring towers far above him. He watched rivers of humanity flow through the canyons of Gotham on their endless journeys out into the wider world.

And he was carried with them . . .

Bruce himself prepares the bed of coals for the fire pit.

First he digs a shallow trench in the earth, three feet wide and twelve feet long.

At Cassandra's direction, he collects a pile of logs and lays them out horizontally along the pit, spaced evenly apart, like railroad ties. Then he stacks other logs across them vertically. Then he lays on another horizontal track of logs.

When he has a mound of wood about twelve feet long and three feet high, she instructs him to pack dry reeds around them.

Then he lights a reed from Cassandra's cooking fire and sets the reed kindling ablaze. It ignites, and, soon, the logs begin to burn.

Bruce and Cassandra talk as they stare into the blaze.

"Pain is a sensation—of body or of spirit. It is one of many feelings that your mind can register. Pain is nothing. It can be managed through strength of will."

Bruce nods. "I know. I've researched the techniques . . . breathing control, hypnosis . . ."

"What of the spiritual nature? Have you researched that as well?"

Bruce doesn't answer.

"The interior is something you'd deny?" she asks.

Bruce shrugs. "No. It's something I control."

"Do you?"

Bruce gazes into the fire. "Does it hurt, Cassandra? To walk on burning coals?"

"Sometimes. For some people."

"Does it scar?"

Cassandra looks at him seriously. "Bruce . . . what pain does not?"

Bruce frowns. "But pain can be overcome."

Cassandra shook her head. "It is the fear of pain that must be overcome. Once you accept this . . . once you are no longer afraid . . . you can do anything. Even walk on fire."

By nightfall, the logs have burned down and collapsed into ash and glowing coals.

As instructed, Bruce rakes out the embers, smoothing them into a glowing ribbon of heat and brilliance. As he does so, the wood of his rake begins to char.

Bruce looks at the glow of the coals. He feels their heat. And he mutters, "I must be nuts to even think of trying this."

"That is the voice of fear," Cassandra says. She slips off her sandals and steps onto the coals. She walks smoothly. Coolly. Confidently. Four steps and she's on the ground. She turns and walks back to him. "Will you let fear rule your life? Will you let it stop you from becoming all that you can be?"

Bruce looks at her. He thinks back to the worst moments of his life. Those terrible instants when fear and pain had overwhelmed him. And the wonderful times when they had not.

He takes a deep breath. A flood of resolve breaks over him, bringing with it a pins-and-needles sensation, a surge of tingling energy that rushes through his whole body. All the hairs on his arms stand erect.

Without a qualm, he steps barefoot upon the glowing coals and feels them crunch beneath his feet. Three smooth steps and he is off the coals and onto the hard dry ground.

Like Cassandra, he turns and walks that glowing ribbon back to the beginning.

He stands beside Cassandra, grinning like a fool, elated by the miracle that he has been a part of.

"The lesson is not that you can walk on fire," Cassandra says as if she reads his thoughts. *"The lesson is that when you control what your mind focuses on, you can accomplish anything."*

She turns from the fire and walks toward the hut.

"Cassandra?"

"Yes, Bruce?" She looks back, catches his eye. *"Ah. You wish an answer to the question that has hung in the air since you arrived.*

"My knowledge was gained through deceit. I came to the fakirs seeking enlightenment, masquerading as a boy. I have no doubt that they saw me for what I really was, but they agreed to show me the path."

"Why?" Bruce asked.

"So I would fail. It became a game for them." She glances at him, one of her rare, mischievous smiles. *"But I didn't fail. And eventually, they tired of the game, cast me out, and I was exposed. They said I had tricked them. I was branded a witch. My family turned their backs to me, as I had caused them great shame. In this village, I am either feared or hated."*

Bruce reaches out, touching her shoulder. *"Why don't you leave?"*

She places her hand over his. *"Because this is where I belong. In your life, is there no such place?"*

Reality shifted.

He blinked. The tropical heat of India fell away and became the dank humid air of the storm drains beneath the streets of Gotham.

Batman glanced down at the small monitor sitting on the apron beside him. Three of the little LEDs were blinking, but only faintly. Croc was still some distance off. But as he watched, the signals became stronger. Then two more LEDs began to strobe.

How interesting, he thought.

All the blinking LEDs were indicating tunnels to the south, toward the river. But Croc couldn't be in all of them at the same time. Perhaps he was moving in some cross tunnel that intersected the others. In any case, the blinking lights were becoming brighter and brighter by the moment. Hunter and prey, Killer Croc was coming.

Batman stood up silently. He didn't know how sharp Croc's senses were, and he was taking no chances.

Without a sound, he folded into the mouth of one of the auxiliary drains on the north side of the vault. He checked his grappling gun, then rechecked the magazine. It was a double-action weapon, but he didn't know how much time he would have once things began to happen.

Very quietly, he cocked the hammer. The first shot might be crucial.

A glance at the monitor told him that Croc was somewhere close by. But his motion sensors were still unable to pinpoint the exact location. The indicators for every southern tunnel were now blinking at full intensity. And several of the lights from the other compass points were blinking now as well. It was as if Killer Croc was coming from all directions. The tunnel behind him was completely silent, but Batman couldn't resist a quick look back down its inky depths.

Nothing.

He peered out of the darkness of the tunnel into an equally black vault. His night-vision lenses turned everything ghostly green, grainy like a bad television set. Despite that, his surroundings were clearly visible.

Then the light around him changed. A quick glance told him that all the LEDs on his monitor had quit blinking. Wherever Croc was, and he had to be quite close, he had stopped moving. Possibly even stopped breathing for the moment.

Batman scanned the empty vault before him, searching for an answer. The LED monitor shone solid red across the entire gird. He had to be here somewhere. Almost within arm's reach. And just before all hell broke loose, he understood. Croc had either gained access to a minor unmapped tunnel or else dug his own. However he had done it, Croc was now directly overhead.

27

Batman glanced up in time to see the ceiling of the vault collapse.

With a terrifying bellow, Killer Croc dropped into the chamber accompanied by a shower of masonry, granite chunks, and dust. The net came down under him. Water splashed everywhere as he hit the pond at the bottom of the vault.

Batman had flipped off his night-vision lenses just as the ceiling gave way. He turned on his xenon spots, and the vault, full of shadows and fury, exploded into brilliance. Croc, momentarily blinded by the light, thrashed about a few feet below Batman's perch, roaring like a wounded animal. In another moment, he'd recover his bearings. And armored though Batman was, he knew from experience that he could ill afford another one-on-one match with the angry monster.

He fired grapnels in rapid succession, arcing his shots all around the vault. The pitons carrying the wires bound to the edge of the net flew in every direction, pulling the ends of the net up and over Croc. Each piton hit the stonework with authority and sank up to its eye. Croc flung himself against the netting as it rose around him but was thrown back. It was made of one of Wayne Enterprises' strongest polymers.

Croc plunged into the water and came up holding a large piece of the granite ceiling. He hurled the broken slab. It caught in the net and rebounded, hitting Croc in the shoulder. His scream of pain and anger shook the vault.

Batman realized that Croc had thrown the missile directly at the mouth of the drain where he was crouching. Croc's eyes had already adjusted to the bright light, and he had located his tormentor.

Batman pressed another stud on his glove, and a small armored extension slid out of his cowl and around his mouth and chin, locking into place. He turned on his compressed air and initiated self-contained breathing mode.

As Croc tore at the net with his great clawed hands, Batman threw an anesthetic grenade against the far wall. It burst instantly, and a greenish gas began expanding to fill the vault from top to bottom.

Batman could see that Croc understood instantly what was happening. He leaned forward, gathered as much of the net together as he could, then leapt backward, pulling the net after him. There was a sharp crack as four of the pitons pulled out of the wall in a cloud of rock dust and masonry fragments.

Batman backed farther into his tunnel, but he was too late.

Croc burst out of the pond, arms extended. One clawed hand wrapped around Batman's left arm and locked into place. Croc brought his legs up against the stone wall beneath the tunnel and bent backward, launching himself toward the pool, pulling Batman out of the tunnel and down into the water on top of him.

As Batman fought for balance, Croc slashed a clawed hand across his chest plate, leaving a trail of silver grooves. But the armor held.

In a frenzy, Croc opened his mouth and bit the lower half of Batman's face, trying to wound Batman as he had done once before. The metal face guard rang as Croc's teeth closed over it. This time, Batman was undamaged, and he brought an armored knee hard into Croc's stomach. The monster grunted, letting him go.

But Croc's thick hide, hard and knobbed, served as armor of his own. Before Batman could follow up any advantage he might have gained, the demon dove headfirst into the water in front of him and grabbed hold of both his legs. He spun around, dragging Batman beneath the water. Batman's head bounced sharply off the edge of one of the trenches at the bottom of the vault. His ears rang, and he realized that he could feel the cold of the frothing water against his mouth and chin. The impact had cracked his armored face covering and broken his oxygen mask.

Croc slammed him time and again against the bottom of the vault. Batman twisted his body to take the brunt of the pounding on his body armor. Croc was literally trying to tear him apart against the stone channeling.

His risk assessment was short and to the point. With several feet of water around him and anesthetic gas in the air above, the outlook in his current situation was poor. Batman had learned a number of yoga techniques, but he had no doubt that if it came down to it, Croc would be able to hold his breath longer than he could. And if he passed out before Croc did, from either gas or drowning, it was game over.

He had to end this fast.

As Killer Croc yanked at his calf to throw him once more against the bottom of the pool, Batman suddenly bent his knees tightly, pulled his own body up against the demon's, and slashed a forearm up across the monster's scaled face. Simultaneously, he pressed the concealed trigger that turned the serrated points along the outer edges of his gauntlets into knifelike blades. These ripped through the softer flesh beneath Croc's eye, nearly blinding him. Croc roared and clutched at his wound, dropping Batman's legs as he did so.

Batman jackknifed off Croc's chest and threw his cape over Croc's head, twisting it and pulling it tight. For a second, Croc was baffled, flailing and grabbing at the cloth. Then he found his purchase and tore the cloak asunder. But that precious second was all Batman needed.

He leapt out of the pond and, with his shredded cape trailing behind him, sprang to the concrete apron once more, then leapt into another of the auxiliary tunnels. He took off, heading east under the main business district of Midtown. He was running at full speed by the time Croc pulled himself into the tunnel after him.

Batman bore off to the left at a branching tunnel. Lit by his small spotlights, the shadows of the ribbed pipe strobed back and forth as he ran. He could hear Croc lumbering through the tunnel behind him.

The side tunnels were smaller than the main branches. From the noise Croc was making, Batman knew that the monster was scraping the sides—perhaps even the top—of the tunnel, too big to run through it freely. A hundred yards down the tunnel, Batman paused and waited. After a minute, the echoes told him that Croc had reached the fork and, seeing the distant light of Batman's spots, had entered the left branch after him.

Batman sprinted ahead again, slamming his feet against the metal pipe, making as much noise as possible. He didn't want to lose Croc now. The floor of the tunnel was climbing by the time he reached the next intersection, a three-way divide. He stopped.

Turning around, he paced off twenty-seven feet back the way he had come. He reached into his utility belt and pulled out a small block with a black sheath around the outside—a shaped charge made of RDX.

Croc was some distance behind him but still coming.

Batman judged the angle and, peeling away the backing, pressed the charge against the wall of the tunnel, some six and a half feet off the ground on the upper arc of the tunnel ceiling. He depressed a small button on the back of the block and stepped away around the corner into the left-hand tunnel at the intersection.

He held his hands against his cowl over his ears and counted the seconds off silently . . . *3* . . . *2* . . . *1*.

There was a muffled bang. Debris, dust and metal splinters rattled against the wall of the tunnel intersection. A moment later, Batman stepped to the newly opened hole in the top of the auxiliary storm drain.

In his studies of the underground structures of the city, Batman had found a spot where this particular storm drain rose close to the surface, directly below the underground electrical grid. He had blown his way into the underground transformer vault directly in front of Rawson Holdings Corporate Headquarters.

It will have to be repaired before the next major storm, he thought, *or there'll be hell to pay with the electrical system in this part of Gotham.*

He pulled himself up through the opening, a short, roughly circular gap, and into a cast-concrete enclosure some thirteen feet long, five feet wide, and six feet high. He saw he had misjudged by about a foot and was a little to the left of center in the small room. The lower part of the wall next to him had been destroyed by the blast. But the cables that entered either end of the room a foot or two above the floor seemed to be intact.

He could hear Killer Croc approaching the breach in the storm drain below, his grunts and growls sounding like curses, like effort and anger combined.

Batman looked the transformer over quickly. It was a GothCon 2500 series. He yanked open the front cover and pulled the safety switch. A red light came on above him. He hoped the many computers in Rawson's corporate headquarters above him had functioning backup systems.

He pulled a small coil of thick wire out of a pocket on his utility belt. Working with lightning speed, he unrolled the coil and strung one end through and around the eye of one of his spare pitons. He spun the loose end around the shaft as tightly as possible.

"Be prepared," he muttered.

The scrabbling behind him told him Croc had found the

opening and was trying to lever himself up through it. Quickly, keeping his back to the opening, Batman looped the other end of the wire around the end of one of the electrical coiled cores inside the transformer.

Out of the corner of his eye, Batman saw Croc begin to pull himself up silently, watched his monstrous shoulders clear the opening and his scaled torso slide into view.

Batman pulled out his grappling gun and snapped the piton into the empty magazine still attached to the side of the weapon.

Croc forced one knee up and over the lip of the opening into the room. He pulled his other leg up after him and began to stand. His right claw reached out for Batman, now only a few feet away.

Batman whirled and fired in the same motion.

The piton struck Croc just above the right knee and stuck. The chamber rocked as he screamed in pain and, at that moment, Batman flipped the transformer switch.

The red light went out. Sparks flew everywhere. Croc ceased roaring and froze, vibrating madly, arms outstretched, fists tightly clenched. Batman dove to the floor on the other side of the room just as the transformer gave off a series of electrical bursts. And shut down.

Croc slumped and slid back into the hole. With a crash, he fell to the floor of the storm drain below and lay there, inert. Batman stood and brushed several live sparks off his legs. He noticed that the red light was on again above the transformer.

He looked down the hole into the storm drain. Croc lay where he had fallen, breathing but otherwise motionless. The piton was still stuck in Croc's leg but the wire had melted completely.

Batman popped the pin on his second anesthetic grenade and dropped it into the drain below. He pulled off what was left of his cape and stretched it across the open hole in the transformer vault, weighting it down with loose pieces of concrete from the damaged wall and floor.

Once more, Batman touched the button near the chin of

his mask. There was a short burst of static in his ear, then he heard the voice of Jim Gordon.

"Batman?"

Gordon sounded surprisingly awake for—what time was it? Not yet morning rush hour, anyway. The streets overhead were still relatively quiet.

"It's over, Jim," he said. "Send a SWAT team along with your MCU detectives . . . and a prison van and the heaviest shackles you've got. Go through the manhole into the transformer vault right in front of the Rawson building. There's a new hole in the floor that leads into the storm drains. Croc's there, out like a light. Tell your boys to bring rebreathing gear. Some of the gas I used on Croc may still be present. I've covered the hole to trap the gas, but you'd better hurry. I don't know how long it'll take Croc to revive, and you need to have him hog-tied before that happens."

"Team's already on its way," Gordon said. "But the Rawson building?" He sounded amused now. "Are you telling me you had something to do with the electrical emergency they called me about a few minutes ago?"

"Perish the thought. Just tell Gotham Consolidated not to send any of their workers down the manhole until the police have arrived and given the all clear. Although if you have any local reporters you don't like, now's your chance."

Gordon laughed at the other end of the line. "Don't tempt me," he said. "You okay?"

"I'm a little scraped up but nothing time spent resting won't cure. I'll be in the area watching until your guys have secured the premises. See you around, Gordon."

As he swung up to the roof of an adjacent building, he thought about the damage he'd left behind to the city's electrical grid. It wasn't major in the scheme of things. Still, it would have to be fixed. A Wayne Enterprises subsidiary could put in a bid to do the repair work. But the notion of being paid to repair the damage he himself had done, however just the cause, did raise certain conflict-of-interest issues. He sighed. Wayne Electrics would be able to do a fine job. Sometimes, the life of the vigilante was a bit more complex than it might appear on the surface.

The Gotham City Police Department SWAT team arrived in several heavy vehicles three minutes later.

By the time Detectives Montoya and Allen reached the scene, the SWAT team had the still-unconscious Killer Croc in wrist and ankle shackles.

Montoya and Allen leaned against their unmarked, just inside the police barricades. Allen watched with interest as the SWAT team began to rig a hoist over the manhole cover to bring Croc to the surface. The SWAT team worked with economy and discipline, their movements almost like a dance.

But Montoya, standing behind him, stared up at the Rawson building setbacks, searching its gables and roofs for a shadow she was certain was up there somewhere.

A cheer went up behind her, and she turned to see the trussed-up figure of Killer Croc being swung out of the manhole over onto a stretcher. He was beginning to awaken and starting to struggle. Though the monster was clearly groggy, it still took eight members of the SWAT team to manhandle him into the back of the prison van. By the time they had the door closed and locked, he was bellowing.

A dozen squad cars flanked it front and back as the van moved off down the avenue amid a light show of flashing red beacons, heading for Arkham Asylum. Montoya could see that the van was rocking from side to side as it traveled down the empty roads toward the Narrows.

She yawned. It had been a late night and an early morning. The eastern sky was lightening, heralding the coming dawn.

And then, as she turned to look at the departing convoy, she saw what she'd been looking for. A deep shadow passed across the brick facade above Lenny's Deli. It was

two stories up and it was gone in a split second, but the silhouette had been unmistakably the one she'd seen through
the frosted glass of Lieutenant Gordon's office. She smiled
to herself as she moved back toward Allen. For just a moment, she had seen the defender of Gotham City about
whom so little was known.

Detective Montoya had finally seen the Batman.

28

There was a fully furnished gym in Bruce Wayne's pent-house apartment. Bruce had begun this portion of his work-out with dumbbells, then moved on to a weight machine. Now he was finishing off his program the old-fashioned way.

Dressed in gym pants, he was doing one-arm, one-leg push-ups. Concentrating on his form, he contracted his abdominal muscles, keeping his torso straight. He had placed his right hand slightly in front of his shoulder and held his left hand behind his back. The toe of his right foot rested on the heel of his left foot. He inhaled, bent his elbow, and slowly lowered his body to within three inches of the floor. Then he exhaled as he pushed back up into the starting position.

. . . forty-three . . .

When he reached fifty reps, he would switch—left hand on the floor, left foot on his right heel—and do it all over again.

A bead of perspiration hung from the tip of his nose . . . then elongated and splashed onto the wooden floor. He was dripping wet, sweating more profusely than usual. His body's way of getting rid of Killer Croc's poison.

He hadn't been 100 percent since Croc had bitten him. His mind kept sliding back into the past.

Into the heat.

The sounds.

The darkness . . .

A crash outside Cassandra's hut jerks Bruce from a sound sleep. Cassandra is awake already and standing.

Another crash. Rocks hurled against the closed door.

Outside, the angry voices of several drunken youths call to her in their native dialect. "Come out, Cassandra!"

"Witch!"

"Whore!"

"Show yourself!"

Bruce stands. "Cassandra?"

"It's nothing." Her voice is soft and calm.

"Sounds like an angry nothing." He tries to make light of the incident, but his heart is pounding.

Cassandra shrugs. "Just boys playing at being men. Remember? I'm hated."

"And feared," Bruce murmurs.

"Wait here."

"No." He takes a step forward.

"Please. It's nothing," Cassandra says again.

She opens the door and goes outside into the small courtyard. Bruce stands inside, watching from the shadows, willing to follow her lead, at least for now. After all, this is her land. These are her people. Perhaps she's right. Maybe she understands them, as he does not.

He sees that the youths outside are members of the gang who eyed him suspiciously while he waited to meet the fakirs. Is he the reason that they're here? Is he the cause of this confrontation?

Cassandra speaks to them firmly in Hindi, in a tone

*their mothers might use. "You shame yourselves, acting this
way." She clearly thinks she can handle herself.*

*"Shame? Us?" The young man's voice was indignant.
"You teach an outsider what is not his to know."*

"You give him what isn't yours to give."

"You are dishonored!"

"The ways of satya *and* shimsa *are open to everyone,"
Cassandra says calmly. "You would do well to abide by
them. Now leave, before your mothers see you."*

"Witch!" The boy strikes her across the face.

She stares into his eyes. Quietly. Defiantly.

He raises his hand to strike her again.

*Bruce steps out of the shadows and grabs his wrist.
"Enough," he says, striving for her calm against the anger
that threatens to overwhelm him.*

*The young man wrenches his hand free from Bruce's
grasp, then swings it at him in a backhand swipe calcu-
lated to send him sprawling to his knees.*

*Bruce ducks his blow and punches—a jab to the gut—
and sends the youth reeling.*

*The others step forward—a pack of snarling jackals.
There are five of them. In a minute, four are on the ground.
One has staggered back, cradling his wrist. The fallen rise,
trying to look threatening, but something in Bruce's eyes
stops them.*

*"Do not mistake me," Bruce says in perfect Hindi. "I
am not like Cassandra. I am like you."*

*Involuntarily, the lead boy steps back a pace. And then,
ashamed that he has done so, he yells angrily and leaps to
hit Bruce again.*

*"Don't!" Cassandra yells, but she is too late. There is a
blur of motion around Bruce's right hand and a sharp crack.*

The attacker stands frozen.

No one moves.

*Then, twisting to his left, the young man falls slowly to
the ground, settling like a rag doll on the dirt before Cassandra's house.*

The others hesitate. Then, ashamed to back down before their peers, they step forward once again.

"Don't be fools," Cassandra snaps. "Take your friend." *She points to the young man sprawled in the dirt. "Leave this place."*

This time they look into Bruce's eyes.

And this time, they go.

Cassandra stands with her back to him. He reaches out to touch her shoulder. "Cassandra, are—"

She pulls away and walks through her door. Bruce follows.

"You need to leave," she says. "Like the fakirs, they would have grown tired of their game. They would have left on their own. Violence begets violence. That is how it grows."

Cassandra kneels, picks up Bruce's gear, and begins to stow it in his backpack. "You have your answer now. You've learned what you wanted to know."

"Yes, I—"

She stands and hands him the backpack.

Bruce takes the pack and slings it over his shoulders. "I've failed you, Cassandra. You're right. It's time for me to leave."

"No," Cassandra whispers, as Bruce disappears into darkness. "I have failed you. Forgive me."

. . . forty-seven . . .

He knew now that there had been no failure on either of their parts. No need for forgiveness. Her answers were fine ones. The best. They simply hadn't fit the questions he had been asking. Rā's al Ghūl had taught him that turning the other cheek wasn't always the answer. Not for him. The corners of his mouth turned up slightly. Nor for Rā's either, for that matter.

Sweat and poison dripped from his pores and pooled on the gym floor.

. . . forty-eight . . .

A year after he left Cassandra, Bruce crossed the border into China's Xizang Province. There he tangled with the Chinese authorities, landed in a border jail, and somehow gained the attention of Rā's al Ghūl.

... *forty-nine* ...

And Rā's—his teacher, his enemy—had honed him and given him the mental and physical toughness to become what he needed to be.

... *fifty* ...

On a San Diego rooftop, a man knelt among the shad-ows, placing an elongated carrying case on the tar paper. He flipped a pair of snaps and opened the case with care. Inside the case, each section resting in its own pocket on a specially molded base covered in black velvet, was a unique weapon. The shadow took out what appeared to be a long rod with a handgrip near one end, and then a short flat box. He began to screw them together. He was assembling a rifle, a unique rifle that had been made in Europe from the owner's design. It was an exceptionally well-crafted piece of precision equipment.

The shadow removed a slender wooden stock, locked the assembled barrel and firing chamber in place. The rifle had only one purpose. It was a perfect instrument for killing. The craftsman who had made the weapon had questioned his choice of stock. He suggested a slender metal rod with a small shoulder pad at one end. Easier to conceal, slightly more efficient.

The shadow had preferred a wooden stock to metal. It was warmer and more . . . comforting somehow. He laughed inwardly at his own conceit, but he had insisted on the wooden stock. The gunsmith—a master armorer really—had acquiesced with good grace. He was being paid well, and the customer was always right.

The shadow slid the bolt into place, clicked it shut, flicked it open with his thumb. It moved smoothly and silently. He preferred a bolt-action weapon. It discouraged the overconfidence automatic weapons often gave their wielders.

But the real genius of the rifle was that the barrel and the firing chamber were single-use interchangeable items. The shadow rotated them in various combinations, then disposed of them. As a result, the killing instrument he held in his hands created a different profile of the weapon each time he used it. It might mock a Russian Dragunov Sniper Rifle, a Hungarian AMD-65, or even an American M16A4.

The shadow's name—the name he had been born with—was Floyd Lawton, the younger son in the wealthy—if completely dysfunctional—Lawton family. The Lawtons were old money allied with a wild, almost manic streak. As a result, they had bought their way out of difficulties for as long as anyone could remember. Most people thought that was a pity.

The Lawtons had lived high, wild, and free since before the Revolutionary War. And the males of the line were expected to be, among other things, fine marksmen. Thomas, Floyd's older brother, excelled in everything except this one skill, where to his everlasting fury, Floyd was untouchable.

Then their mother—driven half-mad by the abuses and infidelities of her husband—had instigated a three-way shoot-out between Floyd, his brother, and his father. The gun battle had left Thomas dead and their father confined to a wheelchair. Family money had stymied the investigation—a terrible accident!—just as it had hushed up young Floyd's role in the incident. It never became a matter of public or private record. But the bullet that had blown through his brother's chest had taken not only his brother's life; it had destroyed Floyd's soul. He discovered that some part of him had reveled in the destruction of another human being. He had found his calling. Nothing would ever be the same again.

From that moment on, he knew what he was.

Deadshot.

An assassin for hire.

An emotionless marksman.

A deadly killing machine.

He snapped a high-powered telescopic sight into place above the firing chamber. At the moment of truth, he found that fixing a target in its crosshairs provided a tremendously satisfying sense of power and purpose. It never lasted long, but it was addictive.

He took a short bipod out of the case and attached it to the front of the barrel, just two inches behind the muzzle.

Finally, he removed a leather slip from the case, clipped it to the underside of the barrel, slipped the loop over his left arm up to the biceps, and tightened the friction lock. He wrapped the sling around his arm and across the back of his left hand and took hold of the barrel's grip. He flipped open the bolt once more.

He was ready.

Deadshot removed a single 7.62mm round from the case. He'd brought several, and a loaded magazine as well. But a single shot was all he generally needed. Magazines tended to unbalance the weapon slightly. More importantly, he felt a magazine's presence diminished a marksman's concentration. If you felt that you needed several shots to complete a contract, you were apt to be a little less demanding of yourself when you fired the first shot. And sometimes, one shot was all you had time for.

Which was, of course, part of the rush.

It wasn't that he was depressed—at least not exactly. But he was frequently overcome by ennui so intense that only the hunt could awaken any passion in him. That—and getting away with murder.

He had designed a costume to flummox the authorities: a dark red and metallic jumpsuit that covered his body completely from head to foot so he never left the tiniest shred of skin or hair at any hit to prove he had been there. A featureless full-head metal mask concealed his face. A targeting device covered his right eye, providing telescopic, infrared, and night vision as required. He favored his custom-made killing instrument, but he was broad-minded. He carried an array of weaponry, as he felt that variety was the spice of life. And death. Depending on the circumstances surrounding the kill, he would sometimes eschew his instrument and opt for a different approach. He wanted nothing to connect one assassination to the next. The bullet that killed his victims was the only forensic evidence he ever left behind.

Of late, he had begun to make it more difficult for himself—choosing tricky angles and shots that would have been impossible for anyone else. Even with this intense stimulus, he was bored, almost unto death, most of the time.

Recently he had added removable wrist-mounted .357 Magnums with silencer capabilities to his costume. They were gross weapons. Fine for short range, but inappropriate for distance shots. Still, the concept amused him. Things did occasionally go wrong. The time might come when he would have to do close-up work. As much as he despised organizational conformity, he thought there was something to the Boy Scout precept "Be prepared."

If Deadshot had looked up, he would have seen the coastal city spread out before him. Bright lights. Palm trees. A hint of breeze wafting in off the Pacific Ocean. But he wasn't here to admire the scenery.

He was studying a nearby hotel roof terrace where a fund-raiser was in full swing. Posters stood on easels—VERICHIO FOR MAYOR written bright and large above an image of the candidate's smiling face—reinforcing the crowd's belief that they were there to back a winner. Red, white, and blue streamers fluttered in the light breeze. Balloons, tethered in cheerful bunches, bobbed decoratively, waiting to be released during Verichio's campaign speech.

The scope built into Deadshot's mask shifted among the partygoers, darting from face to face, focusing for an instant, then moving on. The assassin was searching for Verichio himself, the city DA who had fought forcefully against organized crime and who, as mayor, promised to continue the battle to even greater effect.

Deadshot scanned quickly past the throng who mobbed the bar and started to sweep toward a cluster near the terrace wall. Then a man at the bar took two martini glasses from the bartender and turned, and Deadshot saw the same distinguished face that graced the campaign posters.

Tsk-tsk, he thought. *The candidate should be shaking hands, not belting down cocktails.* He smiled and aimed but a lovely blonde—a campaign worker with whom Verichio was rumored to be having a torrid affair—moved between him and the candidate and blocked his shot. Shooting directly through her was an option, but he hated waste of any sort.

Verichio handed the blonde her martini. She half turned—she had a classic profile; Deadshot could understand the attraction—and smiled up at Verichio. She was still blocking the shot. He decided the situation called for slightly revised tactics. He fished the magazine out of the case beside him and snapped it into place. He peered into the scope attached to the rifle.

Verichio held out his glass and she clinked it playfully with hers.

Deadshot smiled. There was nothing—literally—that he loved better than a challenge.

His first bullet shattered the stem of her martini glass. She jerked back, too startled to scream.

The second bullet sliced through the stem of Verichio's own glass.

Verichio turned openmouthed, looking straight at Deadshot, and the third bullet hit him square in the Adam's apple, ripped through his throat and out the back of his neck, and buried itself in the outdoor carpet.

Verichio was dead before he slammed into the appetizer table.

The blonde was screaming.

In less than a minute, Deadshot had disassembled his rifle and was moving quietly toward the roof exit and the service stairwell carrying his case.

One minute more and he would be in the hotel room where he was registered under an assumed name. In another, he would have changed into business attire. Then he would be out the door to his room, down the service stairs and into the lobby, where he would be just another businessman carrying a leather bag on his way to a late dinner meeting.

His cell phone vibrated against his waist. He checked the incoming text. Another time. Another place. Another city.

Once he was away from the hotel, he would answer the message.

Floyd Lawton lounged negligently in one of the velvet armchairs in the corner of the Shimmering Sands hotel bar. He crossed his long elegant legs and sipped his martini, nodded in approval, then placed it on the low table before him.

Designer sunglasses shaded his eyes against glare as he glanced casually out the floor-to-ceiling windows toward the wharf, where moored yachts and cabin cruisers bobbed enticingly on the high tide.

His Italian suit fit his lanky body well, making him look more slender than athletic. His hair, trim mustache, and goatee were conservative but stylish. He attracted no serious attention. A low-level movie exec. Maybe someone in accounting.

Appearances could, indeed, be deceiving.

The corner where he sat felt dark and cozy against the glare of sunlight coming off of the water. This was the way Lawton liked it. He preferred keeping to the shadows.

He glanced at his watch.

A square-set, heavy-jawed man with a flattened boxer's nose strolled into the bar. His hair was slicked back from a sharp widow's peak. He wore a rumpled linen sports jacket over a garish shirt that was open several buttons too far. The bulge of a shoulder holster was clear to anyone who knew what to look for. Thick gold chains nestled in curly graying chest hair.

The man stopped and blinked while his small eyes adjusted to the gloom. Then he spotted Lawton. He stalked

over, settled into an armchair across from the assassin, and
pulled a thick envelope from the inner pocket of his jacket.
For an instant, he rested it on the low table. Then he slid it
over so that it lay beside Lawton's nearly untouched cocktail.

Lawton picked up the envelope and pocketed it. "Everyone happy?"

The man flashed a grin that was half sneer. The small
gap in his front teeth made him look like an old '69 Buick.
"Yeah. But the cocktail glasses . . . a little much, don't you
think?"

Lawton stretched out a slender hand, snagged the cocktail garnish, and bit a green olive off a red plastic toothpick
shaped like a sword. He shrugged. "Just keeping it interesting."

"This next one, we don't need no flourishes, understand? You got our e-mail?"

Lawton nodded. "Gotham. Again."

"Our Russian associates are having difficulties there.
His removal will alleviate most of their problems. However, this one could get dicey."

Lawton shrugged. "Just another cop kill . . ."

"You think? You worry me sometimes."

The assassin flicked the sword-shaped toothpick. It spun
over the table and stuck right in the bulky man's tooth gap.
"You worry too much."

Lawton downed his cocktail in a single motion, rose,
and strode out the door of the bar, into the bright sunlight.

The large man pulled the toothpick from between his
front teeth and scowled after him. "Someday I'll zip that
arrogant bastard," he muttered.

If looks could have killed, the assassin would already be
dead.

Back in Lucius Fox's lab, Bruce Wayne peered over
Fox's shoulder as the older man screwed the outer casing
onto the revamped gizmo.

"I don't know about this, Bruce," he said with a sigh. "I've cranked up the juice so that any bullet coming in should, in theory, be deflected, and this time, deflected straight down into the ground instead of flying all over the place. But the power needed to deflect that kind of incoming kinetic energy is pretty steep. And redirecting it along specific vector lines is an additional load. I think the gizmo will work, at least for a bit, but any sort of serious attempt to breach its field is going to overload it pretty fast."

"Then what?" asked Bruce.

"Then what do you think? You're no idiot. You can do the math. If there's incoming and the gizmo fails, you can kiss somebody's ass good-bye."

"But it will work for a time?"

Fox nodded reluctantly. "I just wouldn't be accepting any life insurance policies on the user."

"What do you mean, Borya Oleksienko said Maroni's ordered a hit on Lieutenant Gordon?" Detective Montoya said, glancing up from the paperwork piled on her desk in the MCU squad room. The O'Fallon kidnapping and rescue, the disruption in several utilities, and the recapture of Waylon Jones, aka Killer Croc, had engendered enough paperwork to keep her and Allen at their desks until next week. She frowned across the aisle at her partner, who was working his way unenthusiastically through an equally tall stack of documents. "Cris, that's just wrong on so may levels . . ."

"Oleksienko was running a protection racket," Allen said. "We nabbed him. He plea-bargained. That's what he gave us. According to him, that's the word on the street."

Montoya snorted. "And we believe him because . . . ? It just doesn't make sense. The Ronald Marshall investigation suggests Marshall's laundering money for the Russian mob . . . and Yuri Dimitrov in particular. Now Gordon has begun to broaden our investigation to include the Russian. So why would Maroni want Gordon out of the picture? He

should be sending him champagne. And why would Oleksienko roll over, anyway? The Russian's lawyers have
sprung goons worse than him for worse crimes than protection."

"You think it's some kind of setup?"

"Don't you?"

Allen grinned. "Yeah. I bet that's what Gordon thinks,
too. I just can't figure out what it's a setup for."

Montoya glanced over at Gordon's office. "Cris," she
hissed. "I think maybe we aren't the only ones who think
this whole thing is funky."

Gordon swiveled his chair and turned to face Batman.
He reached into his suit-coat pocket and pulled out the ear-
buds. "Thanks!" he said, holding them out toward Batman.
"I expect we won't be needing them again for a while."

Batman took them and slipped them into a pocket in his
utility belt. "Unless it turns out that the Scarecrow escaped
both the explosion and the flood. I went back down into the
underground network, looked around for him. There's no
trace. But he appears to have had a lot of bolt-holes."

Gordon sighed. "At least Croc's in custody. I just hope
he stays that way."

"I've heard Maroni has supposedly ordered a hit on
you," Batman said.

Gordon snorted. "And you believe that about as much as
I do."

"I think *something* is going on," Batman said. "It
wouldn't hurt to play along. Make whoever went to all that
trouble to concoct that story think that you bought it hook,
line, and sinker. Maybe even leak it to the press. Travel
with armed protection. And . . . this!" He pulled the gizmo
from his utility belt and handed it to Gordon.

Gordon turned it over in his hand. "What is it?"

"A kind of invisible armor created by a friend of mine,"
Batman said. "Put it in your pocket and keep the battery

charged. It won't stop a hail of bullets, but it should protect you from a sniper's round, fired from a distance. Which is what you're being threatened with."

Gordon frowned. "I don't like being cosseted."

Batman grinned. "Who does? I'm actually wearing my body armor as a fashion statement." Then he sobered. "Look, you're not being cosseted. You're using yourself as bait. And sometimes, the bait gets hurt."

Gordon raised an eyebrow. "And you'll be the one to spring the trap?"

"Trust me," Batman said.

"Any idea who we might catch in this little trap you're setting?"

"If we're lucky, it will be the assassin who killed Teresa Williams and Anton Solonik. So far they're linked to Marshall and to the Russian."

"Marshall!" Gordon made a disgusted sound in the back of his throat. "He managed to lose the tail we had on him. Just . . . disappeared for nearly twenty-four hours. Suddenly he's back in Gotham. Changed phones, too. Making sure no one can trace his calls."

"The assassin may lead us to Marshall. And beyond."

"That's what I think, too," Gordon muttered. "That's the main reason I'll agree to this charade." He sighed. "Some members of the press have irresponsibly publicized the theory that you and I sometimes work in concert. I wonder if whoever set this plan in motion is using this to draw you out into the open. *You* could be their true target."

Batman's mouth quirked wryly. "Oddly enough, I've considered that possibility."

News vans clustered beyond the fifty-foot no-parking area surrounding Gotham City Police Department headquarters. Photographers jostled for shots of the police snipers who patrolled the roof and scanned adjacent buildings. Several news choppers whirled nearby, cameras trained on the private lot behind GCPD headquarters, where

Lieutenant James Gordon, embattled head of Gotham's Major Crimes Unit, would emerge.

Gordon, decked out in helmet and Kevlar vest, with Batman's gizmo hidden in his pocket, waited as an armored limo pulled up to the bulletproof Plexiglas-shielded rear door. Four SWAT police, wearing Kevlar vests and armed with assault rifles, surrounded him and rushed him to the armored limousine.

Gordon climbed inside the back of the limo, and one of the SWAT team climbed in beside him. Another SWAT cop sat in front beside the driver.

These two—and others—would guard him at home until he was ready to return to police headquarters. He had sent his wife and kids to visit her sister, on the remote possibility there was any real danger, all the while reassuring them that this was just a clever stratagem to catch some bad guys. In the morning, more SWAT police would escort him back to police headquarters.

A squad car pulled out in front of them. A second squad car followed as Gordon's limo pulled out of the parking lot behind it. As it crossed the sidewalk, preparing to turn onto the street, reporters and cameramen rushed the vehicle, shining lights, flashing bulbs, and shouting questions.

"Who informed you of the mob hit?"

"Who ordered the hit man?"

"Is this for real?"

All good questions. He was beginning to wonder. If the sniper was going to make his move, Gordon wished he would just get on with it. He reached under his Kevlar helmet to tug the vest away from his neck.

This had been going on for three days. Gordon thought that if he had to endure three more days of this dubious celebrity, he'd go out of his mind.

29

Batman stood on the roof of the Goyer Button Factory in Downtown's old industrial district, watching as Gordon's motorcade sped down Nolan Street, into the area known as Factory Park.

The days when Factory Park was a major industrial center were long past, though many of the old buildings still housed light industry. Printers existed cheek by jowl with violin manufacturers, furriers, art glass and ceramics makers, kitchen- and restaurant-supply companies, and hundreds of other small businesses.

Other floors in the buildings had been partially converted to living spaces, mostly occupied by the city's artists, drawn to the spacious, rough loft areas with large windows and small rents.

As Batman dashed along the roofs of the old plants that edged Nolan, he noted that trendy shops and restaurants, even a few art galleries, had begun to occupy the ground floors. Soon investment bankers and stockbrokers would move in, drive up area prices, and force the starving artists out to colonize and gentrify another run-down section of the city.

Gotham's artists—the new urban pioneers.

Batman ran along Nolan, shadowing Gordon's limousine. When the motorcade crossed a street, he crossed with it—gliding downward on his cape to land on a shorter, three-story building.

Each day, the motorcade had altered its route, and Gordon had made sure Batman had the itinerary in advance. Still, there were sometimes a few surprises.

Batman ducked beneath the laundry some loft dweller had strung across a rooftop—floral-pattern sheets and several men's and women's paint-smeared T-shirts and jeans. Artists. Didn't need to be a detective to figure that out! He vaulted over a low wall edging one rooftop, landed several feet below on the asphalt roof of the adjacent building, and kept on running.

No matter what route the motorcade followed through Downtown, if Gordon was heading for home, there was one certainty: his motorcade would eventually have to funnel onto the Tricorner Narrows Bridge, which linked Downtown with Tricorner Island and its docks and warehouses.

If an assassin was going to take a potshot at Gordon, Batman figured he'd probably set up somewhere near the spot where the entrance ramp edged upward through a corridor of old factory buildings.

Those aged structures, many decorated with old-world flourishes, offered hundreds of potential perches. Their roofs and windows would provide numerous vantage points for an assassin who needed to get off one clear shot through a car window. And, with the many exterior fire escapes as well as roof access hatches down to interior stairwells, there were literally hundreds of escape routes.

But Gordon's motorcade had come this way for the past three days. The fact that the hit man hadn't made a move suggested to Batman that Gordon wasn't his real target. They could be betting Gordon's life on that supposition. The gizmo in Gordon's hip pocket was their insurance in case they were wrong. Up ahead, the police motorcade slowed to a statelier pace as it turned onto the entrance ramp.

Batman hit the cross street at a run and fired his grapnel up at the next building. It hooked on the facade. A moment later, he was running across the roof. He climbed up over the wall . . . and nearly tripped over rooftop lovers entwined on a blanket. They let out startled squeaks as Batman leapt over them.

On the ramp, traffic slowed even more.

Batman trotted to the far edge of the roof and looked toward the bridge. Up ahead, he could see a long line of bright red brake lights flashing on. Horns began to honk. Exhaust from stopped cars poured into the streets, fouling the night air. Traffic onto the ramp and bridge itself was almost at a standstill.

Anything could cause a slowdown across the Tricorner, from a minor fender bender to an overturned tanker dripping toxic chemicals onto the pavement.

He switched on the antenna, hidden in one of the ears of his cowl, and began scanning the police radio bands. A car was stalled, blocking both lanes of the entrance ramp, pouring smoke from beneath its hood into the hot night air. Traffic was snarled on all approaches. A tow truck was on the way.

The event could be suspicious. Or it could mean nothing. But if he were the hit man, he would have engineered a traffic jam that would stop the motorcade and trap Gordon where he wanted him.

Batman scanned the area from his rooftop vantage point. The silhouette of the Tricorner Narrows suspension bridge loomed dark against the Gotham night, silhouetted against the clouds. It rose above the rooftops with their jumble of structures—access sheds, water towers, billboards, old signs, air-conditioning units, air vents. All good places for a hit man to hide. The assassin—if there was one—could be on either side of the ramp or somewhere up ahead, planning to fire through the windshield.

He moved across the rooftops, activating the nightscope and telescopic lenses built into his cowl, as he searched the shadows.

Nothing.

He switched to infrared, but the roof asphalt still held the heat of the day and made his heat scope useless.

Finally, he switched on his high-gain microphone. Maybe it would pick up the whisper of movement on one of the surrounding rooftops.

He turned slowly, scanning the buildings that rose beside the ramp. And noticed something odd. Yesterday and the day before and the day before that, there had been a lit sign on a rooftop partially cantilevered across the road about halfway up the ramp—massive red, white, and blue letters that spelled out the name KANE. Tonight, that sign wasn't turned on.

Like the stalled car, it could mean nothing.

Or . . .

He glanced at Gordon's limo, then across the ramp at the Kane building. That sign would make a perfect blind.

Moving rapidly and silently across the rooftops, keeping to the shadows, using every available means of cover, the Dark Knight slipped silently toward the Kane building.

He ducked behind a small water tower, then peered out cautiously, aiming his high-gain mikes directly at the great sign.

At first, he heard nothing. Then, as he was about to move again, there came a soft *clink*, followed by a slight rhythmic ringing. Batman realized he was hearing pieces of metal being screwed together. There was another soft *clink*, then silence.

Deadshot crouched behind massive letters that spelled out KANE in bold block capitals twenty-five feet high. Normally the letters that decorated the roof of the sheet-metal factory would be brightly outlined in red, white, and blue neon—Robert Kane, the factory's owner, was nothing if not patriotic. But Deadshot, with no small degree of amusement, had temporarily pulled the plug on the man's egotistical display.

Doing the factory owner a favor, actually. Up close, he

could tell that the letters were rickety, and the roof beneath them was rotted with water damage. It was a miracle the sign still worked. Even more a miracle that the whole building hadn't gone up in an electrical fire.

He lay in darkness, rifle resting on the crossbar of the A as he used the nightscope built into his metal helmet to scan the rooftops of the neighboring buildings. Then he turned his head to check the access ramp to the bridge.

Deadshot was becoming increasingly irritated with this assignment—both by the publicity surrounding it and by the lack of access to his target. There were just too many variables, and he was too little in command. After three successive nights of waiting for the right moment, he had set up the roadblock, hoping to apply some pressure and give himself the time he needed to spot his target before Gordon had gone.

But, for all his planning, the target had yet to appear. The blare of horns and the stink of exhaust were adding to his irritation.

He frowned as the limo inched around the curve toward him.

He twitched a muscle in his cheek—he controlled his optical sight through fine motor movements—and a section of the limousine was enlarged telescopically. There Gordon was, in the backseat, looking almost as irritated as he himself felt. For a moment, Deadshot thought about pulling out, about reconfiguring his entire approach and starting over.

Suddenly he wanted to wipe that scowl off Gordon's stupid face.

He switched eyes, looking now through the crosshairs of the telescopic sight on his rifle, aiming through the clear glass of the windshield. He had chambered his own self-loaded specialty round. A bulletproof windshield was no problem.

Using danger to Gordon as bait hadn't been a bad plan, as far as that went. But perhaps the rumor of danger wasn't going to be enough to lure Batman out into the open. Perhaps . . .

Deadshot sighted on the space between Gordon's eyes, right below his Kevlar helmet, and squeezed the trigger.

James Gordon sat in the backseat of the limousine, staring out at the line of cars that had come to a standstill.

"Blasted traffic jam," Gordon grumbled. "I'd get home faster if I got out and—"

Crack!

A hole appeared in the windshield.

There was a pinging sound from the gizmo in his pocket—the shield Batman had given him.

Then something small and hard slammed into the carpeted floor not quite six inches from Lieutenant Gordon's left foot.

The bullet had smashed a hole in the windshield. Through his telescopic sight, Deadshot could see clearly where the round had penetrated. Small cracks radiated out from the point of entry.

Yet there was Gordon, sitting in the backseat of the limo, yelling something at his driver, clearly shocked, but definitely alive.

Deadshot forgot that he was simply creating a diversion to bring Batman out into the open. He forgot everything except that, for the first time ever, his clear shot had missed. Snarling, he snapped a loaded magazine into place.

He aimed and squeezed the trigger once again.

Batman was a couple of rooftops away from the Kane building and on the other side of the ramp when he heard the first faint *puft!* followed by a soft *crack*.

The sounds were unmistakable—silenced rifle . . . snapping glass.

He whirled—saw cracks appearing in the limo windshield—then heard another distinctive *puft!* And another soft *crack!*

Without his high-gain microphone he might have missed them altogether.

Two rounds, he thought. *Two hits.* The gizmo could handle that many. He didn't want to give the hit man a chance to fire a third round.

Throwing aside all hope of surprising the assailant, Batman ran full tilt and launched himself off the edge of the roof and into the air above the ramp. He activated the glide mechanism, caught a thermal, and soared like a kite over the road toward the roof of the Kane building.

30

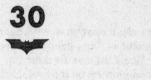

For a split second, Deadshot didn't register what was happening. Below him, sirens were starting to wail. And above him, a dark shadow seemed to be filling the sky. He snapped out of it, cursing the precious moments he'd lost. His ploy had worked! Batman had leapt finally, heroically to the rescue—and into the path of a bullet earmarked for him, personally! There was still time to finish the job. He swung the muzzle of the barrel around to his left.

Forget Gordon! Forget everything! Concentrate on the mission!

Batman was already so close that the telescopic sight was useless, a hindrance rather than a help. But Deadshot was a master of his craft and at this range, accurately firing from the hip was duck soup.

Deadshot aimed the rifle—such an easy shot, hardly worthy of his skill—and pulled the trigger.

Pft! Pft! You're dead!

He would worry, later, how Gordon had survived his first shot. On the second, Gordon had fallen sideways. He—

Batman was still coming at him!

He cursed his broken concentration, tore the scope from

the rifle, and brought the gun up to his shoulder. There was still time.

Deadshot pumped out three more rounds—one at Batman's heart, one at his throat, a third one at his head.

He was close enough now to hear the quiet *pft!* without the benefit of high-gain microphones. He felt the bullet punch like a fist into his chest.

He was almost on the roof. He threw up his arm and—

Pft! Pft! Pft!

One bullet slammed into his chest, a second blow almost on top of the first, nearly knocking the wind from his lungs.

One hit the arm he had thrown up over his face, leaving it feeling bruised and numb.

The third round sailed past his head and up over the Gotham skyline.

Batman collapsed his cape and dropped bonelessly onto the Kane building's roof, landing behind a huge commercial air-conditioning unit.

He lay on the asphalt, struggling to catch his breath. Thank heaven for his Kevlar armor. He wondered what the assassin had been firing. Because it felt like several of his ribs were broken.

His chest was on fire.

Cassandra had taught him about fire.

He smiled through clenched teeth.

A man who could walk on fire could do anything.

Behind the sign, Deadshot waited.

There was no movement. No sound. Batman had fallen behind the air-conditioning unit. He was dead. He had to be dead.

But after Deadshot had failed to kill Gordon with the first bullet . . . after he had hit Batman at point-blank range and Batman had kept coming at him, his confidence was shaken—just a little. He needed to make sure.

He set down his rifle, pulled his wrist guns from the case beside him, and snapped the weapons onto his forearms.

Click snapt!

Click snapt!

He toggled the switches to fully automatic.

As distasteful as he would normally have found the notion, there was something reassuring about the idea of filling Batman's body full of lead. In other circumstances, he might have smiled at the cliché, but this time, it was different. He was feeling something he didn't recognize at first. Something that both troubled and excited him. As he stood up, weapons at the ready, he realized with a start that what he was feeling was fear.

Soon . . . very soon, the police would figure out where the bullets that struck Gordon had come from, and they would be all over the building. He needed to collect his equipment. He needed to disappear. He needed to vanish into the night like all the times before. But most of all, at this moment, he needed to be certain.

Warily, he edged toward the air conditioner . . . then whirled around it with his arms extended in firing position, almost desperate to see Batman's bleeding corpse.

The roof before him was empty.

A small object rolled into view coming from the other end of the steel air-conditioning structure. Deadshot turned away just as the grenade exploded, blowing tear gas in every direction. He'd avoided the direct blast, but his eyes were tearing slightly when he heard a whirring hiss behind him! A *klang*, then a *snapt!* He glanced upward in astonishment. With the sound of rending metal, the massive sign that said KANE began to topple toward him.

Batman had recognized the clinking sounds of metal parts being assembled. Given the profession of the gentleman on the other side of the roof, it was easy to surmise that whatever he was doing, it wasn't something designed to augment Batman's health.

He had heard the rustling shuffle as the hit man stood and began to walk stealthily toward where he lay.

Slowly, silently, as the hit man was approaching one side of the massive air conditioner, Batman had edged cautiously, silently, around to the other side, until he was facing the sign.

He rolled a gas grenade at the assassin and, as it went off filling the air with obscuring smoke, he fired a grapnel at the top of the sign. It caught with a *klang!* on the top of the giant letter *N*.

He hit the retractor, and the monofilament jerked him upward. Ten feet. Fifteen.

Then, to his shock, the massive sign began to topple forward—slowly, inexorably. The entire structure was coming down!

Batman released the monofilament cable, dropped onto the roof, and sprinted for the edge, racing to evade the falling letters. The assassin was in front of him and to the right, running like a madman.

Deadshot looked back in shock and amazement. Batman was behind him, closing fast. He threw back his left wrist and wildly fired off a burst on full automatic. The sign was gathering momentum; it was almost upon them. There was no way out.

Batman dove low, tackled the assassin from behind, and drove the two of them over the edge of the building. Behind them, the sign crashed onto the asphalt roof, smashed through the low safety wall, and came to a stop, cantilevered out over the Tricorner Narrows Bridge access ramp.

Holding the assassin with one arm, Batman fired a grapnel up at the fallen sign. It caught on the edge of the *N* and held. The cable went taut, and he felt as though his arm were being pulled from its socket. He almost lost the hit man, who was, he realized belatedly, wearing some sort of costume.

Batman and the assassin swung like a pendulum back toward the building. The brick wall was coming up fast. Batman released a little more cable, and they crashed through one of the floor-to-ceiling windows and sprawled together on the floor amid flying shards of glass.

The hit man kicked free of Batman, catching him in his broken ribs.

Batman groaned and rolled beneath a conveyer belt toward a heavy piece of floor-mounted machinery.

"Thanks, Batman. Much obliged," the hit man shouted as he scrambled to his knees, firing his wrist guns after Batman at point-blank range.

Batman huddled, teeth gritted, behind the giant machine as the assassin's bullets ricocheted around him. "No good deed goes unpunished," he muttered. *That will teach me to save crazed killers from being crushed to death by falling signs.*

He rolled farther back and saw the words ADONIS MFG. For a moment, he was afraid he was having another flashback . . . this time to Malaysia. Then he realized that what he was seeing was real. He was looking at an embossed metal plate bolted to the machine he was sheltering behind—an Adonis metal-stamping press, used to mold sheet metal into a number of useful shapes. During his time in Malaysia, he had worked briefly in a similar factory on a machine just like this one.

The ambient light from the city shone through the huge windows and threw the interior of the factory into stark relief. He could see a half dozen Adonis machines standing in a line across the floor. Great rolls of sheet metal hung from the ceiling, and smaller pieces of equipment were everywhere. They were in one of the few industrial factories left in this part of Gotham.

Batman thought of Venus and hoped that she would extend her protection to him as he huddled beneath the

Adonis while a hail of bullets bounced all around him. He rolled his eyes. Maybe his system hadn't completely cleared itself of Croc's hallucinogens, after all.

The firing stopped abruptly. The hit man's clips must be empty, Batman realized. But the killer was too far away to rush before he could reload. Batman pushed himself farther behind the stamping press, farther back into the shadow.

Deadshot covered the sounds of reloading by calling out, "I heard you don't use guns, Batman. Why not? They give you a much longer reach."

He felt high, energized by the notion that in a few moments, he was going to kill the only thing he'd felt afraid of in years. He was about to become the number-one hit man of all time—the guy who killed Batman.

He fired short bursts at random, blasting around the factory, enjoying the power, not shooting at anything in particular, just feeling out the place.

"Guns are beautiful, Batman," he shouted. "Scary, too. All that noise." He fired another short burst. "And bullets are cheap." And another.

"It's like being God." He laughed in triumph, emptying another clip down the length of the factory.

He stopped; glass crunched under his feet. He looked around as he flicked his wrists, ejecting used magazines. He reached behind him to reload again. "You spoiled my record, Batman. I haven't missed a target in fifteen years, and you made me miss. But we'll just keep that between us, shall we?"

Looking around, Deadshot noticed a few drops of blood on the floor where the two of them had first landed. Blood smudges and drops led away back under the nearest machine.

Deadshot looked into the darkness and smiled.

He stopped, listening. Waited. His wristbands smoked. There was a noise.

Batarangs flew out of the darkness, arcing gracefully to-

ward him. Shifting to single-shot mode, Deadshot blew
them apart, each in turn. "One, two, three, four, five . . .
Like skeets, baby."

A whisper and more came soaring toward him.

"Six, seven, eight. Bang. Bang. Bang."

He was laughing. "You know what they call me, Batman? Deadshot! Because that's what I am!"

A ninth Batarang looped around, coming straight for
Deadshot. He aimed almost casually and fired.

The bullet hit . . . and the Batarang exploded with a white
light that filled the room. Deadshot recoiled, shielding his
eyes, momentarily blinded. As his sight cleared, he glimpsed
a bat-winged shadow flying across the room above the machinery.

In a panic, he sprayed bullets in its direction, without
thought or concentration.

The dark shape swept across the press frame and dropped
from sight.

Deadshot raced around the corner of the stamping press,
firing as he went.

He caught Batman against the wall behind the metal
press and fired round after round into his back.

Bullets slammed into his nemesis, shredding his cape.

How could Batman still be standing?! It was as though
the force of Deadshot's own firepower were keeping the
Dark Knight upright.

Deadshot reloaded each gun in turn, keeping up an almost constant barrage. The barrels of his guns began to
smoke. His wrists ached from the strain of taking the re-
coil. He was yelling.

Why wouldn't Batman fall? Why wouldn't he die?

As Deadshot ceased firing, and the air cleared, he saw it
was not Batman behind the press, but only his cape. Now
almost completely shredded, it hung limply, attached by
several Batarangs to the factory wall.

"Game over," said a quiet voice in his ear. Before he
could react, an elbow to the back of the neck knocked him
off his feet.

Deadshot fell forward, extending his arms to try to break his fall. They came to rest on the press bed.

Batman hit a foot control on the floor beside the metal press. The ram came down, crushing Deadshot's hands and arms, briefly setting off the wrist guns, which fired on their own until they were empty, spewing bullets across the far end of the factory. Deadshot jerked and pulled helplessly.

He screamed and fainted.

Batman stood over him. He'd stopped the ram a few inches above the bed. They wouldn't have to amputate Deadshot's arms. But his wrists and probably his forearms would be broken.

He could heal in jail.

"The illusion of godhood," he murmured. "To take lives, to deal out death. Simple stuff for anyone with a gun. Until you achieve the power to *give* life, you're not a god. You're just a punk with a weapon."

Batman flipped on his communicator, spoke into the microphone. "Jim?"

There was a momentary bustle at the other end of the line. "Batman?" He heard the strain in Gordon's voice.

"Jim, are you okay?"

"That creep's last shot went through my forearm. I'm being bandaged up even as we speak. Your little science-fiction gizmo fried a round too soon. My ass'll be getting over that burn for a week. So tell me what I want to hear."

"I'm on the eleventh floor of the Kane building. Come and get your assailant. He's stuck in one of the metal stamping presses up here. And mind that whoever releases the press knows how to raise the ram. He . . . uh . . . he's wearing a costume. Calls himself Deadshot."

Batman could almost feel Gordon rolling his eyes at the other end of the line.

"Reinforcements are on the way. Better make yourself scarce. If Detective Montoya gets there before you're gone, you'll be signing autographs all night!"

31

Detectives Allen and Montoya walked down the hospital corridor, toward the room where Anton Solonik had died. The MCU had arranged that special placement, hoping that the irony—and threat—of it would not be lost on Floyd Lawton.

"Floyd Lawton, aka Deadshot. Hit man for hire. A real piece of work," Montoya said.

"You want to be good cop or bad cop?"

"Bad cop," Montoya said. "It's my turn. You got to be bad cop when we interviewed Ronald Marshall."

"That wasn't any fun. He lawyered up faster than a rat down a drainpipe."

Montoya grinned. "A . . . what . . . ?"

"Southern idiom, Renee. You can't beat Southern idioms."

"Cris . . ." She rolled her eyes. "The point is, our pal Deadshot doesn't know Marshall hasn't dropped the dime on him."

As they walked into Lawton's hospital room, the TV was tuned to the news. The story of the arrest of the hit man who called himself Deadshot was the lead story on the

newscasts of every Gotham station. Following that was the
shorter, secondary story regarding the arrest of developer
Ronald Marshall on charges of money laundering and
bribery. Other charges were pending.

It had been a productive couple of days for Gotham's
Major Crimes Unit.

Deadshot lay in bed, his arms in casts up beyond his elbows. Montoya, the grim-faced, tough bad cop read Lawton the Miranda warning.

"Floyd Lawton, you have been arrested for the attempted murder of Lieutenant James Gordon of the
GCPD. You have the right to remain silent. Anything you
say can and will be used against you in a court of law. You
have the right to have an attorney present during question-
ing. If you cannot afford an attorney, one will be appointed
for you." She loomed over him, assuming a dominant
position.

Allen pulled up a visitor's chair beside his bed and sat,
putting himself on Lawton's level.

Lawton glanced away from the TV, over at Montoya. "A
formal interrogation? Of course, I want my lawyer present."

Allen glanced at the window—the same one through
which Lawton had fired the bullet that had killed the Russian *vor*. "Choose your lawyer carefully; that's all I'm saying. We'll keep the blind shut and a guard on your room the
whole time you're here. But you'll be out soon . . . part of
the regular prison population."

Lawton glanced up at the TV, which was reshowing the
picture of Ronald Marshall being driven into the police-
headquarters parking lot.

Allen leaned close. "Look, you might as well know.
When Ronald Marshall hired you for that hit, he set you up
to die. Batman was supposed to kill you. Must have heard
us coming before he could finish the job. Of course, Batman's still out there."

Lawton nodded, as if the idea had already occurred to him.

"And then there's the Russian," Montoya said coldly.
"He knows you're in custody. He already wanted you dead.

And he's paranoid as hell. His spies will have seen us come in here. Probably already hired someone to do to you what you did to Anton."

"Look," Allen said. "We just want to give you a chance to tell your side of the story."

Lawton frowned at Allen. "Since *she's* still standing, I presume that means *you* must be the good cop. Still, there is some truth in what you say. The Russian is notoriously unforgiving. I can give you Marshall . . . and maybe the Russian. But I want a deal."

"Do you think the Russian really wanted Batman to kill Lawton?" Montoya said as they walked away from Lawton's room.

Allen shrugged. "Doesn't matter whether it's true or not, as long as Lawton believes it."

"And his deal?"

"He's probably off the hook for attempted murder of Gordon. But there's still the Teresa Williams case. Or the Anton Solonik murder. Not to mention a number of unsolved homicides on the books with his MO—or lack of one—in other cities."

Montoya nodded. "San Diego wants him. Apparently they think he offed an antimob mayoral candidate. And we've had a couple of calls from Chicago." She shrugged. "We got what we needed—Marshall and the Russian on a platter. If the Russian didn't want him dead before, he certainly will now. Lawton's ass is grass, no matter how you cut it."

Allen considered this as they entered the elevator. He punched 1. "Maybe," he said. "But I'm thinking that if the Russian is going to try to off the creep, he'd better do it before Lawton's arms heal."

"So the Russian's in jail," Batman said. **"Congratulations."**

"Without bail," Gordon said. "Considered a flight risk. Of course, we still have to get through his trial."

They were standing on the roof of the GCPD headquarters, side by side, staring out over the city. The air was clear for once, and they could see a few stars overhead. There was a hint of fall in the air.

"How's your arm?"

"Nearly good as new," Gordon said with a laugh. "They gave me a medal."

"Maroni is still out there," Batman said. "And probably, so is the Scarecrow. And there are other Arkham escapees."

Gordon shrugged. "Problems for another day."

Batman smiled slightly. "One thing you can say for Gotham cops—they'll never be out of work."

Gordon grinned. "One thing you can say for Maroni—he has yet to put on a costume."

Soft laughter drifted out across the city.

It was one of those crisp mornings that augur fall. The Bill Finger Country Club golf course was pure pleasure as Bruce Wayne stepped onto the beautifully manicured twelfth green.

His ball lay close to the same spot from which he had missed the hole during the Ronald Marshall Invitational. The difference was, this time the game was actually golf and the stakes were no higher than who bought a round of beer back in the clubhouse.

He putted, striking the ball with the correct force at just the right angle. It rolled forward, looped dramatically—just as he had intended—and dropped into the cup.

"Bull's-eye!" Bruce said.

The three other men in the foursome—Lucius Fox; tall, balding Nikolas Wilsom III, shipping magnate; and short, stocky Clay Carter, heir to the Bonaventure fortune, grinned their congratulations.

Wilsom wrote down the score, shaking his head. "Well, you're having a day."

Carter chuckled. "Lot better than the one at Marshall's tournament."

Bruce plucked his ball from the hole. "Something about Marshall threw me off my game."

Carter rummaged in his golf bag. "Did you hear he was arrested?"

Bruce raised his eyebrows. "I heard something about it. No details."

Carter leaned forward. "Apparently Marshall arranged the Teresa Williams murder. Among others. And he was laundering money for the Russian mob."

Bruce's eyes widened. "Amazing!"

"Now the cops have gone after Yuri Dimitrov," Carter said eagerly. "He's the goon who orchestrated the Little Roma bloodbath. They call him 'the Russian.'"

"Good for the cops," Bruce said.

Fox sank his putt and smiled. "You gotta read the papers once in a while."

As the foursome walked to the clubhouse, Bruce said, "I guess this means an empty spot on the planning board."

"Yeah," Carter said. "You interested?"

Bruce shrugged. "Maybe. You've already got some other new guy, don't you? What's his name? Coddlecot?"

"Cobblepot. Oswald Cobblepot." Carter chuckled. "He's a character. Got a beak on him like a penguin."

"Count me in," Bruce said. "Sounds like someone I'd like to meet."

High above the city, perched on the old dirigible mooring post atop a tall skyscraper, Batman crouched, watching. The moon had set, and the wind was freshening from the east. The crisp sea air blew through Gotham's steamy canyons and lifted his black cape so it billowed out behind him like a pennant snapping in the breeze.

Batman watched as the lights of his city winked out, and

the faces of the buildings began to reflect the rosy warmth of the rising sun. Far below, trucks and vans rumbled and jounced along the city's streets, making their early morning deliveries to restaurant row and the garment district and Gotham's newsstands.

The black cape snapped again and, a moment later, the Dark Knight was gone.